Today's Most Daring Erotic Fiction by Women

"MY DATE WITH MARCIE" *by Serena Moloch*
Two archenemies—a straight-A student and a sexy high school "bad girl"—are startled to see each other on a double date, but their surprise turns to pleasure when they make up with more than just a handshake.

"ABOUT PENETRATION" *by Catherine Tavel*
A married man who tries to remain faithful to his wife by refusing to penetrate his mistress discovers exciting, alternative ways to fulfill his mistress' desires.

"TENNESSEE" *by Pat Williams*
In the South, where the stars hang down beside your head and the snakes slide out of their skins, all is not what it seems—as a teenage girl realizes when she falls in love with an alluring, enigmatic woman.

"TRUST" *by Mary Maxwell*
Trust is the ultimate test in this tense tale where anything goes—including making love on the cutting edge of a knife.

... And 22 Other Deliciously Voluptuous Stories

SUSIE BRIGHT is the charismatic and much-quoted sex educator and author of *Susie Bright's Sexual Reality* and *Susie Sexpert's Lesbian Sex World*. She is the editor of *Herotica* and *Herotica 2* (Plume), and of the annual *Best American Erotica* series. In addition to her groundbreaking work as editor of *On Our Backs* magazine, she has written frequently on the role of sexuality and erotica in our culture. She lives in San Francisco with her four-year-old daughter, Aretha Elizabeth.

HEROTICA 3

A Collection of Women's Erotic Fiction

Edited by Susie Bright

A PLUME BOOK

PLUME
Published by the Penguin Group
Penguin Books USA Inc., 375 Hudson Street,
New York, New York, 10014, U.S.A.
Penguin Books Ltd, 27 Wrights Lane, London W8 5TZ, England
Penguin Books Australia Ltd, Ringwood, Victoria, Australia
Penguin Books Canada Ltd, 10 Alcorn Avenue,
Toronto, Ontario, Canada M4V 3B2
Penguin Books (N.Z.) Ltd, 182–190 Wairau Road,
Auckland 10, New Zealand

Penguin Books Ltd, Registered Offices:
Harmondsworth, Middlesex, England

First published by Plume/Meridian, an imprint of Dutton Signet, a division of
Penguin Books USA Inc.

First Printing, June, 1994

10 9 8 7 6 5 4

 REGISTERED TRADEMARK—MARCA REGISTRADA

LIBRARY OF CONGRESS CATALOGING IN PUBLICATION DATA:
Herotica 3 : a collection of women's erotic fiction / edited by Susie Bright.
        p.   cm.
    ISBN 0-452-27180-0
    1. Erotic stories, American. 2. American fiction—Women authors.
3. Women—Sexual behavior—Fiction. I. Bright, Susie.
PS648.E7H475   1994
813.008'03538—dc20
                                                            93-42996
                                                            CIP

Printed in the United States of America
Set in Caledonia

PUBLISHER'S NOTE
These stories are works of fiction. Names, characters, places, and incidents either
are the product of the author's imagination or are used fictitiously, and any resem-
blance to actual persons, living or dead, events, or locales is entirely coincidental.

BOOKS ARE AVAILABLE AT QUANTITY DISCOUNTS WHEN USED TO PROMOTE PRODUCTS OR
SERVICES. FOR INFORMATION PLEASE WRITE TO PREMIUM MARKETING DIVISION, PEN-
GUIN BOOKS USA INC., 375 HUDSON STREET, NEW YORK, NEW YORK, 10014.

*This collection is dedicated to
the memory of Jane Longaway*

Contents

Introduction

I collect sexy stories: erotic fiction, dirty books, porno, sensuous reading, you name it. I started acquiring these stories when I didn't have any name for them, except *Don't Let Anyone Find Out About This*. I collected them underneath my bed, in the back of my underwear drawer, in the knothole of a tree on my way to school.

I accumulated my stories in secret—finding them in other people's underwear drawers, or at garage sales where I could lift them without anyone noticing, or in the back of baby-sitters' cars, where I sat while they went out for cigarettes. After puberty, I started writing my own stories to arouse myself. I'd enter elaborate fantasies in my diaries in code, or rip out the pages the next day.

My collection matured over time. These days I buy erotic fiction without hesitation in any bookstore in town. Moreover, I publish many of the sexiest stories I can find. I have been editing erotica for ten years now. I get interviewed by journalists, grad students, and fellow travelers regarding my sex fiction collection and expertise. Inevitably, the conversation turns to politics. The reporter leans into me and states the question as if drawing a line in the sand: "Are you a feminist?"

Each time I'm asked, I pause for a moment, because if it's a one word answer they're looking for, it should be as plain as the nose on my face. Isn't it obvious?

Tragically, feminism is perceived as "down on sex" and against pornography. "Feminist pornography" is considered a contradiction in terms; "feminist erotica" only marginally less so. Women's liberation is always being counterpoised to erotic freedom, despite the fact that sexual liberation has always been a cornerstone of modern feminism. One of the oldest feminist challenges is to eliminate the double standard, to move from barefoot and pregnant to orgasmic and decisive.

So why isn't the sex field treated by feminists as just another Old Boys Club that needs to be shaken up and infused with a woman's point of view? Feminists have zapped other male-only institutions from construction sites to the halls of Congress.

Sex is different. It's different because our culture is so puritanical that we can't even discuss sex publicly without our worst fears and fantasies rendering us mute, embarrassed, inarticulate. It's not about Equal Pay for Equal Work, it's about Different Strokes for Different Folks. Those differences are unpalatable to some, unspeakable to others. We haven't been honest about sexuality—we've denied it. Our prudery turns us into liars, yet despite all these factors, sex is compelling. Women's desire does not change through fear of condemnation.

The women claiming the erotic frontier are woman-centric, no-compromises, read-my-lips Amazons. They're the women writing sexual fiction, the women publishing it, the scholars teaching it, the entrepreneurs selling it, the politicos on a soapbox debating it. If they have one thing in common, it's that one day they picked up a sexual story and said out loud to themselves, "I like this." Then they said the same thing to their lovers, their families, over dinner, to audiences. They are risk takers, women who say yes to sex as forcefully as they've been raised to say no. Any woman who confesses enthusiasm for erotic writing or visual materials is on the erotic frontier. Why is the existence of these women so hard to believe? Because we're a minority? It's true there aren't a lot of politically active feminists who go public with their erotic adventures, but we've been vocal and inspiring enough to make an impressive dent.

Sexual liberation for women is certainly not all jolly and climaxing with happy faces. In many years of teaching and talking sex, I have never had a man come up and say, "I don't know where my penis is and I've never had an orgasm." It never will happen either. It's feminists who have put the clitoris on the map; now we're concentrating above the neck.

Why do the anti-porn feminists still dominate the public perception of feminist views on sexuality?

I've often participated in debates where some woman "against pornography" tells me that a woman is being raped every ten seconds, and that my work is at the core of this devastation. An entire women's studies class picketed my lecture on lesbian erotica in history, passing out a leaflet that said, "First slavery in the Roman Empire . . . then the Holocaust . . . Now, Susie Bright comes to the University of Minnesota campus."

This last example may have pushed the argument to its surreal limits, but the U of M protesters' sentiment reflects the more comprehensive statements by anti-porn leaders like Andrea Dworkin, Catherine MacKinnon, or Robin Morgan. Their position articulates the anti-erotic lock on feminist ideology. On the one side they incite the visceral female reaction to male violence; on the other, they play to traditional middle class Anglo-Saxon prejudices within the women's movement. And all this controversy exists within a national climate of sexual ignorance defined by religion and superstition, so that even with the best intentions, we know so very little. Eros is a universe, and we haven't even gotten off the launch pad.

The feminist "sex wars" have been going on since the early 1980s, from the first bloom of the women's erotic renaissance. It has always been exasperating for me to articulate my anger with the feminist status quo. It now seems that a lot of my pro-porn arguments of the past have been as superficial as the prejudices of the anti-porn feminists and even more defensive. It may sound reassuring to say, "Fantasies shall set you free, nothing you imagine in your mind can hurt you," but these are only feel-good sentiments, Dale Carnegie with a vibrator in his hand. There's often

a long and unpredictable road between our fantasy and consciousness.

Feminists worry about the effects of written and visual
expressions of sexuality in the same way that parents worry about
violent TV programming, or that consumers worry about sensa-
tional advertising. How much effect does it have on us? How easily can we be swayed? Why is it that I can stay up all night with
insomnia, watch a four-hour infomercial about molecular hair
curlers, and race on down to the mall to buy a set the next day
even though I have never set my hair in my entire life, yet when
asked if men get the idea that all women become whores by reading *Playboy*, I reply, "Don't be ridiculous."

It's not a ridiculous notion that we get ideas and inspiration
from the media or the arts. It's not news that you can be suckered
by anything. But we also find ourselves skeptical of these same
images or inventing our own interpretations that may be quite the
opposite of the producers' intentions. Certainly I learned to look
for lesbian associations and sympathies in Hollywood movies
when I knew in reality that they never meant to speak to me.
Most women's entire experience with pornography is taking material that was made for men's tastes and manipulating it to our own
purposes.

There is one thing for certain about the effect of pictures and
words on our minds: Sexuality has been preposterously singled
out as the most vile influence around. I am hardly the first person
to point out how we are inundated with violent images from our
earliest fairy tales and cartoons. Nearly everyone sees Hollywood
movies and network news shows and the violence they contain.
Relatively few people see hardcore pornography, yet this is where
all of our law enforcement, legislation, and political condemnation
is focused for attack. How can we think we are assessing sexual
expression fairly when clearly we have a knee-jerk reaction to it?
Our attitude toward sexually explicit materials is riddled with hy-
pocrisy and second guessing, and feminist attitudes towards it are
no exception.

The first time I heard Andrea Dworkin, the most charismatic
anti-porn orator of all, speak about what men do to women, it

turned my stomach. I was one of many young women in the audience, most of us either crying, pale with anger, or shocked. Her descriptions jarred memories of events I'd love to forget. My thoughts turned to my teenage years and the soldier who came back from basic training and raped me. My nails raked bloody scratches down his back, but they didn't stop his cock from moving in and out of me like a piston. I have fractured recollections of a drunk who followed my mother home and broke into our house. I hid in the closet with my roller skates clutched in my hand to bean him with if she couldn't succeed in talking him out of the room. I remembered, not so long ago, the young kid who held a knife to my breast and stuck his dirty hand in my pants before he fled with my purse.

Every woman around me at the lecture must have recalled her own catalog of male cruelty, sadism, and indifference. Inside each one of us who loves a husband, father, or son is a wound of resentment that can be opened every time she is reminded of the bullies, the pigs.

Feminists are accused of man-hating, the implication, of course, being that they are infantile, as stubborn and undiscriminating as two-year-olds who hate their bedtime. But hating one's oppressor, hating the bullies, is entirely natural. What's unnatural is for women to deny that we feel so strongly. Any minority that has successfully stood up for itself has had to address hating whoever has hurt its members. You can't just "hate" sexism and racism without contemplating the individuals who enforce that ideology.

But my memories weren't the only thing upsetting me the night I saw Dworkin speak. She took the anger of her audience, an audience charged up with humiliation, guilt, and titillation at her explicit descriptions, and she turned them all against a culprit that most of those young women had very little first-hand experience with—pornography.

I could not find my release down that path. I know my friend who joined the Air Force was not acting out what he saw in a magazine when he raped me. He was a virgin when I met him, tender and open; after nine months in the service, he became hardened and mean. I don't think that drunk who harassed my mother had been looking at anything but the bottom of a bottle

for a long time. And the babyface with the switchblade in his
dirty hand—I don't know who his role models were, but I think
they were closer to him in flesh than celluloid.

Dworkin's explanation of pornography as a rapist's tool is unbelievable to me. The idea that dirty pictures mixed with testosterone equal a time bomb doesn't add up. It's as though she pulled
only one worm out of the whole squirming can.

My dread of male violence is only a single thread in my need
to know why human cruelty exists in the first place, why some
people lose control, and how unexpected and vicious those man-
ifestations are. My questions are given little reassurance by the
limitlessness of erotic imagination—but I'm not looking for a pat
on the head.

It's not that sexual fantasy is so incompatible with feminism; it's
that politics—any political philosophy—does not adequately address sexual psychology.

Close your eyes for a moment, and remember the last time you
had an orgasm. At the moment of climax, how many of you were
thinking about a lovely walk on the beach, or a bouquet of balloons? Be honest. Beach walking is a really nice romantic fantasy,
and so are sunsets, dinners for two, and a bearskin rug in front of
a blazing fireplace. But as erotic fantasies that get us off, they
don't often come up. The highest levels of arousal are often
reached with thoughts that frighten us, anger us, overwhelm us.
What is awful, what is forbidden, what is taboo, what is dreaded,
is *exactly* what is erotic—up to a point. In fantasy, nothing can actually harm you. And the point at which a particular thought or
image goes past that point and becomes *anti*-erotic is as individ-
ual as your fingerprint.

Look at one example of a common fantasy—the anticipation of
getting caught having sex. The titillation might be the small
chance of being seen or heard. The bedsprings squeak too loudly.
You can't stop, you're with the lover of your dreams. The phone
rings. Someone bursts in. Your mother. No, your ex. With a gun.
With an accomplice. And an alibi. Does the bed still groan under
your sweating bodies? At what point in this scenario does the heat

turn to fear, the hard-on go limp, the wet pussy turn to dry mouth? This is what different strokes are all about.

Scientists, sex researchers, psychotherapists—none of them knows why we have the fantasies we do. That's right, they *don't know,* and most of them admit that in public.

Of course, sexual fantasies can be interpreted, but not easily or reductively. A sexual fantasy of a homosexual experience does not mean one is queer. A lesbian who fantasizes a tryst with a man is not living a lie. A rape in fantasy is certainly the antithesis of a rape in reality, where nothing is under the subject's guidance, limits, or control.

From the time we are small, we develop a very strong sense of what is make-believe and what is reality. I learn from watching how my own toddler has grown; sometimes she defers to others' boundaries and at other times she gets to act as if she were omnipotent.

My kid's idea of ecstasy is being tickled—very popular at her age. I call it the original S/M activity. She loves to run around saying, "Catch me, catch me!" and playing hide and seek. When I find her and get my fingers under her arms she laughs and shrieks, "Stop! Stop!" as in the original *Perils of Pauline.* But the moment I stop tickling her, she is absolutely certain to take a big breath and cry out, "Again!"

On the other hand, when I really lose my temper at my daughter, there's no mistaking the pain. She cries, I swear and steam, and there's nothing consensual about it. My daughter, like every other child, is learning about boundaries and trust, long before the media gets to her.

When we are face to face with a grown-up who doesn't see limits, for whom there is no line between pretend and real, we are not dealing with someone who just has naughty sex fantasies or who reads too many *Hustlers,* or who takes Madonna's latest pop tune the wrong way. We are dealing with a pathological lack of compassion and empathy that overrides fundamental adult Dos and Don'ts.

Historically, men as a group have been chauvinistic, egocentric, accustomed to gaining entrance. But if every man who had an aggressive rape fantasy acted it out, we would be living in a state of absolute barbarism. The sexual sociopath our society dreads is not just a villain of feminism or women's rights; his beliefs and preferences are superseded by a lack of conscience, a drop from reality, a failure to feel guilt or accountability that goes beyond conceit.

The Unstoppable Testosterone Rampage is a very popular mythical stereotype, and it's ironic that there's also an opposite stereotype with a ring of truth to it. It is that men specialize in keeping their feelings under tight control. The successful man is always putting his sexuality aside in consideration of other ambitions, saying, "No, I can't do this now, I don't have time for my family, I don't have time for my sex life, I don't have time for my body, I don't have time for desire." Men struggle to express themselves sexually with any kind of sensuality, or gladness.

If men are capable of exercising tremendous control in every part of their lives, and routinely stifle their sexual desires, then why should we believe the sulking Casanova who insists, "She looked at me like she wanted it, *and I couldn't stop myself*"? Is this the one moment when a man becomes a wild animal, not able to use his masculine discipline to respect another's limits? This is in itself a sexist prejudice. Men's sex is supposedly out of bounds without a leash, while women are deemed incapable of impulsiveness, passion, or just plain horniness.

We hear the same clichés over and over again: men are turned on by porn, women are not; men look at a sex act, then run out and start imitating exactly what they saw. Women, on the other hand, supposedly find satisfaction with soap operas and a big box of chocolates.

Men and women will be separated by artificial notions of sex and romance as long as we cling to traditional gender roles. Fears of violence and chaos will haunt us as long as we struggle with the notion of civilization. Beyond both of these debates is one constant that defines the most important differences in erotic appreciation. It is the element that absolutely dominates the feminist anti-porn position. It is something that Americans in particular are loathe to talk about—our class values and how they define our rules of sexual propriety. The feminist sex wars have

not been routinely defined as class wars—and it's time that they
were.

What are middle-class values regarding sex? They are based
solely on this question: Am I doing the right thing? The right
thing is very important because of the middle-class investment in
a secure future, which depends on deferred gratification. If we
deny immediate gratification, and suppress spontaneous feeling,
the future may seem more promising, i.e., secure.

These values are not only perpetuated by the upper class but
are also the values everyone else is encouraged to adopt. That's
why a lot of people who don't have any money or social standing
whatsoever think this way.

Of course sex is often a matter of immediate passion, impulsive
actions. If it *feels* right, then it is right; this is the motto of the
body. Sexual fantasies are led by our unconscious, not by our su-
perego. Our erotic impulses don't follow a schedule, they don't
care what anybody thinks.

Since everyone has sexual feelings, the degree to which one
controls those feelings will often be reflected in one's economic or
cultural background. The expression "going native," or slumming,
is the juicy evidence of the Dr. Jekyll and Mr. Hyde dual life that
many middle- and upper-class people assume in order to handle
their sexual (and other) desires, which they believe are inappro-
priate to their milieu. Occasionally these people are exposed, and
it is truly grotesque to see the contrast between what they prac-
tice and what they preach. J. Edgar Hoover and Jimmy Swaggart
are some of our most recent outrageous examples. No one has yet
unearthed the pervert masquerading in a feminist anti-porn
crusader's clothing, but it's only a matter of time.

Women of every class are brought up to circumscribe their
sexuality on a different threshold than men. Some manage to suppress their sexual yearning to such a degree that they don't allow
themselves to fantasize, masturbate, or make love with another
person. Our society is so puritanical and materialistic that this
self-control is actually lauded. Women will brag about being celibate as a "choice," but not about being fertile or lusty.

In such a sexually repressive society, state power stays central-
ized at the top. It should not come as a surprise to anyone that

the most powerful religious and right-wing demagogues use "feminist" anti-porn rhetoric to defend their anti-erotic, sex-negative campaigns. The feminist status quo has defined itself by these same upper class values since its origins. There are endless historical examples of the women's movement excluding and alienating others who deviated from upper class, white, and heterosexual (or discreetly closeted) values.

Sojourner Truth electrified a nineteenth-century women's rights convention when she criticized the white suffragettes:

> I think dat 'twixt de Niggers of the South and de women
> of de North all a talkin' 'bout rights, de white men will
> be in a fix pretty soon. But what's all dis here talkin'
> about? Dat man over there say that women needs to
> be helped into carriages, and lifted over ditches, and to
> have the best place everywhere. Nobody ever helped *me*
> into carriages, or over mud puddles, or gives me any
> best places . . . and ar'nt I a woman? Look at me! Look
> at my arm! I have plow and planted and gathered into barns,
> and no man could head me—ar'nt I a woman? I could work
> as much as a man (when I could get it) and bear the
> lash as well—and ar'nt I a woman? I have borne 5 chil-
> dren and I seen 'em most all sold off into slavery, and when
> I cried out with a mother's grief, none but Jesus heard—and
> ar'nt I a woman?*

The more privileged, wealthy, and discreet elements of the women's movement have prevailed in public policy. The same is true of gay liberation: Angry Puerto Rican drag queens may have been the street fighters of the Stonewall rebellion, but they are not the ones advising the President on gay rights.

Erotic language is the language of the streets, the one-on-one revolution that happens every time one lover speaks plainly to another. Sexual fiction, especially, is often an autobiographic statement—it tells a private story, a story of the body, surrounded

*Robin Morgan, ed., *Sisterhood is Powerful: An Anthology of Writings from the Women's Liberation Movement* (New York: Random House, 1970).

by the most important aspects of the lover's life. The stories that
evoke the most controversy over political correctness are those
that raise fears of violence (sadomasochistic material like *The
Story of O,* for example) or stories that evoke an atmosphere that
is "sleazy," "tawdry," "coarse," or "animalistic." Henry Miller's
work was a perfect example of class-conscious censorship in his
time, and Erica Jong's in hers. The *Herotica* series has received
the same type of criticism. All those belittling adjectives are eu-
phemisms for saying that such stories are not in the upper-
middle-class comfort zone. While they may titillate many who
live there, those same people will do their best to keep these rev-
elations from public view.

In recent years, the comfort zone has been seriously shaken up
into an "Every Woman for Herself" zone. Feminists who pursue
erotic inquiry are not only lifting a veil, they are among the insti-
gators of a new wave which can only be described as the democ-
ratization of kinkiness.

I won't turn my back on sexual exploration even when I sense
darkness there. That's exactly what keeps me pushing. I am making a different kind of "investment" in the future, one with such
intimate riches that it cannot be deferred ultimately; one that we
cannot hold back, disguise, or deny.

Susie Bright
San Francisco, August 1993

Serena Moloch

My Date with Marcie

Queens, New York City

So get this. This guy David, David Josephs, who is in my AP Bio
and English classes, who I've sort of been seeing for a while, he
calls me up and says, "Oh, do you mind if we make tonight a double date?" "No, I don't mind," I tell him. "Who with?" "Keith
Welz and Marcie Loewenstein," he tells me. "Oh God," I say, because I *hate* Marcie Loewenstein too much to even begin to describe it in this paragraph, and I'm not too eager to fritter away
my swiftly passing youth in the company of Keith Welz either.
"Do we have to?" I moan. "Lighten up, Barbara," he says. "Don't
be so neurotic." "Oh fine," I say, "well, fine. So what time are you
picking me up?" So here I am, about to go out on a double date
with Marcie Loewenstein, which is absolutely positively totally
unbelievable.

Let me explain, even though I can't, because it is just beyond
belief. How can I begin to tell you how much I despise, detest,
loathe, *excoriate* Marcie Loewenstein? (My SAT teacher made
me learn all those words. I hate my SAT teacher, but not as
much as I hate Marcie Loewenstein.) Marcie Loewenstein is a
muskrat. She has bleached blond hair and wears a ton of
makeup and spends all her time in classes freshening up her
lipstick; she has a big fat mouth that takes up most of her face.
The only part of her I can tolerate looking at is the part of her

hair where the roots show all black. They contrast so well with her nasty pale skin. She's short and not that developed, really, but she wears extremely tight clothes—you can count the change in her pockets. And it's pretty obvious to anyone who looks that nothing comes between her and her Calvins. *Or* her Jou-jous *or* her Sassoons.

Marcie does not mix with the likes of me and I do not mix with the likes of Marcie Loewenstein. We are the Cold War of our high school. I'm considered a brain. This offends me, but I'm not going to start failing classes so that people will realize I have a body just like everyone else. Marcie Loewenstein is willing and eager to play dumb to make boys like her. And they do. But behind her back they call her a slut. I call her one of the Purple People—purple eyeshadow, purple suede fringe boots, purple Cacharel jeans, purple underwear if she ever bothers to put any on, which as I've mentioned I'm pretty sure she doesn't. I think we would have noticed a panty line by now.

Marcie smokes in the bathroom, where she shows off her inhaling skills and blows smoke rings in everyone's face. Mainly mine. Which is what she did the time she cornered me in the girl's bathroom and started up with me. I mean maybe a little bit of it was my fault. I was smoking with some friends (other nerds like me, we get the urge to be bad sometimes too, just like the Purple People; a woman has needs) and we lit some toilet paper on fire by mistake, but we were putting it out, and laughing and screaming, and Marcie Loewenstein and her purple cronies came barging into the stall where we were, like they were the fucking security guards or something, yelling "Okay, who's starting a fire?" And Marcie Loewenstein came up to me really close and stuck her face in mine so that I could see her beige foundation and the layer of blush caked up on top of it and I could smell her second-hand smoke and the grape bubble gum she chews incessantly and the Love's Baby Soft she slathers all over herself. She snarled, "You're trying to get us in trouble, aren't you? You know they'll just blame us if anything happens here." I mean, she had a point, not that she gave me a chance to apologize or clean up the mess or anything like that.

Also, she completely ignored my two friends who were doing their best to fade into the toilet bowl.

So then she goes, "You want to smoke, huh? Well, if you want to smoke, let's see you smoke." She took out a cigarette and lit it, and then drew in this huge breath and sucked smoke down for at least five minutes. Much as I despised her, I was impressed. Then she exhaled through her nostrils, just like Bette Davis (not that she would know who Bette Davis is) and said, "Okay babe. You wanted to smoke. Go ahead. Smoke." She handed me a Marlboro and I was at this point pretty scared and the way out of the stall was blocked by Marcie's purple sweater and purple pants and all I could do was try to stare down her purple-rimmed green eyes— snake eyes—while I lit the cigarette with my hands shaking. And of course I lit it at the wrong end which just amused everyone *immensely*, including my supposed friends, and when I finally did light it properly of course I couldn't inhale without choking and she made an utter fool out of me, which you think would have satisfied her. But no, next thing I know it's a week later and she's starting up with me in the hallway. "You stepped on my foot. Don't you say excuse me? You're so rude." That whole routine. And I hadn't stepped on her foot; I don't know why she's so obsessed with me. The whole thing ended up with me talking into the air going, "She's having delusions, she's insane, she's mentally impaired," and with her hissing at me, "You are so rude," until finally a teacher stepped in.

So then she has to tell me she's going to get me after school. These people are obsessed with "after school"; it's like it's their special imaginary friend, Mr. After School. So there she was, true to her word, after school, following me down the street and sort of poking at me with a whole crew of spectators trailing behind her.

I'm not very good at fighting so I just ignored her until she started announcing, "I'm going to slap her face." So I turned around and said, "Marcie, give it up. I didn't do anything to you. Why are you bugging me? I'm flattered that I'm so important to you, but you mean *nothing* to me. Why don't you just ignore me?" Not very effective really, but I was trying the gentle art of verbal self-defense.

So she goes, "I don't want to leave you alone. I want to bother you."

So I say, "Well, I'm too busy to be bothered by you. You bore me."

I started to walk away but she grabbed my arm. I happen to have very strong arms, even if I can't do the number of push-ups required to pass the Presidential Fitness test (but then I bet the President can't do them either), so I shook her off really hard and kind of twisted her hand in the process. She changed her tune then. "I know boys who wouldn't mind beating a girl up for me, you know."

For some reason I found this statement really pathetic, so I just snorted and said, "That's great. I'm really happy for you, Marcie. Tell them to call me so we can make an appointment for them to beat me up," and walked off and that was the end of that and we haven't spoken since, except that when people make fun of her in class I laugh really hard and when people make fun of me in class she laughs even harder. This is why I hate Marcie Loewenstein. This is the girl I am going on a double date with tonight. I can barely contain my joy.

Well, this is even more unbelievable, I mean even more unbelievable than the concept of my going on a double date with Marcie Loewenstein was what actually happened on this double date. I mean, you're not going to believe it, and the only reason I believe it is because never in this world could I have imagined it. I mean, it didn't start out unbelievable, it started out like a perfectly normal horrible double date with Marcie Loewenstein. Marcie was dressed, or should I say undressed to the nines, in royal purple of course: purple halter top, purple short shorts, and purple Candies which made her about two feet taller than me. You could totally see her nipples through this top. I felt pretty boring in my jeans and chenille top; I knew I'd look good in the clothes Marcie had on, but my mother wouldn't have let me out of the house in them.

I sat in the front of the car with David, and Marcie sat in the back of the car with Keith, and I didn't say a word and neither did Marcie, though her wad of gum was speaking volumes: *snap*,

snap, snap about every ten seconds. I looked at her in the rear view mirror and got some genuine insight into her eye-makeup technique but absolutely none into how to start a conversation. The boys were wrapped up in talk about sports teams I had never heard of so Marcie seemed like my only option, but she wasn't biting.

Somehow we ended up at a Chinese restaurant. Marcie was still refusing to communicate with me directly. "I wouldn't mind Indian food," I said to David, who said to Keith, "How do you guys feel about Indian?" So Keith goes, "Yeah, I don't know, you like Indian, Marcie?" "No, I hate that shit," said Marcie. Back reports to front: "Marcie doesn't want to eat Indian." Front confers. "How about Italian?" You can see how it all took some time.

They don't card at this restaurant so we all had drinks, the kind with pink plastic ferns in them and names like Zombie and Killer and Sloe Comfortable Screw. I'm not allowed to drink—who is—but my parents are always asleep by the time I get home. I was well into my third Sloe Comfortable Screw and feeling pretty sorry for myself for being on this miserable double date when Marcie said to me, "Come with me to the bathroom."

"What?" I said. I would have liked to have a snappy reply but I was too soaked in self-pity to be anything but shocked that she'd spoken to me.

"I hate going to the bathroom alone. Come with me."

I trailed behind her purple butt like a puppy, following her into the bathroom. It was all ornate with a dressing room when you first come in, and the stalls and sinks in a separate room. We stood in the dressing room and I felt my head spinning.

"What are you afraid of the bathroom for?"

"I just hate going alone. Just wait out here, okay?"

"Yeah." When she went in to pee, I looked in the mirror. It was smoky gray and had light bulbs all around it. I looked at my face in gloom. I kind of got lost in contemplation and took out my hairbrush and started to work on my hair when all of a sudden Marcie was saying, "Can I use your hairbrush?"

My English teacher always says everyone has several hygienic principles that they break constantly and one or two to which they are excruciatingly attached. I sit on toilet seats without covering them with toilet paper, I don't wash my hands after I go to the bathroom, I even share tissues—but no one touches my hairbrush.

So I said to Marcie, "Sorry, I never lend my brush out."

"I guess I'm not good enough for you," she snapped. "You think I'm dirty, right?"

She seemed genuinely insulted, which surprised me, but all I said was, "No, I just never lend it out." I started to walk to the door, but she grabbed my arm from behind.

"Why are you so snooty to me? You think you're better than me?"

"No, Marcie, I don't," I said wearily.

"Yeah? Well, then prove it."

"What do you want me to do? Lick your feet?"

"Maybe," she said, moving closer to me. "Maybe I want you to suck my face. Come on. Kiss me. Kiss me right here on the mouth." She moved even closer. "Come on, you let David do it. Don't you think I'm good enough for you?"

"That's sick," I said, "I'm getting out of here." And I ran back to our table where my fourth drink was waiting for me. I dove right into it. She followed and sat down like nothing had happened, but we kept sneaking looks at each other, staring when we didn't think the other was looking. I felt edgy about what was going to happen when we got back in the car and started making out, which is always how these double dates end. I didn't want her to watch David kiss me.

But we didn't end up in a car. We ended up in a motel near the expressway because David had his father's credit card, and I guess his father's permission to use it to take girls to motels and try to fuck them. You know how fathers are with their sons—go ahead, son, enjoy yourself, wink wink, you take after your old man. It had been a while since I'd had sex—the last time was four months ago, right before I broke up with Jed—so I figured, what the hell, I'll live it up tonight. I didn't have to be home until two.

We found ourselves in a tiny room in the Kew Motor Lodge, Marcie and Keith on one of the beds and David and I on the other. I was still pretty drunk and I was really enjoying what David was doing to me. Okay, this is what he was doing (I feel like such a pervert for writing this down): He had my pants off and my top pushed up to my neck and he was rubbing his chest, which has lots of really nice hair, against my breasts and grinding his . . . his I don't know what, his *loins* into me; it felt good and I kind of moaned.

Most of the time my eyes were closed but when I opened them I couldn't help but see Keith and Marcie. They were a lot further along than we were; she had all her clothes off and so did he; she was lying on top of him with her legs apart and her head thrown back, and she was sticking her fingers in his mouth and watching him suck on them. Once in a while she took her fingers out of his mouth and played with her breasts, circling around her nipples, getting them really big and red. It all looked very bold and I got even more excited looking at her, but I was afraid to be caught staring, especially after our scene in the bathroom. So I concentrated on David again, who'd started stroking my thighs, moving his hands up and down and kind of pushing my legs apart as he did it. I felt my underwear get hot and wet from me, and I reached down to his crotch and rubbed my hand over his penis, which felt all fat and hard and was leaking, I bet, just a little bit at the tip. They explained that to us in health class—the pre-ejaculate. That's why I kept my underwear on, because of the pre-ejaculate. He slipped a finger into my underwear and rubbed it around in my wet, then he got a thumb in and started stroking my clit. It felt really good. I got my hand into his shorts and wrapped it around his penis, which I started jerking off, real slow—I've done that a lot and I think I'm getting good at it. My last boyfriend said I had nimble fingers.

I looked over again at the other bed where Marcie was still on her stomach on top of Keith, but reversed this time, so that her head was between his legs. I could see her shiny pale butt moving up and down, like she was humping him, and then she started rooting around in Keith's crotch with her mouth. She'd pulled out his penis and was licking it up and down, and then sucking just the first inch or so in and out of her mouth while her hands bunched up around the bottom of his thing to hold it steady.

When her mouth got free for a second she'd go "Umm, good" in a really sexy voice. Keith was writhing around but Marcie kept pushing his hips down. I threw my legs around David and twisted around his fingers, almost forgetting to jerk him off I felt so close to coming. I made little noises in my throat even though I really wanted to scream. I had my spare hand around David's neck holding him tight against me, and from what I could hear Keith was about to come all over Marcie too. David had three fingers up me and was working them in and out hard and slow, his other hand was under my butt, squeezing my cheeks, when all of a sudden Marcie pulled away from Keith, flicked on a light, sat up, tossed her hair and said, "Let's watch porn flicks."

Keith groaned and tried to pull her back on him but she swatted his hand away; David and I had both broken stride and had taken our hands off each other. I pulled my shirt down and hiked my underpants firmly back up. "Come on, Marcie," Keith said, pointing to his penis, "come back here and finish what you started." He's always been kind of a pig, ever since elementary school.

"Oh, I will," she said, "but first I want to watch some porn movies. Come on. They're really cheap, and there's a big selection. What do you want? 'Wet Nurses'? 'Pretty Pink Pussies'? 'Hot Rods'? 'Lesbo Lust'? Or 'Tittie City'?" She looked straight at me. "Come on, what's your vote?" I looked down at my fingernails. It's one thing to all be in a room naked when the lights are down and you're just paying attention to the person you're with. Of course the turn-on is knowing the other couple is there, but no one really cops to that. It was different to have Marcie staring at me when all I had on was a shirt and soaking wet panties, and she was totally naked with the biggest nipples I had ever seen staring me right in the face. I noticed that her pubic hair was a lot darker than the hair on her head. I remembered how she'd looked when she wanted to suck my face, but I couldn't tell if she'd already forgotten about that.

Keith and David answered before I had a chance to, and their vote was unanimous: "Lesbo Lust." I didn't feel like exercising veto power, so we switched the TV on to cable and got the channel. We all crowded onto the bed right opposite the TV and watched.

"Lesbo Lust" was a real revelation. In it these three women were making a porn movie but the man who was supposed to be in it was late, so one of them started playing the man. She was a petite blonde and she put on this cute deep voice and started telling the others, "Come over here and fuck me, babe," which they did. One of them had a huge silver vibrator which she slid in and out of the other and they were all licking each other's breasts and going down on each other and moaning and whispering a lot too, a constant stream of whispers: "Suck my cunt," "Come on, lick my hole," "That's right, yes, yes, fuck me." I think it was the whispering that got to me; I felt it all under my skin and in my ears and I got so excited. I had never been so excited before in my life without being touched at all. The same went for everyone else in the room and pretty soon David and Keith developed the bright idea of having Marcie and me put on some kind of show. "Come on," David said, prodding my butt with his hand, "you two show us. Do what they're doing in the movie."

"No," I said.

"Be nice," Keith said. "Do it for us to be nice. You're never nice. Don't you want to do it, Marcie?"

"Yeah," David said, "you want to do it, don't you, Marcie? Marcie will do anything," he laughed. "I heard about Marcie in the back of that car with Steve and Alan and Paul."

What a mistake. Marcie's face got really mean and really smart. I thought she was almost baring her teeth, she looked so ferocious. "Oh yeah," she said, "really? I'll do anything, huh? You guys think you're so smart, maybe you should put on a little entertainment for me." She leaned over the edge of the bed, grabbed a belt, lashed David's hands behind him and looped the belt around the bed frame before he could do anything about it in his drunken state. Hey, I thought, hands off, that's my date; but I kept quiet.

"What are you going to do to me?" he chortled. "Make me lick your pussy or something? Yeah," he snorted, "that would be a big punishment. P-U," he sneered, "you smell."

It was getting ugly now. I mentally berated myself for not having brought enough money to take a cab home.

"No," she said, "you're going to put on a show. You and Keith. 'Hot, Homo and Horny.' You're going to sit there while he sucks your cock. Because there's nowhere for you to go, is there?" She flicked her nails at his penis and he inched away as far as he could, but she'd immobilized him pretty well. She turned to Keith. "Well," she said, "let the show begin."

"Very funny, Marcie."

"I'm not kidding," she said. "Get on with it. Do you need instructions? You were pretty sure about what I should do. Just do unto others, asshole. Love thy neighbor. You'll be fine."

"We're not going to do this," he said.

"Yeah," David echoed. "We're not going to do this. Get me out of this thing, man."

"You wanted us to," I said. "Why shouldn't you?" Marcie looked surprised but nodded in appreciation. I was beginning to think we girls had to stick together. And I was curious to see what they would do.

"Yeah," Marcie said, and threw in the refrain from her theme song for the evening, "aren't we good enough for you?"

"We won't do it," said Keith.

"Yeah," David said, "we won't do it."

"Okay," Marcie announced, "fine. But if you don't do it, I'll spread it all over school that you did do it. I'll tell everyone that you're a pair of faggots, and you'll be lucky if you make it out of homeroom alive. And just think," she said, "what would your parents say?"

It was a pretty weak threat, if you ask me, and maybe they secretly really wanted to do it, because they didn't call her bluff. So the next thing we knew, they were both swigging tequila to get their courage up—Keith had to hold the bottle for David because David was still tied up—and then Keith was down on his knees, his hands pulling David towards him, then holding David's penis while he kind of tentatively cupped his mouth around it. David jerked wildly when Keith touched him.

"Come on," Marcie said, "use your tongue, lick him, take it in your mouth and suck it, really get in there."

Keith was turning red but he dipped his head down and David's penis disappeared all the way into his mouth, and he sucked on it hard, moving his mouth up and down over it. Then his hands slid down to David's balls and stroked those—pretty inventive, I thought. David strained at his bonds and thrust his hips up so that he could push his penis further and further in. Eventually they worked out a rhythm where David pushed up and Keith drove down, then David pulled back while Keith sucked up. David strained and twisted when Keith's hands roamed and grabbed David's ass and then Keith's head was deep in David's crotch and he was pulling David's ass toward him. From the side, I could see David's penis bulging in Keith's mouth as he sucked furiously. In the meantime, Marcie got behind Keith and started jerking him off while he sucked, and in two seconds David came all in Keith's mouth and Keith spat it out all over David's legs and then Keith came all over Marcie's hands and the pink patterned carpet. But as far as I could tell, Marcie hadn't come, and neither had I, though I was very, very close. I was almost tempted to take advantage of David by sitting on his face and making him eat me, but what with the tequila and all, he and Keith basically passed out seconds after coming.

Which left Marcie with come all over her hands and me on the bed squeezing my thighs together under a sheet, wishing she'd go away so I could masturbate fast and then just go home. Not knowing what else to say—it was definitely an awkward situation—I decided to be helpful.

"You should be careful about that sperm," I told her. "You can get pregnant, you know, even without having intercourse."

She stared at me in disbelief. "You are such a nerd, I can't take it," she said. She came over to me and yanked my sheet off and started wiping her hands all over me. I tried to struggle away from her and all of a sudden we were wrestling and she pinned me down fast and rubbed her hands on my stomach. "It dies within three minutes," she informed me.

"I didn't know that," I said politely, always happy to add a new fact to my arsenal of contraceptive information. She kept rubbing my stomach, in almost a sexy way. Part of me felt good. Part of me wanted to start talking about the weather so we could get back to normal again.

"You're such a nerd that you're kind of cute," she said, grinning. "Maybe we *should* put on a show together. Look—we can see ourselves in the mirror." She pointed at the huge mirror over the dresser. "But you could see us better if you took off your top." She was like a hypnotist, talking slowly in a husky voice, moving her hands up me very steadily, taking my top off, pressing her cheek against mine to turn my head towards the mirror. I couldn't look. I slipped my face away and said, "No way, Marcie, no mirrors." She looked pissed and moved her hands away; they'd felt good and she'd felt good and it almost felt like we were getting to be friends so I said,

"Anything else, but no mirrors. They freak me out."

"Anything? You wouldn't have the guts."

I may be a nerd but I can't resist a dare.

"Is that a dare?"

"It isn't even a dare. It's a half-dare, a quarter-dare, a—"

"—mere infinitesimal fraction of a dare!" we both yelled at the same time. We were in the same math class and our teacher was always using that expression.

"No, look, dare me," I said. "I'll even bet you."

"What?" she laughed. "The savings from your piggy bank? Okay, I dare you. I dare you to lie on top of me and put your tits on top of mine."

Tits, I thought to myself; she sounds like the women in the movie. I pushed her onto her back and got up on top of her and carefully laid my breasts on top of hers. Mine were bigger. I held my face up away from hers.

"Not like that," she snorted. "Act sexy. Like this."

And she arched her back and started rubbing her nipples against mine. I could feel them hot and crazy and a huge flush started going all over my body. She grabbed my face and started kissing me, and before you could say Roseanne Roseanna Danna our tongues were all over each other. Her body was amazingly hot everywhere, even her tongue felt hot and my mouth went all warm sucking on it. She circled my ear with one finger and her other hand stroked my hair.

"You feel good," she whispered to me. "Bite me."

"Bite you?" I whispered back.

"Yeah, give me a hickey."

I pressed my teeth against her neck and started sucking. She was so soft, I'd never felt anyone like her before. So much soft hot skin and her hand grabbed the back of my neck as I nipped her. She put one of her legs between mine and we started rocking and rubbing against each other. I could feel her wetness against my thigh and all of a sudden I really wanted to put my fingers inside her; I'd never thought of doing that with another girl, ever. I started moving my hand down. We moaned as loud as we wanted because there wasn't anyone awake to hear. But she pushed me up so we were sitting, her back to me, and now we were in the mirror. There she was, all blonde, with her raspberry nipples jutting forward, and she grabbed my hands and put them on her breasts. I didn't exactly know what to do, but I remembered her circling around her own nipples before, so I did that. "Harder, harder," she moaned, and so I pinched them more and more and watched her face in the mirror, all ecstatic. I stopped for a second to give her a break—her nipples were so hard I was afraid they were going to explode.

"You're so pretty," I told her. "I'm excited."

"I know," she said. "I'm going to go down on you. Just touch me a little more first."

"I'd like that," I said, my index fingers teasing her nipples. "But I want to go down on you too."

"Okay, let's sixty-nine."

"What's that?"

"God, I can't believe I know something you don't. Sixty-nine is when two people go down on each other at the same time. The numbers look like what you're doing because the nine is like, flipped over, sucking the six."

"Well, don't be so conceited about it."

"I'll be even more excited after I make you come all in my mouth." We were grinning. From enemies to X-rated Bogart and Bacall all in one night.

"You or me on top?"

"Whatever—it doesn't matter."

"Here goes," I said. I pushed her down, put a pillow under her to support her neck, and turned myself around on top of her. I started kissing her thighs, she opened her legs and I saw her vagina. I don't look at mine very much, so the sight was kind of unfamiliar, but I started getting acquainted real fast, working my way down to kiss her there. I wanted to taste her. She was pulling me down over her, and with no work-up at all I felt her tongue flick against my clitoris—just that little touch was more incredible than anything I'd ever felt before. I hoped my legs wouldn't start shaking uncontrollably. She smelled really musky and good and I started licking her, hoping I was in the right place, trying to concentrate on her while she was driving me crazy on her end. I loved how her hairs felt, all swirly and wiry. I put one finger, then two inside her, she was real soft and tight inside, pulling on my fingers, moving up and down them while I clamped my mouth to her clitoris and sucked and licked it. I was pushing myself all over her face, and things got wilder and wilder, and then she came—I actually made her come and I could feel it all around my fingers. I took my mouth away and I just stayed over her on all fours. My arms were tired but I stayed like that while she kept licking me and fucking me with her fingers and then I came too, and then we both collapsed on each other, holding each other and trying to get our breath back.

Things got a little awkward then, the way they always do after you've had sex with someone for the first time, even when it's normal sex. (Maybe especially when it's normal sex, boys can be so weird.) We got dressed and stuff but we didn't act really romantic. I mean, we both date guys. I don't know.

We concentrated on unbuckling David and trying to dress him and Keith. I kind of wanted to ask her if she thought they'd remember what happened, but I wasn't sure we wanted to remember what we'd just done, so I didn't bring it up. We shared a cab home; it turns out she doesn't live that far from me and she'd been smart enough to bring some money with her—but of course we couldn't talk about anything in the cab.

So I don't know what's going to happen, but today is Sunday and I thought maybe I'd give her a call and we could go shopping or to the movies, but what if she's really obnoxious to me on the phone?

If this were a book report I'd have to state the main idea. Maybe I'd say the main idea is to stay away from double dates; they seem innocent but they can really get out of hand, like a journey where you've lost the map and forgotten your destination. My English teacher would like that. She's really into analogies.

Lenora Clare

The Boy on the Bike

The black straps of her garter snapped against the back of her thighs in a slight off-rhythm with her stride. She was angry—the set of her jaw and the pace of her walk made that clear. The man beside her kept talking. A bead of sweat rolled down her back and the lace of her panties rubbed against her.

"You know it's the best thing for the firm." The man was wearing a gray suit, nearly identical in fabric to hers. They were continuing the argument they'd had at lunch. The Florida sun hit the metal of his wire-rimmed glasses as he turned to her, still speaking. "We've got the votes. It's just a matter of whether you're with us or not."

"You don't have the votes. If you did, you wouldn't have taken me to an early lunch and been your most persuasive, charming self." Looking at him now she had the uncanny feeling that he was her male clone. Same age, same glasses, malcontents, lawyers, new partners in the same firm. Until now, the same goals and philosophies. Same hometown. That still meant something to both of them.

"Depends on whether it's straight majority or voting shares of partnership stock," he said.

"Either way. I did the math, okay? I know you've got to have my vote and my stock to win this battle."

At a basic level, she knew his way was the best for the firm. But she also knew his motive was his own ambition, and that made her stubborn, unwilling to give in. Pausing to stare at Hank, she caught a quick reflection in the glass window behind him and turned suddenly back to the street.

The boy on the bike was pedaling by. She saw him almost every morning on her way to work as she drove her expensive, gold, Japanese sedan down the causeway. She would see him riding his bike: shirtless, cut-off jeans, heavy construction boots, with a tool belt and box tied to the back of the bike. Every time she saw him she watched until he was out of sight. A teenager, he was tan and muscular in the way slightly built young men could be despite their thinness. "God," she thought, "I'm lusting after a boy I could have given birth to."

When Hank laughed, she realized he had followed her stare. "So, Janis, that's what you like. Young construction workers. All this time I've been wasting my efforts." His quick perceptiveness made her uneasy.

"You've never made any effort," she snapped at him. He was married to a thin, beautiful woman, probably not much older than the boy on the bike. "Don't give me grief when you've got the same thing waiting for you at home."

The boy was gone. She glanced back at Hank, and, looking past him into the glass storefront, saw her reflection. Dress-for-success suit, silk blouse, pageboy hair with a touch of gray, strong jaw: a face still handsome but showing its age, showing the first pattern of lines and slackness to come. It scared her sometimes to see how serious, how tough she could look.

She was not the sort of woman the boy on the bike would ever want, and knowing this felt like a physical blow to her stomach.

"If you want my vote, earn it. Make me feel like I'm eighteen, beautiful and desirable. Make me feel like that boy could make me feel."

Hank, she saw, was plainly startled, and he laughed nervously. "Janis, you *are* beautiful and desirable."

"Then make me feel it, by God, make me feel it."

* * *

They walked back to the office without speaking; intense, fast paced. Once inside, they found the office was nearly deserted. Hank had deliberately taken her to lunch well before the regular noon hour, so they could sit without interruption or worry about who was at the next table eavesdropping. Her secretary was gone from her desk.

Janis went resolutely into her office, Hank trailing. When Janis turned briefly toward him, she thought he looked unsure. He shut the door and stood looking at her.

"Don't look so scared, it's not flattering," she said. Without waiting for a response, she went behind her desk, pulled out a small purse, cupped something in her hand and returned to the front of her desk. Hank had not moved from his perch by the door. "Lock it," she said. He did.

She took off her jacket and threw it on the couch with an un-characteristic lack of concern. Janis unbuttoned her blouse and left it draped open, revealing a lacy camisole with pearl buttons that strained just a bit across the top of her bra. Leaning back-wards until the desk supported her at her hips, she opened her arms to him.

The kiss startled them both. Janis pulled back with a gasp, as if she had been shocked by a small electric current.

"Take off your shirt and tie," she commanded, "and hurry." As Hank obeyed, she slipped off the blouse, unhooked the bra, and pulled it off from under the camisole, which she left on.

Under the sheer material of the camisole, she finally exposed her breasts to him. All the years he had sat next to her at meetings just to peek down her blouse, he had never caught a glimpse of anything more than a lace border. She was not the sort of woman to let cleavage show at the office. Now, as she let him, he looked at her breasts, perfect, round, firm, neither too large nor too small. She wondered why she had never used such an as-set before. Hank's obvious admiration made her appreciate her own breasts, the perky way they stood up to his touch, the almost adolescent pinkness of the tips. Just a peek now and then, a care-less bend over a file with a round-necked dress, and she could have won over the men in the firm a lot sooner, she thought.

"Don't just look," she said. Hank, as if waiting for permission, dove into her, licking her breasts through the silky camisole, tasting the faint salt and smelling the clean scent of perfumed soap still clinging to her skin. He sucked each nipple in turn. The lacy fabric that covered them became wet from his tongue; it became only the thinnest damp touch of silk against her breasts. When he pulled his tongue away, the silk still clung to her, mimicking the sensation of his mouth on her skin.

While his lips were on one breast, his hands were on the other. He reached under the silk to touch the bare skin of her pink nipple. Pinching too hard, he made her gasp and pull back suddenly. He backed up and looked at her, at the red imprint he had made on her skin. While he stood back, Janis slipped out of her skirt and stood facing him in only the camisole, her lace panties, her black garter and stockings. She didn't flinch at his study of her body, his obvious appraisal.

"My God, you really are still beautiful," Hank said. Janis knew she had a certain appealing roundness, a softness that would seem very womanly to Hank, although he bragged about liking skinny women. When Hank moved toward her lushness, Janis knew he had momentarily forgotten the taut, weight-lifting body of his wife.

Janis pushed his head down to her panties. "Take them off with your mouth," she said. Hank caught the top edge of the panties in his teeth and pulled them down. He could only get them as far as the hooks on the garter straps that held her stockings. When he reached up with his hands to unhook the garters, she pushed his hands away. "Use your mouth, your teeth," she said.

After a brief struggle, he managed to unhook the garters using his tongue and teeth. This freed him to pull her panties down to her ankles so she could step out of them. The stockings, still clinging to her slightly damp skin, stayed in place with the garter belt cinching her waist.

Hank was hard. Janis laughed, tauntingly, as he struggled out of his gray woollen pants as if he were about to explode. He rose from Janis just long enough to undress. When he approached her again, she held a condom she'd gotten from the purse in her desk. Without speaking, she tore open the package with her teeth and pulled it out with her mouth.

Cupping his buttocks with her hands, using only her mouth and her tongue, she put the condom on the tip of Hank's penis. With the soft, wet skin of her lips, she slowly began to unroll the condom down the length of Hank's erection. Halfway on, she stopped and used her tongue to tickle the uncovered part, to dart and tease and forage into his hair and about his balls. Then she sucked and pulled on the covered part. All the while her hands were moving, probing, touching, exposing.

Slowly, she began again to roll the condom on the rest of the way, backing up now and then to tease and suck upon the tip of him. When she finally had the condom all the way on, Hank was flushed and breathing hard. For a moment she had the full length of him in her mouth; she gave him a smooth, tight suck at the back of her throat before he pulled out.

He pushed her against the desk and entered her, pushing too hard and too fast. Janis had intended to make him explore her, taste her, make her come first with his tongue, but when she took him deep into her mouth, she had felt his urgency. She'd have him make it up to her later if she required it, she thought, as he pushed deeper into her.

Like the sudden disconcerting kiss, this too caught them off guard with a power they had not expected. Janis was moaning without control, without regard for the possibility other people might be returning from lunch. She realized vaguely, somewhere in the back of her mind, that someone might hear them. For once, she did not care.

Janis lifted her feet off the floor and wrapped her legs around Hank's back. She was balanced on her buttocks on top of the desk, with Hank holding her waist. The stronger and more urgent his pushing, the further back on the desk she was forced. Finally, with a grace that amazed her in later reflection, Hank used a chair for a boost up and, without ever uncoupling, was up on the desk, his knees on the hard rosewood, scattering loose papers.

Janis felt the imprint of a small dictation tape in her back. Under Hank's pressure, she heard the plastic covering crack under the movement. It was a small pain, vaguely recognized. Nothing was going to break them apart now.

She moved her stocking-covered feet up and down his legs.

Under his hands, the skin on her hips, stomach and buttocks felt like silk. As Hank stroked her bottom she was seized with a new idea. Pushing him out of her with an odd roughness, to his protest, she shoved him off the desk and jumped off too. She turned her back to him and bent at the waist over the desk, the black line of her garter belt over the pale cream of her ass, her thighs, faced up at him. Bent as she was, her buttocks were thrust out toward him like an invitation.

"Do it," she said.

He pulled open her buttocks, and using a finger, then two, explored the narrower entrance. With the fingers still in, still moving in rhythm to Janis's movement, he entered the now familiar, wet entrance he had just left. Within minutes, Janis came with a definite convulsion of inner muscles she knew he could feel both with his fingers and his penis. Her coming was the permission he needed; he came in her with a quick, sure violence that left him panting. Her legs were quivering.

On the way home that night, Janis saw the boy on the bike along the side of the road. He was dirty. A red handkerchief was rolled and tied around his head to keep sweat and his hair out of his eyes. There was a flush of sun on his face and shoulders. She slowed the car as she drove next to him. The wetness between her legs returned. Keeping her car slow enough to pace herself with his pedaling, Janis studied his young face. If he noticed, he gave no indication.

Janis thought of Hank and their noontime scene at the office. All the irritation and anger had left her when he took her on the desk. Firm politics didn't matter. This boy didn't matter. Suddenly she laughed. Youth wasn't everything. She hit the gas pedal and drove off, still laughing at Hank and the fun they'd had. A bargain is a bargain, she thought. Tomorrow she'd give him her proxy, and he could vote it anyway he wanted to. But tomorrow and for days, months afterward, he would pay her back, reward her. That was his promise, her desire, when he had left her office that day.

Pat Williams

Tennessee

I loved Rohn because she was neither a woman nor a man.

She wasn't black, but she wasn't white either. She wasn't crazy, and she was not sane. She was pretty and she liked to fuck. I was fifteen and that was ideal.

I first met Rohn in the summer down South. The weather was hot and the air was close and heavy with dry grass and small dead rotting animals. Snakes slid out of their skins.

Before I met her I had seen her up at Bell Eagle Esso, the little grocery and filling station that our landlord owned. Sometimes she was with her mother, a thin, pale woman who wore big hats to keep the sun off her face, and who, whenever she spoke, mumbled. I did hear her speak once, and she sounded funny. My grandfather said that she was a foreigner. She usually had Rohn by the arm. Or Rohn was with her older brother, the one most like the mother. People always looked at them funny.

The day I met her, she was astride a big roan mare.

She had a black cowboy hat on, pulled low so that it shadowed her eyes. Her thick red hair fell down onto her shoulders.

We were in the middle of a pasture. Over by a pond some cows

Previously published in *On Our Backs*. Reprinted with permission of the author.

stood still as if they'd been painted there. I was walking home
from a neighbor's house, where I'd gone after school.

I kind of stepped backwards because the horse was so big.

She grinned, flashing her dark face under the hat's shadow.

"How you t'day?" Her drawl was soft and gentle. It wasn't
high-pitched and evil like a peckerwood's, so it didn't scare me.
I said, "I'm all right."

She pushed her hat back and I saw that her eyes were green
in gray. Her brows arched with the grace of a bow. I think my
heart did something.

"You wanna ride home?" She told me later I had a kind of half
smile on my lips to make her wonder.

I climbed up and she pulled me the rest of the way onto the
horse. From up there I could see the tin roof of my folks' house.
Smoke was coming from the chimney, going straight up. Grandma
was starting supper.

I wedged into the saddle between her thighs. Her arms encircled me and she rested her hand holding the bridle on the horn
between my legs. Her breasts were small and firm and pressed
against my back. I was too shy to move.

She asked me what grade I was in, and did I like going to
school in town, and she bet I didn't like arithmetic. I thought, at
the time, that she was a senior in high school or maybe already
in college. We rocked in time to the horse's movements. I felt her
arms tightening about me and the horse walking slower.

"You got a boyfriend?" she asked me, and I said no.

"You want to go for a ride?" she asked, and I said yes.

I knew I would get scolded, but I could no more have refused
than turn down strawberries and ice cream. We turned away from
the sight of my house. The cows came back into view. A big or-
ange and black butterfly hung in the air. The sky was clear.

"Hold on," she said. When the horse sailed over the fence, I
thought my heart would shoot out of my mouth. My terror evap-
orated in her laughter, and then her low chuckle brought another
feeling altogether. She was holding me so tight still.

Rohn loosened the rein some more. She put her face down next
to my cheek. I heard her breathing and felt her long fingers moving on my body, as if they were gently searching for something

just under my clothes. I stopped breathing for a minute. She smelled of Ivory soap and the heat of the day. Once, her hat brim brushed my face; it felt soft as cotton.

"Can I touch your breast?" she whispered.

I managed to say yes.

With just two fingers and a thumb she rubbed softly in circles. Around and around through my blouse, from the fullness of my breast to its tip. She did it softly and once she squeezed the nipple a little. Her hand held the reins on my bare thigh where my skirt had come up.

She put her whole hand over my breast and kneaded it. I noticed the wetness between my legs. I tried to open them wider and they pressed against her. She kissed my cheek. The dampness her lips left there cooled in the air.

She kept squeezing and playing with my tit, and I think I moaned or gasped or something because she kissed me again. I turned my face toward her. She took off her hat and gave it to me to hold.

She unbuttoned one button of my blouse and slipped her hand inside. It was warm, dry and smooth. Her hair fell against my face, and it felt like the silk scarf my aunt had sent my grandma from New York.

She held my tit hard and then she pinched the nipple a little. The small pain heated my whole front. Her mouth was on mine and I thought I would die. It was warm and wet and I thought I would starve before I moved away. I opened my mouth and she pushed her tongue in. She licked the inside of my mouth, inside my jaws, the roof of my mouth. I took her tongue and sucked it.

Her hand, pressing my breast, pinched the nipple more, and each burst of pain filled me enough to almost lift me. And she was kissing me harder and spit was all down on my chin.

She pulled away suddenly, breathing hard, and I came awake. Her gray-green eyes were soft and heavy, but they started to clear until they had the depth and transparency of a cat's eyes. I tried to smile, but she had looked away. One of the cows lowed, a long, deep chest sound. I heard birds which had been there all along. She took her hat and put it back on, pushed up this time.

"I'ma take you home. All right?"

I didn't say anything. It was hot. My blouse was damp from sweat and there was moisture on the back of my hands. If I tasted them, they would be salty. Rohn read my mind, the first of many times. "It's all right," she said, "you didn't do anything wrong." She kind of smiled as if there were something on her mind. I smiled back.

Southern nights are full of stars and crickets and mosquitos.

The stars hang down beside your head. The crickets are inside your head. The mosquitos bite. They are there for the purpose of reality, I imagine. If they don't often find their way into romantic stories, it is not their fault.

I used to sit out in the front in my rocking chair after watching "Amos and Andy" or "Ozzie and Harriet," until it was well after dark. I used to look up at the stars and try to fathom how far away they were. It was hard to comprehend that the light I was seeing from a certain star had started from there eight years ago. I thought of furnaces bigger than the earth. I thought of people who'd been alive eight years ago and weren't anymore. I heard somebody quietly call my name, or thought I did.

I listened and I heard it again. "Pa-tri-ciaaa." I walked around to the side of the house.

She was standing not more than six feet away, as quiet as a haunt. I grinned in the dark and I think she smiled. She didn't have her hat on, and her hair was all tousled. She had on jeans and a man's big plaid shirt.

I stood close to her, and we whispered, because the house was right there.

"Can you go for a ride? In my car? It's right down the road."

"Naw, I don't think so."

"How about a walk?"

I shrugged. "It's late. Grandma won't let me."

"Just inside the pasture. Over that fence. Just over there."

I waited a minute. I wanted to so badly.

"Okay," I whispered.

Then she was touching me, lightly, her arm around my shoulder. We were about the same height because I was tall for my age. She smelled of some odd perfume; I learned that it was her mother's.

We walked through the garden, stepping across the rows of turnip greens and the tomato vines. It was a new moon, and everything was dark blue. She held the barbed wire apart while I climbed through, and I did the same for her. She slipped through without touching it anywhere, like she'd done it a lot.

We sat on the ground, close enough to feel the warmth of each other. I pulled out blades of grass and waited. There was nothing to hear but the crickets. She lay back, her hands folded behind her head.

"I bet I know what you were doing. Looking at the stars, huh?"

I nodded. I felt her smile.

"Bet you were sitting out there, trying to think how they could be so far away?"

I giggled.

She reached down and gently tugged me down beside her. She could read my mind. It felt good, like somebody else in there with me. I have never waited for anything as hard as I waited for that first kiss.

She pulled me onto her so that my breasts touched hers for the first time. Then she pulled my chin down with two fingers and gave me a lingering taste-kiss right on the lips. It was better than the kisses two days before on the horse and I might not have had one like it since.

She ran her tongue across my lips. I opened my mouth and she started kissing me harder. Soon it was like the other day with her tongue halfway down my throat. We rolled over slowly until she was above me. She was on me with her legs straddled, when I felt something I shouldn't have. It woke me.

"Rohn . . .?"

She laughed low and deep in her chest. "I told you I wasn't like other women. Didn't I tell you that?"

But she was soft. And her voice was a woman's. And her breath was a woman's. And her breasts. She kept kissing me and pushing down on my body and grinding her hips into me until I responded.

I had on jeans that night. My blouse was already open and now she started to undo my pants. I helped her and we got them off.

Then she was up on her knees, still straddling me and doing something with the zipper on her pants. She took her penis out. It was warm and hard and at first she rubbed it back and forth against my clitoris. It made me lose my breath. I pulled her toward me and she told me to open my legs wider and I did.

At this time I was still a virgin. She was big for me and it hurt going in. I squirmed and she covered my mouth with her own.

It hurt but I kept pushing up to her and trying to open my legs wider. So we lay there, twisting and rutting on the ground. I came. I'd never come before with something inside me. And my bud between my legs filled up until I felt ready to burst. I was panting and she seemed to suck the air right from the center of my body. Taking my breath.

I came again and then she did. We were wet and sticky and a mess. My grandmother could call any time. Rohn held me.

I wanted to ask her, "How can you be?"

I could not comprehend.

Later that night in bed, I kept waking just at the edge of sleep, warmed by the soreness between my legs.

Carson McCullers wrote about "freaks" and "misfits." Faulkner wrote about freakish habits, and then there was Huck and Jim. There is a strange kind of tolerance down South when it comes to personal habits. Just don't involve politics. Just keep it behind closed doors so that it can be gossiped about. Fantasized about. Keep it under cover of night so that tales can grow.

I was your basic black adolescent tomboy with pigtails everywhere and a pointed chin. I looked from beneath long-lashed eyes without raising my head and gave tight-lipped secret smiles and rakish grins. I shrugged off the impossible.

What was nasty was funny to me and I smelled of sweat and my jeans had grass stains. I masturbated to movie magazines and let boys feel me up because it felt good. My experiences had, in some twisted way, prepared me for Rohn.

I was told that I would burn in Hell if I did practically anything. I was inevitably going to Hell, but I was too terrified of that fact to give it much thought. So I ran wild like the heathen I was, amid flowers with odors sweet and heavy enough to drug you; ran with dogs and other beasts that copulated when the spirit struck through the tall grass on hot summer nights. This was as real to me as Bible verses. So Rohn was real to me.

Rohn was the bill for some long ago charge that her mother—or her ancestors—had run up. Her mother accepted her as such.

She had not been made to go to school. Legally they got her declared an idiot or something. She was taught at home, better than the schools around here could teach her, most likely, because her mother was educated.

Her mother and her elder brother were the only ones who had anything to do with her. The others despised her. She told me that her younger sister had twice tried to kill her with rat poison. Her father beat her whenever he came home and found her there without the mother or the brother.

She told me later, after I was allowed to go riding in her car, that she was always afraid somebody would tell my grandparents some wild tale about her.

But she also told me that when she was in her teens, her mother took a turn to her. The same bed that she had nursed her in. Her mother, convinced that Rohn would never find a lover, took her in. This time, instead of opening her blouse to nurse Rohn, she opened her legs to her. Anytime she wanted it, she said.

I was in love with Rohn by then. I figured that she had to like me more than most, else she would never have told me those things. On the other hand, they could all have been lies.

One Sunday she came by in her '56 Chevy; it was green and white and shiny.

I ran out to the car and leaned on the window. "Hi."

She smiled. "I just came by to tell you how pretty you are." Which she knew would make me grin.

"Can you go for a ride?" she asked.

I shook my head. "I don't think so."

"Ask."

So I ran back in and asked, and was told no, I couldn't go for a ride in anybody's car, and what was I wanting to go for a ride with Miss Rohn for anyhow?

I ran back out and told her. Her smile changed to somewhere between sad and disgusted, and she nodded. "Oh, well." Then she looked at me and winked. "Maybe some other time, okay?"

"Yeah maybe."

"You take care y'hear?"

"All right."

Never occurred to me to say ma'am to her, ever.

I was up at the store to get some things for Grandma. It was getting near to evening. Rohn's car was there.

I'd never felt this way about a real person before. I felt about her like I only felt about fantasy movie stars.

She watched me approach the car. She was sitting with her back to the door, one leg up and her arm stretched across the back of the seat. She half smiled.

"Hi."

"Hi."

I explained about my errand; I'm not sure what there was to explain. She looked at me quietly. I think that she knew what she was doing. Driving me insane. So I took my leave and went inside.

When I came out, she offered me a ride home. Her eyes darted toward the store and then she opened the car door. She set my groceries in the back.

We pulled out of the station. Dark was falling and the bright Esso sign came on. We sped past my turn-off road. I sighed in relief.

She cut the radio to the black station from Memphis, WDIA. It had already been set on the signal dial. At home I could listen to WDIA only three times a day, when the gospel programs came on. Now some sister was singing about not having enough meat in her kitchen.

We drove across the railroad tracks and pulled off a dirt road near a stand of trees. We didn't have much time. Already I was wet.

We walked into the woods and she pulled me to her and kissed

me. We kissed a long time. I began moving a little bit, and I felt
her growing big. I wanted her inside me and I kissed her harder.

But she had other plans.

She undid her zipper and told me to get on my knees. Halfway
down I realized what she wanted.

I'd never done it before, I'd never even read about it, but it
seemed a natural thing to do.

She took my face between her hands; her hands were smooth
and they felt hot. The sky was still light though the wood was
dark. One dead tree without any leaves stood in front of the others. There was an old sack or something caught in its high
branches. "Don't use your teeth none, hear?"

I opened my mouth. It was like a fat sausage, tasteless except
for a little salt. I slid my mouth over it, like she told me, against
the plump vein underneath. And I let her shove it against the
back of my mouth. I squeezed her hips firm in my hands and she
massaged my cheeks and my throat with her thumbs, and ran her
fingers all in my hair and on the back of my neck. She rotated her
hips slowly. And then faster and harder I sucked until my tongue
felt like lead, but it had begun to taste so good. She twisted real
slow, and I grabbed and sucked. Time was passing. Grandma was
waiting. Time was, I think, standing still. For us. A sheriff on a
horse with a posse could have come out of the trees and we
wouldn't have known. Or two boys could have been watching us.

She came. I jerked my mouth away and spat, but some of it got
on my shirt. Rather, my grandfather's shirt.

I was hot, too, and between my legs was very sticky, so we lay
on the ground and dry fucked with our pants up until I came. She
was hard again, I think. But she said that she would go home to
her mother.

We sped away in the car. The wind felt good. The slide guitar
from the radio drowned out the crickets.

I had a playroom. It was just a curtained-off place between the
kitchen stove and the wall where I kept all of my magazines, and
where I went to read them and to fantasize.

One day I was sitting in there when I heard Rohn's voice. My
grandfather said something back to her and then called my name.

I went to the door. She was wearing a white shirt and old jeans and loafers. Rohn didn't look like a boy and she didn't look like a girl. I was afraid that my grandparents would see what I saw. If they did, they'd take it away from me. But Grandma kept on working in the tomatoes and Grandpa went back to help her. Only the dog followed Rohn over, sniffing her.

"Hi."

I asked her into my playhouse. The curtains could be pinned closed and I could hear footsteps on the wooden steps if need be.

Her shirt smelled of starch; it was a white so new and clean that it had a bluish tinge. I kissed it. I kissed her. Her teeth touched my tongue. She sucked it. She had such a fine mouth. We hardly ever talked. I knew what she wanted from me, and she could have all she wanted. That particular day she was going to take much more than I'd ever imagined she could.

We pressed against each other, all our clothes on, and I felt her soft breasts pressing mine. I breathed in, and pressed against them more. It's the feeling I still like best when I'm with a woman. Those round soft tits pushing.

We lay on the floor tight and moving just a little. She kissed, with her lips parted slightly and soft and moist, first my mouth, then my cheeks and my nose and my throat.

I started to pull down my shorts. She grinned; sometimes she just did that, out of the blue, like a Cheshire cat. I wonder what went on in her mind.

I kneeled in front of her and she cupped my buttocks in her hands and squeezed them. She put her mouth on my shoulder, right at the stem of my neck and sucked a bit until I had more of a welt than a hickey. She bit me, and I drew in the pain like a scorching breath.

I had my hands all in her hair. In the silk and the curls. I loved that hair. I felt it on my hands when I awoke in the night. Outside the kitchen door I heard the dog give a loud yawn and then, I think, he turned around and lay down.

We kissed. She worked her hand around in front and slid it right between my vulva lips. She wriggled her finger a little and I groaned and squeezed her to me. Her other hand was still squeezing and rubbing my behind. She kissed my neck, rubbed her mouth up to my ear and stuck her tongue in. I laughed and pulled my head away.

Then she moved her finger from around the front and stuck it up my asshole. It was hard and sticky, and I jumped. She pushed it and it hurt just a little, so I sucked my breath in. I'd never tell her to stop when she was hurting me because I liked the deep kisses that she gave me when she did. She always kissed me like that when she was hurting me somewhere.

We kissed deep and slow and she kept working her finger deeper up my asshole. Every once in a while I would whimper. We stopped kissing and she buried her face in my neck and pressed me to her, moving herself into my pussy and rotating her hips. I creamed. She was hard. We twisted and rubbed; I got the lips of my cunt over her dick and stroked up and down, and rubbed up and down, streaming across my bud and covering her joint with cream. Her finger was still there, I don't know how far in it was. She groaned.

She eased her finger out and chuckled; I felt the laugh in her throat. "Do you have any Vas'line?" she asked.

We had just a little, so I brought back the jar of bacon grease that was sitting on the stove to go with it.

She eased me around so that my back was to her. I felt her lips and tongue on the back of my neck. For a moment her hands cupped my breasts.

She told me to bend over and spread my legs as far apart as I could. I said she couldn't, that it was too small. She said we'd manage. She wiped the grease on me.

So I did what I was told and I told her to be careful. She dipped her finger a few times in my cunt and I shuddered.

I was spread so wide I could already feel the pain. I held my breath. She told me to relax.

I did, except for biting my lip when I felt the tip of her joint probing around where it shouldn't. I told her again to be careful. I was scared, but the fear was part of what was making me sweat and tremble. She pushed and immediately I felt the impossibility of the whole thing. But it didn't change anything.

She rubbed my clitoris again with her finger, just barely skimming it. I was already on the brink of coming. I opened wider and she pressed in more. It hurt.

A fraction of an inch by a fraction of an inch. She pushed and I gasped. "Relax. Relax, baby." I felt her voice.

"Come on," she whispered right in my ear, her voice more like wind or dry leaves.

"I love you. I love you. I love you." I said it every time I gasped.

She gathered me in her arms, crisscrossed like a straitjacket, and buried her face in my hair. I could hear her carefully placed breaths like somebody measuring something just so. My ass began to burn.

She pushed, she held me so tight I could hardly breathe. Something started to fill up my ass; it felt good, and at the same time I felt I was going to rip. My clit was swollen; my clit wanted to swell up big and long as my tongue. She started a regular pump now and I think I whined. The burning was a red-hot rod sliding into moist pink flesh. Mixed in with her gasps loud in my ear were groans as if she were in a little bit of agony. She touched my clit and I jumped. She pushed a finger up my vagina. Two fingers. I covered her hand with mine to make her take it out, but she didn't. My hand lay on hers, softly, as if it were helpless.

The pain was so intense I was almost dizzy; I moaned a little, like I was getting the shit fucked out of me. I'm sure that the dog, psychic as he was, raised his head. With one finger she stroked my bud and the pleasure made me call her name.

I started to squirm, we moved like wrestlers; she was inside me and all over me. I loved it and I couldn't bear it. She might have had it all the way inside my body. We wrestled and knocked over a stack of movie magazines. We tore and twisted their pages, and they carpeted the hard linoleum beneath us.

I felt saliva covering all of my chin and strings of it wet my nose when I lowered my head. There was something wet and warm moving on the back of my neck. She came.

I felt as if I was going to explode, as if steam was building up in my bowels. She held me tight, still and silent for a minute as we both trembled. We relaxed and she pulled it out through my raw flesh. Right after, a brownish egg-white liquid streamed out of my asshole like the runs, and covered the movie stars' eyes and mouths. I expected it to smell but it didn't.

Her face was covered with sweat and around her temple a few curls lay flat and darkened with moisture. My shirt, which I'd left on and open, was wet and my breasts glistened. The playhouse seemed close, steamed. Then sounds came back. A truck passing on the road; from far away, my grandfather's voice. That was all.

She took me in her arms and kissed me gently on the mouth and face. There was blood on my bottom lip; she licked some off. I held her weakly. I kissed her back softly. We kissed for a long, long while.

We laughed a little and I noticed something warm still running down my neck and I patted it with my fingers. It was blood. I twisted around and it was all over the collar of my shirt. Then I realized that my breasts hurt; I touched them and they were tender and bruised. I felt like I had been in an accident. I felt like . . .

"I love you," she said.

She knew just what to say after putting me through a meatgrinder. I was so thankful.

The next night at church was the Lord's Supper.

It was a night full of stars that I didn't want to leave to go inside. But I filed back into the building with the other girls. A sweetish yellow light filled the church.

The preacher got up and, in a conversational tone as if he were down among us, said what he always did about eating the flesh of the Lord with sins on our conscience. We would burn in Hell if we did. I broke out in a sweat. If I had died since the last Lord's Supper, I knew that I would be in Hell.

But then something happened worse than Hell. Rohn left me. She was just gone.

I didn't see her at all the week following the Lord's Supper. I thought that maybe she had gone somewhere with her mother. But she didn't come back the next week either.

The Saturday night following the second week I knew that something was wrong. I cried a whole night so silently that my grandmother, sleeping in the same bed, didn't hear me.

I learned, mostly by listening, that she had indeed disappeared. Rohn had disappeared and so had Fauna Dipman.

Fauna Dipman was a light-skinned girl with freckles. She went to the Baptist church. She had just gotten married that past spring. I'd never paid her much attention and Rohn had never mentioned her. I heard somebody saying that Rohn was crazy and Fauna was probably dead. Fauna's young husband walked around like somebody had hit him on the head.

One day I went to a small hollow down past our garden at the edge of the woods. It was another of my secret places and I had taken Rohn there. While I was there, something made the hair on the back of my neck stand up. It was just a feeling.

She had already started haunting me. I ran out of that hollow so fast I had a stitch in my side. I still run from that place in my dreams. I wake up sweating and feeling the hollow, not as empty as it should be, at my back.

I didn't see Rohn again for twenty-eight years.

I lived up North then, and one spring I went to visit a long-distance lover who lived in New Orleans. On the morning of the day I was to leave we drove to a shopping area where there were a lot of small craft shops just opening. It was early and there weren't many people about. My friend, Emily, had run back to the post office for something and I waited near the car, under a huge oak tree. I hardly paid attention to a car that drove up and parked just a few yards away.

Rohn got out of that car.

I had no doubt it was her. Her dark red hair was shorter and slicked back. She'd put on a little weight. She wore men's trousers. Her face was quiet and mature.

She walked into a little candle shop. I could not move. Burst after burst of light was going off inside me. Rohn.

I looked at her car. It was a long, blue, shiny Oldsmobile. A car for adults. And I looked at the woman in the passenger seat. It was Fauna. Fauna, as the young wife would look almost thirty years later. With her lipstick and her powdered cheeks and her hair pulled back. Her contented smile as if she were happy. Or at least was that morning.

I tried to think of all the things that I would say to them. I imagined the scene. I thought of dinner that night. When Rohn appeared at the door of the candle shop I didn't move.

I stood there concealed by the large tree and I did not move. I stared at Rohn. I stared as hard as I could.

She was handsome. She had long, dark curving eyebrows. A one-sided trace of a smile on her face. Sideburns. And she seemed to walk with just a bit of a limp. What happened, baby?

I let her get back into the big Oldsmobile. It tilted slightly at her weight on the seat. Closed the door. Backed out of the little drive. I saw Fauna laugh at something Rohn had said. And drive away.

I watched the car go further and further until it disappeared.

When Emily came back we got into the car. Emily is beautiful. She is a dark, honey-skinned New Orleans woman with amber eyes. She is all woman.

I was still seeing Rohn and Fauna. I still saw the point at which their car had disappeared. Emily threw her arm across the back of the seat and playfully tugged at my hair. She was just turning back to start the car when I said, "I love you."

She raised her eyebrows and smiled. She thought it was meant for her.

I leaned closer to her and she reached toward me and took my hand in both of hers. We kissed. She brushed my upper lip with her tongue and then she brushed my lower lip. She kissed both sides of my mouth just a taste and my mouth opened just slightly and she licked the insides. I took her tongue and sucked and sucked and we kissed and kissed . . . but my mind was on Rohn. God, she must have done something powerful to me. If Emily had been like Rohn, there is no way I would live nine hundred miles from her.

There's a certain kind of woman I can never resist, no matter what she does. A certain hair color that makes me want to touch it, a certain slow swagger that I'll turn around on the street to look at, a certain accent; that combined with a tone of voice I remember, can make the hairs stand up on my neck.

Rohn was on my mind and I let Emily touch me where she wanted to. But it was Rohn making me feel so weak, nearly thirty years later, sucking all my breath away.

Mary Maxwell

Trust

She lies curled on her side, facing away from him. The window is open, and he hears the sounds of the city outside: a bus, sighing to a stop at the curb, rap music blaring from a car, two drunks arguing on the street corner. He can't make out the words, but the tone is unmistakable. Summer in the city.

"Did you come?" he asks her.

She doesn't move. "I'm okay." Her voice is flat.

"But you didn't come."

She turns onto her back. Light from the streetlight shines through the thin curtains and he can barely see her face. "Why does that question always sound like an accusation? Like it's some affront to your manhood that I didn't come."

"I just wanted to know. If there's something I could do better ..."

She shrugs, the slightest movement of her shoulders.

"I'm willing to try if you give me a chance. What can I do? What do you like?"

She is silent, staring at the ceiling.

"Look, just trust me a little. Tell me what I can do."

"Do you trust me?" she asks him.

"Sure I do. If I wanted something, I'd tell you."

"Yeah." Her voice has an edge of doubt. "You trust me."

"Why shouldn't I?"

"No reason. I was just asking." She turns her head to look at him, and her face is in shadow. He can see the glitter of her eyes. "I just wanted to know."

"Why?"

"I had an idea . . ." Her voice trails off.

"What idea?"

"You wouldn't be into it." Her tone dismisses him.

He leans forward, wishing he could see her expression. "Try me."

"I like knives," she says. She casts off the sheet and sits up suddenly, turning so that she faces him. She is naked, sitting cross-legged on the rumpled sheets. "That's all. I like knives."

"What about knives?" he says hesitantly. "You want me to hold a knife or—"

"Oh, no." Her tone is amused—how could he have misunderstood her so? "I hold the knife."

"You hold the knife?"

"Sure." She reaches into a drawer in the bedside table, turning momentarily into the light. Her face is flushed, excited; her mouth a little open, her eyes bright. From the drawer, she takes a knife. The blade is as long as his hand, curved slightly, like an erect cock. "This knife," she says.

He doesn't move, watching her. "You're serious."

"Yes."

"What do you do with the knife?"

"Just hold it. I've never hurt anyone. Here—feel it."

He holds out his hand for the knife. She doesn't hand it to him; instead, she grasps his wrist with her other hand, warm skin against his, and rests the blade lightly against his wrist.

"It's cold against your skin, isn't it? It takes your warmth away. It takes your breath away." She strokes his wrist with the flat of the blade. "Go ahead and breathe. There's nothing to be afraid of." She stops stroking his wrist and slowly turns the blade so that the edge rests against his skin. "Even now, as long as you don't move, it won't hurt you."

After a moment, she lifts the blade away and releases his wrist. The skin where the blade had rested tingles from the chill of the metal. His wrist is a study in heat and cold: hot where her hand had held him; cold where the blade had touched.

She watches him, the hand with the knife held loosely in her lap. She lifts the knife and touches one of her bare nipples with the flat of the blade. "I can feel the warmth of your skin in the blade. I like that."

With her free hand, she reaches out to touch his leg, running her fingers up from knee to inner thigh. A delicate touch, so soft and tender. He shivers.

"You're cold," she says. "I can warm you up." Her fingers move on his inner thigh, the back of her hand gently tickling his balls. "You know I can." She brings her legs together and shifts to a kneeling position beside him. Her hand cups his balls, and the tips of her fingers caress the sensitive spot just behind them.

He can still see the knife in her right hand. The blade glitters in the streetlight.

"Why knives?" he asks.

She laughs quietly. "You might as well ask why tigers have teeth, why scorpions sting. It just is." Still on her knees, she moves her leg to straddle his thigh. She leans in and kisses him, her tongue soft against his lips, darting into his mouth. Her hand squeezes his balls gently, then fondles his cock. Her fingers are warm and persuasive. He feels his cock grow hard.

He keeps his eyes on the knife. While she kisses him, the blade traces patterns in the air, catching the light and reflecting it onto the ceiling, the walls.

She sits up and glances at his face. "It's beautiful, isn't it?" she says. "Don't you think so?"

Not waiting for an answer, she kisses his chest, sucking lightly on his nipple while her hand strokes his cock, moving up and down the shaft with increasing urgency. She moves against his leg, and he feels the wetness of her cunt. He closes his eyes. A moment later he feels the flat of the knife blade against his nipple. The warmth of her breath; the chill of the knife. He feels the chill all the way down to his groin. He opens his eyes, looking up at her. Light shines full on her face, her bare breasts. Her nipples are hard.

He reaches up, meaning to lift the knife away from his body, but her hand strokes his stiff cock, and he reaches for her breasts instead, caressing the warm flesh.

She smiles at him, shaking her head. "No," she says. "I told you: Don't move." With the flat of the blade, she pushes his hand away. "I'll move." She leans closer, bringing her breast to his lips, and he sucks on her nipple. She brings the blade back to his chest, and he feels the cold metal, but it no longer seems important.

"That's right," she says. "Yeah, that's it."

She lifts the knife away from him and kisses the spot where the blade had rested, warming his skin. Her body slides down beside his until he feels her breath on his thigh. She kisses his balls, then runs her tongue up the hard shaft of his cock, taking the tip into her mouth.

"Oh, yeah," he moans.

Her tongue swirls around the tip of his cock, each circle bringing a new level of sensation. He feels the chill of metal against the shaft of his cock, and the breath catches in his throat. But her tongue circles again, warm and urgent, pressing against the head of his cock. He tenses his thigh muscles, resisting the urge to lift his hips and push himself deeper into her mouth. He feels the cold touch of steel on his belly. For a moment, she lifts her mouth away from him. "Don't move," she says.

"Please," he says. "Please."

She laughs and once again takes his cock into her mouth, moving so that he is deep inside her, pressing against the warm wetness of her tongue, her throat. She positions his leg between her thighs, and he feels her wet cunt rubbing against him.

He cannot move, he knows that. He aches to grab her head and push his cock deeper into her throat. He feels the chill of the knife as she moves it to touch his ass, his thigh, his chest. He is afraid of the touch of the knife against his balls. Does he trust her? Why not? Does it matter? What matters is the heat of her lips on his cock, her hand on his balls. The chill of the knife on his chest, his side. Her mouth moving faster, sucking him harder, again and again, with hot-lipped urgency. He moans, trying to form a word. "Please . . . ," but he doesn't know what he is asking for. He knows nothing but the heat of her lips and the touch of her hand and the chill of the blade. "Please . . ."

She takes his cock deep and he feels the chill of the knife against his balls as he comes, frozen into stillness by the touch of the blade, his hands in fists at his side, moaning as she swallows his hot cum.

He lies very still, feeling the sweat drying on his chest. She lifts the knife away. "You can move now," she says.

Marcy Sheiner

~

Two Guys and a Girl

When I moved across the country for a prestigious new job, I was forced to leave behind one of the best, and certainly the most avid, lovers I'd ever had. I begged Jack to come with me, but he had his own career, his own life—and besides, we'd never even been monogamous. We saw each other an average of every other weekend—not much, but with Jack, that's all I needed. That entire weekend was spent in bed, fucking and sucking, sometimes all through the night; we'd try to sleep, but one or the other would invariably wake up and claw at the other.

Now, in sunny California, I was seeing Brian, a younger, adventurous guy who was willing to play out just about any sexual fantasy, at least verbally. One of my favorites was to be with two men at once, something I had never managed to pull off. I'd been with women, by myself or in threesomes with men, but I had never been able to find two men at the same time with whom I felt comfortable enough to engage in a threesome. What's more, half of my girlfriends, all of them far less sexually adventurous than I, had managed it, and reported that it was exquisite.

Brian indulged my fantasy; that is, we talked about it during sex, pretending another man was with us. Sometimes he used a dildo on me while I sucked his cock, and was pretty good at creating the illusion of another man being there. What Brian didn't know, however, was that not only did I want two cocks at once, but I also wanted to see them get it on together.

Years ago I had discovered a fascination for male-male love through gay men's magazines. I'll never forget the rush I got the first time I opened one of them and saw two extremely large dicks rubbing up against each other. For days I couldn't get the image out of my mind. I began reading and watching gay men's porn regularly; it turned me on because men turn me on, but also because it's the raunchiest, most aggressive, down-and-dirty form of pornography around. These reading materials, needless to say, were kept hidden from Brian, who expressed no interest in being with men at all.

One day Jack called to say he was coming to California on a business trip. My pussy juices began flowing immediately; there was no way I wasn't going to sleep with him. But I worried about Brian—we hadn't really decided whether we were monogamous, and an old lover is always a threat. Then suddenly it hit me: maybe I could finally fulfill my fantasy.

It would be tricky: neither man had ever been with a guy, and both had more than a touch of machismo in their personalities. One night, I waited until Brian was pumping his cock into my pussy, on the brink of orgasm, then whispered, "Wouldn't you love to see me get fucked by another guy?"

Brian, of course, thought this was just our usual fantasy play. "Oh, yeah, baby, I'd like to see you with six or seven cocks jackin' off on your face, on your tits . . ."

He didn't get much further—we both came.

Later on I casually mentioned Jack's upcoming visit, gradually sharing the information that I'd like to try a threesome. Brian was understandably hesitant, but over the next few days I worked on him, describing visions of a cock in my pussy and one in my mouth, while gently stroking his organ, coaxing him into cooperation. I didn't reveal any hopes that he and Jack might suck and fuck each other; I figured I'd cross that bridge when and if we got to it.

Brian valiantly agreed to let me see Jack alone the night of his arrival, so I could feel him out on the subject. After a year apart, we immediately fell all over each other—clawing clothing, biting flesh, sinking into old familiar rhythms. When we were finally sated, I asked Jack if he remembered how I had always wanted to be with two men. He did. Then I told him about Brian, and asked if he was up for it.

He agreed. The next night found me on my knees in front of a full-length mirror, sucking Brian's cock while Jack fucked me from behind. The sensation was indescribable—like being totally filled, totally satisfied.

After a while I took Brian's dick out of my mouth and said innocently, "Honey, I'd really love it if you'd lick my pussy while Jack's fucking me."

Both men did a double take, but shrugged agreeably. We moved onto the bed and I lay down on my back. Jack climbed on top and resumed fucking me, while Brian knelt and put his mouth near my mons. He slowly licked my clit and my outer lips while Jack's cock slid in and out of my hole.

"Down lower," I murmured, gently pushing Brian's head down between my legs.

He moved down hesitantly, to where he could no longer avoid the cock furiously pumping in and out of me. He tried, but just as I had hoped, excitement finally overtook him, and soon he was licking Jack's prick as it made its journey in and out. I watched Jack's face and saw he was excited, and with one neat movement slid myself up and out of the way.

For a moment that seemed like hours, we were suspended in time. The men realized what was happening, and I wondered if they'd let it go further. Then the moment passed, and Brian took the whole of Jack's cock down his throat, sucking eagerly, his fingers kneading Jack's large balls. Jack pumped in and out of Brian's mouth just the same as if it were mine.

Brian sidled his way around so his cock faced Jack's mouth, and Jack stroked and squeezed the head, finally taking the pulsing meat into his mouth. I lay back and began stroking my pussy, feasting on the sumptuous vision before me.

Feelings of lust coursed through me, along with a little bit of jealousy. The men became so involved in sucking each other, they forgot I even existed. I reached into my bedside drawer, grabbed my trusty dildo, and began fucking myself. How ironic, I thought.

Here I've got two flesh-and-blood men in bed with me, and I'm using an artificial organ.

I fucked myself with my dildo while I watched them sixty-nine, and my orgasm coincided with both men shooting hot cum into each other's throats. As their hard-ons withered and they returned to reality, both men looked at me with a mixture of embarrassment and apology. They broke apart to lie on either side of me.

"That was so hot," I finally said.

They both let out a sigh of relief. After a while I reached down and took a cock in each hand, stroking and kneading them until they were again erect. Eventually I sat up and pushed their cocks closer together, rubbing the head of one up and down the other's shaft. I knelt and licked each of them, then took both inside my mouth, though I could only fit an inch or two. We were all breathing heavily. Interestingly, while I had always expected I'd be a passive partner in this kind of triangle, I was orchestrating all the action. The men wanted to get it on with each other but were too inhibited to do so without my encouragement.

And encourage them I did. I told Brian to lie on his belly, then directed Jack's cock to his asshole. I lubricated the head and Brian's hole, then gently guided the cock inside. Brian moaned, spreading his ass cheeks as Jack sank it in inch by yielding inch. He began to fuck Brian, slowly at first, then faster, until Brian was on all fours, pushing against Jack's dick, silently begging for more. I slid beneath Brian and spread my legs. He entered me easily as Jack thrust in and out of his asshole without missing a beat.

I thought I'd die of pleasure right then and there. I have always loved the sensation of having a man's weight on me, pounding me into the bed, dissolving all my tension; now I had the weight of two men on top of me. It felt as if Jack's cock reached right through Brian, and both men were fucking me. Jack was grunting, making animal sounds I'd never heard from him before, and Brian was sighing in ecstasy, having totally surrendered. I felt his cock stiffen and I gripped it hard with my pussy muscles. As he shot his load into me, spasms rocked my cunt. At the same time, Jack let out a loud grunt that was almost a lion's roar, and the three of us shook together as one organism, holding onto each other for dear life. I felt as if we'd just experienced a minor earth-quake.

We collapsed in a sweaty, exhausted heap. After a while I got up and made us something to eat. I chattered on about the experience, talking about everything I had felt and learned. But boys will be boys: though they had managed to break through some heavy cultural barriers, Brian and Jack remained locked in masculine silence when it came to talking about their feelings.

Jack returned to the East Coast but left a lasting legacy: Brian and I have added a new dimension to our sex life—we watch gay men's porn together. Though he isn't cruising gay bars, the memory of our threesome infuses our lovemaking, and I expect it to be with me for a long time to come.

Magenta Michaels

Sileni: A Moonlit Tale

"A tail?" she grinned up at him, repeating his words, delighted at the outrageousness of the notion. "You have a tail?"

They were packed in against the crowded bar; flame-haired Samantha in her witchiest, clingingest, this-is-the-night-that-we're-going-to-do-It black dress, and this starkly beautiful dark-haired man, their shoulders jammed together beneath the arcing green of potted palms and the low jeweled light of Tiffany lamps that made up Henry Africa's: The Watering Hole.

"Is it soft and fluffy like a bunny's," she teased him, "or does it have a little pom-pom on the tip, like a poodle's? Can you hold things with it? Does it wag furiously when you're happy? Did it give you complexes as a child?" She ran out of breath and stood beaming as she waited for his response. He had remained silent during the whole barrage of questions, smiling down into the amber lights of his drink as he drew circles with the base of his glass through the wet spot on the bar.

"You must be serious about this," he chided her through soft Italian syllables. He reached out to smooth a stray lock back from her face. "I'm trying to tell you something."

Samantha flipped her wild red crinkles from one side of her face to the other. She eyed him as she considered. It was true that she had wondered at the oddness of his halting gait, and she had

puzzled over the full, almost old-fashioned cut of his obviously expensive suits. But she had finally dismissed these things as Italian
"style" and Continental eccentricity. A tail had not been one of
her considerations.

"Can I see it?" she demanded, smiling over the rim of her
glass, enjoying what her question implied.

"Yes," he responded, after a time.

They readied themselves to go.

It took them twenty minutes to pay the check and find a cab,
and another twenty to get to his ritzy, uptown address; during the
whole of the ride, the subject of his tail didn't cross her mind
again. She was busy congratulating herself on her great good luck
at having found such a treasure. He was polished, he was European, he seemed to have money, he was sexy and he was beautiful. She turned to his profile. His beauty was impossible,
immaculate; not the virile, masculine good looks assigned to western cowboys, but rather the finely chiseled, almost inbred aristo-
cratic beauty that a mother might wish for her only daughter. He
turned to find her studying him, and he captured her hand, bringing her fingers to his lips. So it was only when they stood before
the wide door of his apartment, her stomach leaping in anticipation of what lay ahead, that the floating remembrance of his talk
of a tail bubbled to the surface of her mind. But then he was
pushing open the door, and she was following him inside, slowing
her step in the wake of his peculiar walk, her feet sinking down
into the thickly padded carpet.

He asked her to wait in the entrance hall as he went ahead flip-
ping on the lights, and she stood in the echoing semi-dark, listening to him move around the apartment.

"Come," he said finally, holding out his hand to her, now the
perfect host, "let me see to your comfort." And he took her arm,
leading her blinking into the light.

It was not the vastness of the room nor the richness of its ar-
chitecture that made her draw in her breath. She had seen high
vaulted ceilings and mahogany-paneled doors and floor-to-ceiling
French windows that banked an entire wall before. No, it was that
the grandeur of the room in which she stood had been turned
into a wooded grove, an enchanted forest brought indoors.

No ordinary man lived here. It was as though the most sumptuous furnishings, the most beautiful objects had been collected
onto the face of a brilliantly patterned Persian kilim and set down
carefully in the midst of a perfect forest glen. Trees of different
leaf and size grew clustered, sometimes three or four deep, their
limbs and leaves overlapping, their containers hidden by small
granite boulders and lengths of dried branches scattered among
their bases. White garden roses, voluptuous in their antique
vases, covered every surface, filling in the spaces between the
piles of handbound books and the collections of whimsical arti-
facts from every century, every corner of the world. A domed silver bird cage perched atop a freestanding stone column, the
column itself spiraled with small dark ivy, the burnished floor of
the silver cage littered with rose potpourri and crushed gold leaf.
Soft deep sofas covered in white-on-white silk vied with the
graceful curves of upholstered chairs that offered tapestry seats. A
tall, beveled mirror in an ornate gilded frame nestled among the
foliage of a cluster of trees so that in passing, it seemed that one
saw oneself reflected in the Garden of Eden. The room stood
poised, alive in its vibrancy.

He took her coat and then busied himself mixing drinks while
she wandered around the room, examining the masks and sculp-
ture and fingering the spines of ancient books. She came to stand
before a muraled wall, its haunting scene done in trompe l'oeil so
that it spilled over onto the curved ceiling and surrounding walls,
creating the illusion for the viewer of being part of the artfully
done painting. The scene was a depiction of a wild and thunder-
ous falls, its ocean of falling water beginning a half-mile in the air.
And at the crest of the cliff where the waters began their descent
perched a lone medieval castle, its dark stone towers and
landward-facing battlements rising up from the very edges of a
massive granite shelf that jutted out from the living rock over the
turbulent water's fall.

"What is this place?" She spoke in a whisper, awestruck that
such a scene could exist, even in an artist's mind.

He came to stand beside her, pressing a drink into her hand.

"It is beautiful, is it not? I was born in the great forests behind
the fortress that you see. The castle is my family's. Over the cen-

turies we were pushed to the edge of this terrible water by those who were not like us. I am of the Sileni. We are not as ordinary men."

"Ahh . . . ," she said as she smiled at him over the rim of her glass. "Of course . . . the tail."

She took a sip from her drink. It was frothy, smelling of roses, but had a slightly bitter bite.

"A potion," he answered her before she could ask, "so that my tail does not deter you." He led her away from the mural to a low sofa, bending to kiss her after she had settled herself among the cushions. His breath was wonderful, strange, bringing up odd, swirling images behind her closed eyelids. She arched up to his kiss, parting her lips, but he slid his mouth away, pressing it instead to the ridge of her throat and the base of her ears, drawing the lobes into his mouth and then softly letting them go. He sniffed at her skin as though delighting in the scent beneath her cosmetics and perfume.

After a while he knelt before her, biting softly through her dress at the surface of her thighs moving upward, his teeth finally finding her risen nipples through the thin fabric of her dress. His arms rested on the sofa at either side of her hips and he burrowed his face into her lap, kissing her fingers out of his way as he gathered her skirts up and up until they lay in a soft heap around her hips. Then he pulled her hips to him, pausing a moment before he pressed his face to her crotch. It was as though he could not get enough of her smell, pulling her essence into his nostrils with slow deep breaths. He rubbed his nose up and down on either side of her clitoris as it pushed outward, swollen, against the silk of her panties. Then he opened his lips to her, dragging his tongue in wide, slow strokes over the lace-covered lips of her vagina, soaking the fabric with the wet of his tongue and making her hips push upward toward his mouth; aching for the lace to be pushed away, aching for the softness of his tongue to curl bare around her dark-hooded kernel of flesh.

"Let me see you . . . let me see how beautiful you are," and he stood up to help her with her dress.

In a moment she was naked, except for her panties, but she

stepped away from his hands when he moved to slide them from her hips.

"Let me see your tail first," reminding him even now of the words that had gotten her here in the first place. "I want to see your tail."

"You are certain?" He searched her face, and when she nodded yes, he rose without speaking, crossing the room to the far wall where he slowly lowered the lights until there was nothing left but a rectangle of moonlight, spilling its many-paned shadow across the carpet floor.

He approached her now from across the darkened room, stopping just outside the puddle of moonlight, his eyes on her face as he stood before her, removing his shoes, unbuttoning his shirt in the dark. She lay her head back against the sofa, listening to him unbuckle his belt, unzip his trousers. And when she finally heard him step from the cloth, dropping the garment to the floor, she raised her head to look.

Even in the dimness she knew that the deep coloring of his lower body had nothing to do with suntan. It was as though his torso and arms floated bottomless, white and reflective in the dark.

And then came the movement behind him. It was more of a sound coupled with something, something she felt with her skin rather than a thing that her eye had identified in the dim light. There was a short cracking noise, and a whooshing sound, as though the air behind him had been moved and cooled by the fierce hard snap of cloth or hair.

A low vibration began in the muscles of her forearms and the fronts of her thighs as she stared at him, her eyes searching the velvet space around the dark half of his body.

He stepped toward her, directly into the puddle of moonlight, pausing in mid-stride to give complete illumination to what the pale light revealed. His lower body was that of a horse. Not a deformed man, not some pitiable creature of twisted limbs and crusted skin, but a clear and exquisite creation unto himself, the bones of the horse half enabling a gait that nearly mimicked that of a man. He stood before her in all his magnificence, the thick muscles of his rump and thighs knotted and rippling beneath the glistening dark brown of his coat.

He turned for her slightly, just so she could see the tail. It developed out of the base of his spine, lying tight against the top of his buttocks. Full and wild, it was not a romantic version of human hair, but made up of hard black strands, as coarse and strong as those that made up the tail of any barnyard animal. It dropped headlong past the v-shaped backs of his veined legs to stop just before his hooves.

He took a step toward her, this time out of the moonlit box. The wonder of the tail was now shadowed by the mystery of his unsheathed sex. It hung heavy before him, a pink speckled shaft as thick as her wrist, its weight not allowing an upward curve. She could not take her eyes from its dark tip. It rose as a lure, baiting her eye, its color as deep as the dark brown of his coat. He took another step toward her, knelt before her, tugging gently at her panties, easing them over her hips, his eyes never leaving her face. He placed one of her legs and then the other over his shoulders, and finally, dropping his eyes from her face, he bent once more to the triangle between her thighs.

It seemed to her that she floated from her body, that she watched their coupling from a high corner of the room; she found the scene breathtaking and beautiful. She saw moonlight streaming through the tall French windows, over the paleness of the low couches and her own naked shoulders, over his head moving ever so slightly as he bent to his work, and finally over the dark glory of his tail as it spread behind him like an open, finely etched fan. She watched how her hips lifted to his kiss and how he eased her knees down from his shoulders to wrap her legs around his waist, her heels crossed and propped at the base of his tail. He was pulling at her now, gathering her to him as he slid her thighs onto the tops of his own. The backs of her legs were prickled by his ruffled coat as she slid forward against the natural grain of his hair. Their faces were inches apart now, his nose and mouth glistening from his labors. He lifted his cock from between his legs and lay it between them, against her belly. It poked dry and immense, nothing like any man could ever be. He took her hand and closed it around the girth of him. When she did not shrink from its weight and size but opened and closed her fingers along its length, he fitted the dark head of it to her opening.

"Do you find me a monster?" he whispered against her lips, his breath smelling of her pussy. She found herself responding, her self now back in her body, as she wound her arms around his neck in answer. He gathered her onto him, a little at a time, allowing her wetness to ease his way. And when finally they sat belly to belly, his cock curved hard within her, he rose with her, his hands filled with her buttocks, and walked to the tall gilded mirror among the trees so that she could see herself impaled upon his animal sex.

"Let me down," she murmured, and she slid from his hard flesh to a pile of sheepskins spread before the mirror. She arranged herself on her knees, offering him her backside. He curved his torso over her back, parting her cheeks with the head of his member.

She stiffened, thinking he would enter her there, but he did not, instead rubbing his tip slowly up and down against the slick puckered mouth of her anus. Then he slid it under and into her, stretching her sides as he began to rock, a small thrusting, as he waited for her to respond. Finally, she matched his movements with her own, and he climbed to the rounded hooves that were his heels to begin his animal thrust.

He rode her, he rode her, his hips scooping under and up, then shuddering into her; a cadenced rhythm marked by the loud squishing sound of his dick as he stroked. Her naked sides were stinging from the wicked slap of his tail, which whipped furiously behind him. His balls slapped against her as the weight of his flesh pulled her inner lips downward, yanking the hood over her bursting clitoris.

She was wild with her need, grunting with her need, her legs lifting from the floor as time and again she rammed herself backward onto the impossible girth of him, her hips whipping ovals in the air.

Then came her release; the creeping wave of it rising up from her calves and spreading quickly over her like gooseflesh, as her body ignited and she bucked against him unchecked. Whimpering, she sought only to satisfy herself, her face pressed hard into the sheepskins, her hands now claws that kneaded the rugs. Her back arched itself and her toes cramped as every part of her body coiled, impelling her toward her finish.

When it was over, it was she who lay exhausted, and he rose to tend to her, rubbing her back, kissing her buttocks and covering her with a silken afghan drawn down from a chair. Unable to keep her eyes open, she snuggled down into the lushness of the musky rugs, nearly asleep with floating dreams of being mistress of the castle above the waterfall. She heard, as she drifted off to sleep, the clip-clop of rounded hooves stepping from the padded carpet to the marble tile of the bathroom floor.

Catherine Tavel

∽

About Penetration

It was simple. Thomas just couldn't penetrate Diane. Or more specifically, he wouldn't. But Thomas had his reasons, his own personal rationalizations. In a way, they made perfect sense to Diane's mind, but not to her body. And definitely not to her heart. They were married, only not to each other. But really now, what difference did it make whether or not he stuck his tongue into her mouth or his cock into her pussy? Adultery was adultery, whether you technically penetrated someone or not. Right? Of course it was.

How did they meet? If Diane had told anyone about his existence (which she hadn't), she wouldn't have had the nerve to be honest. But the truth was that she and Thomas met on a lonely Saturday night in May. Only they didn't actually meet. Their voices met. You see, he phoned her that night, dialed seven anonymous numbers because he was feeling empty and alone. He wasn't seeking sex, even though the first thing he said to Diane was, "I want to eat your pussy."

Why hadn't Diane hung up the telephone then and there? She frequently received phone calls of this nature and, as a rule, would hang up. But there was something in Thomas' voice, something that sounded just as sad as he felt inside. Something in his voice seeped into her skin. And that was that.

Diane had been in a bad frame of mind that night. Her husband was out and she was transferring documents from disk to disk on her word processor. She simply wasn't in the mood for cunnilingus. In fact, when she finished her chores, she was seriously contemplating settling down for a nice long cry. That's when the telephone rang.

Diane was by no means an easy lay, even over the phone. She was bitchy. She was smart-assed. She was abrasive. But still, Thomas wouldn't give up. He kept talking smut; she kept trying to change the subject to decipher what kind of person he was beneath the raunch.

"Come on, touch your cunt for me," Thomas said.

And Diane wondered aloud, "Are you married?"

"Yes," was his answer.

"For how long?" she prodded.

"Three years."

"Where is she now?" Diane pressed.

"In New Jersey visiting her sister with our daughter."

"How old is she?"

"Three weeks old," Thomas admitted. Diane was surprised that a woman would venture away from home with such a young infant, but this said a lot about Thomas' wife. She was always leaving—if not physically, then mentally. That's probably why Thomas was on the phone with Diane after all, now, wasn't it?

There was a long pause, then Diane asked, "Why did you marry her?"

After an even longer pause, Thomas responded, "Because we were compatible."

Diane burst out laughing. "Computers are compatible. There has to be much more between people."

That's how Diane and Thomas began speaking of other topics—their lives, their childhoods, their beliefs, their unfulfilling marriages. The parallels were uncanny—their mothers had the same first name, each of their spouses were Jewish while Diane and Thomas were raised Catholic, Diane was five days younger than Thomas' wife, and Thomas was now living in the neighborhood where Diane had grown up. And they were both unhappy. Then Thomas and Diane started to talk dirty again, and both of them faked orgasms. Maybe they wanted to get back to plain talking.

When it happened again, the sex part came naturally. Thomas told Diane to get her vibrator and she fucked herself with it. Diane told Thomas how much she loved to suck cock, that to her, semen tasted fresh and clean, like the ocean. Thomas chuckled even though his dick was hard. He called her many names. He called her a whore, a slut, a cunt. No one had ever called Diane those names before, but for some reason, she liked it. She liked it a great deal. And Thomas liked calling her those names, even though he respected her and sensed she was actually a good person. She called him a bastard and a motherfucker even though he sounded like a very sweet man when he wasn't cursing. Thomas and Diane uttered the kind of words they couldn't say to their spouses, no matter how intense it got. Besides, Thomas needed something, something for himself. Only he wasn't exactly sure what it was. He thought he found it in Diane's voice.

When Diane and Thomas climaxed, it was for real and it was together. They called out each other's name. Now, the same old names sounded different, special. Diane almost cried, which was what she did when she came hard and strong. The crying was almost involuntary, like sneezing, only it frightened some men. It frightened Diane, but she had learned to accept it, to embrace it, simply because it was hers.

After the orgasm, Thomas and Diane talked more. He waited patiently on the line while she ran off to pee. Diane didn't think Thomas would be there when she returned—and she didn't want to lose him, not so soon anyway—but he was there, waiting patiently. Thomas admitted that he didn't remember what number he had dialed at random. It was 332-something. Diane told him the last four digits, 9610, because she wanted him to phone again.

Next they described themselves to each other. Diane told him how small her breasts were, even about the gray flecks in her black hair. Thomas told her his height, weight, and how big his dick was. Later he confessed that he'd lied—he was only five foot eight. She thought this fabrication odd because most men would have lied about the size of their genitals, but Thomas was more sensitive about his height. Since Diane was only five foot five, it didn't matter. But it wouldn't have mattered anyway.

So Thomas and Diane talked. And talked. They talked until she heard her husband unlock the front door. And after she softly clicked down the telephone, Diane noticed that she and Thomas had been speaking for more than two hours.

Diane existed in a sort of euphoria for the next few days. She couldn't sleep that night, but she smiled restlessly in the blackness, still giddy from her orgasm. The thought of two strangers reaching out to each other in the middle of the night was such a romantic notion. Was it fate? Was it destiny? Perhaps it was the luck of the dial. Would Thomas ever phone her again? Something about that prospect scared her, but something else about it made her long for him. An empty hole of emotion had somehow been filled by the sound of his voice. What would she do if he never called again? How could she live with a cavern inside her chest?

Two days passed. And two nights. Diane's mood peaked and ebbed constantly. Her heart rose each time the telephone rang and it plummeted whenever it was anyone else but Thomas. Her husband noticed nothing different in Diane's behavior because he was so tangled up in his own ghosts. Plus, her odd attitude shifts were not unusual for Diane. When she had sex with her husband (which had always been frequent and calmly satisfactory), she imagined what it might be like to make love with Thomas. His words rang out in her head as she had orgasms with her husband, and it was good.

But then he called. Thomas actually called! Her heart dropped, and then floated upward at the sound of his voice. They made plans to meet a few days later. In the morning. At a nearby park.

Thomas was not what Diane had pictured, although she hadn't really pictured anything. Thomas, on the contrary, said that Diane was exactly what he had imagined. But how could anyone have imagined eyes so chestnut brown, so knowing, yet so starkly innocent? Diane was afraid to look into Thomas' eyes, which were green and as piercing as broken glass. It almost hurt when he studied her. It was as though he were cutting through her, digging for something that she was desperately trying to hide. Diane had to turn away at first.

They stood in the middle of the playground, between the swings and slides. It was too early for anyone else to be there yet. (Diane had told her husband that she was going out for a jog, and Thomas had told his wife he had to be at work early that day.) They just stared at each other, and then held each other. Thomas felt odd in Diane's arms. She gazed into his eyes, like a child about to ask a question, and then he said, "Don't."

She didn't.

At first, Diane was afraid to get into Thomas' car. She asked him to show her some identification. Right there on the sidewalk, he opened his wallet. Besides his driver's license, Diane saw Thomas' wedding picture. She certainly didn't need to see that. It gave her a chill in her stomach, but she got into the white Toyota anyway. Thomas tossed the car keys into her lap, in case she still didn't trust him. She tossed them back because she did.

Thomas and Diane sat there getting used to each other. She didn't know what to say. They said it all on the telephone, but in person, face to face, they were strangers. She knew things about him that few people did. For example, she knew what he sounded like when he was coming. But then, she didn't know things that everyone else did. And she wanted to know everything.

Thomas had a scar that sliced through his right nostril. Diane thought it was curiously sexy. She reached out and touched it. "How did you get this?" she asked.

"In a car accident," Thomas said, quite matter-of-factly. "I went through the windshield."

"Oh."

So, Thomas and Diane did what they did best. They talked. And talked and talked. Then, for some reason, Diane said, "I'm so wet," and blushed. She didn't know why, she just had to say it. She wanted him to know.

All Thomas did was smile. Then he moved as close as he could in his bucket seat to Diane. "Touch yourself," he whispered. "Touch yourself for me." It was broad daylight. People were passing the car, walking their poodles. But Diane did as Thomas said. She touched her pussy through her black, lace-trimmed Spandex shorts.

Thomas wouldn't touch her, though. Diane didn't think too

much of this at first. Perhaps he didn't want to bring home her pungent scent to his wife, or else he was playing an erotic game. In any event, Diane tried to satisfy herself with his voice. It drifted to her ears from the other side of the Toyota. It tickled her eardrums, then oozed down to her crotch, where it tickled the tip of her clitoris. Diane's panties were soaked. She could feel it through her clothing. The seam of her shorts dug into her slit. Her fingers pressed the seam into the crack of her cunt even deeper.

"No," Diane kept saying over and over again. Even though she meant "yes." She didn't want Thomas to see her face turned inside out, her limbs trembling, her lower lip crumbling, her eyelids fluttering, yet in another way, she did. In her mind, Thomas *had* to see everything. Even the ugly things.

But to Thomas, nothing about Diane was ugly. Not the tiny cobweb of cranberry-colored veins on her left thigh. Not the nose that was far too large for her delicate features. Not the callus on the middle digit of her right hand, which was now shoved into her cunt. Nothing about Diane was ugly, because it was real.

Thomas reached over and caressed her thigh. He would later tell Diane that her skin was as soft as his newborn daughter's cheeks. And in the future, that would make Diane smile many, many times. Thomas' hand felt very big and warm and strong as it stroked Diane's smoothness. His hand traveled up past the lace leg band of her shorts and stopped at the outside of her panties. But he would not go any further.

Thomas leaned forward and opened the glove compartment. He took out a plastic cigar case. Printed on it were the words IT'S A GIRL in fancy script. Thomas slid the cigar holder up along Diane's leg and under the elastic of her panties. It slipped easily into her pussy. Diane gasped. Thomas looked into her dark eyes. He wiggled his finger inside the plastic casing which wiggled inside Diane's cunt. She felt as though she would climax immediately, but she didn't want to. Then he would see. He would see everything.

Thomas took a second cigar case and fit it onto another finger. There were now two plastic tubes wedged in Diane's pussy. It was perverse. It was almost funny. It was intense. It was silly. But whatever it was, Diane was going to come. She turned her face toward the car door and bit into her lip and came.

Afterward, Thomas smiled again. Diane was near tears. She needed more of him and she wanted to make him come. Only he wouldn't let her touch him. He wouldn't even kiss her. Yet, when he grasped her nipples, he knew how she liked to be touched. She liked to have them squeezed. Hard. Very hard. And no one, except herself, did it right. Up until Thomas.

It was getting late and Thomas really had to get to work. He left Diane on the curb, not unlike an abandoned puppy. Well, she did have those abandoned puppy eyes. She felt full and empty at the same time. Would Thomas ever call again? Would she ever see him again? Probably not, Diane told herself.

But Thomas called the next day. And a few days after that. And so on. They shared stories and secrets and laughed and came together. He told her things that he told no one else, things so private they can't even be mentioned here.

Another time, Thomas disappeared for six weeks. She counted the days, the weeks. He didn't meet Diane in their place by the park. He didn't even phone her. Diane thought it was over, but then, she always thought it was over. "Why is it," she once asked Thomas, "that whenever I see you, it feels like the last time?" Thomas wasn't sure what to answer.

Those six weeks had been almost unbearable for Diane. Thomas wouldn't give her his telephone number and it was unlisted anyway, so she couldn't look it up. She started checking the obituaries, even though she didn't know his last name. During that period, Diane asked herself many times whether it had been worth it, meeting Thomas. Worth all the pain. Worth all the rejection when he wouldn't touch her. And many times, her silent response was the same: "Yes."

Thomas resurfaced, safe, with no real explanation. It was ridiculous. It was pathetic. It was love. It was hate. It was anger. It was acceptance. It was all of the above and more. Diane convinced herself that she was psychotic, obsessed, immature, insane. Then she realized that she was only human and she was probably just in love.

Diane and Thomas continued to meet in secret places. Sometimes they would talk. Others, they would sit there and sigh. Diane would always try to touch him and he would constantly push her away. Why did Thomas do this? And more important, why did Diane accept it? First, it was a challenge. Second, she harbored the hope that her sensuality would triumph over his will. It was an erotic power struggle of sorts. Sometimes Diane did win, but only partly.

"Not in the car," Thomas would say. Then the next time they were in the car, he would jerk off and splatter semen all over her pussy while she fingered herself into a frenzy. "Never again in the car," he would swear, but then he would stroke his prick and she would struggle to lick the jism as it shot onto her face and neck. He stroked with one hand and held her face away with the other, not even permitting her tongue to make contact with the head of his cock. Diane was confused. But perhaps Thomas was even more confused than she was.

One night, they sat in the car in the parking lot of Seaman's Furniture store. They studied the stars. "What's your favorite ice cream flavor?" Diane asked.

"I hate ice cream," Thomas said.

"But what if someone put a gun to your head and made you choose?" Diane wondered.

"Then I'd have to say vanilla," Thomas admitted.

After a few moments, Diane wondered, "And your favorite color?"

"Yellow," Thomas said.

"Yellow like the sun or yellow like gold?" Diane prodded.

"Like the sun. And yours?" he asked.

"Blue," Diane stated most emphatically. "Blue like the sky."

Thomas nodded. "The sun and the sky."

Diane couldn't decide what her favorite song was. There were so many. His was "Turn the Page." Magically, it came onto the radio. She lay her head in his lap and listened to the words and tried to figure out why he liked it so much. There were chills moving up her spine during the saxophone solo. Somehow, she understood. She understood perfectly.

Thomas looked into Diane's eyes. Then, he held her head in his hands and rubbed it against his cock. He began getting hard.

Diane moved her head of her own accord. Suddenly, Thomas said, "No," and made her sit up. The magic was broken because Diane had tried to take control of the situation. Thomas liked to believe that their silent lust was actually under control and he was only an innocent bystander, swept away in the undertow. There was less guilt that way.

Sometimes Thomas and Diane talked on the telephone and watched television together, each in their own apartment, miles away. This was very nice. Diane cuddled herself beneath a blanket and pretended that they were in bed together. Sometimes they would flip channels. Other times, they would switch to comedians or movie classics and comment on how beautiful Elizabeth Taylor was in *The Last Time I Saw Paris*. Diane rented Thomas' favorite movie, *Cinema Paradiso*. She saw it alone one night, hoping her telepathy would make him phone her. But it didn't. When the movie was over, the ending touched Diane so deeply that she cried for half an hour. And cried bitterly. She cried because she understood why Thomas loved that movie so much.

Finally, one day, Thomas explained why he couldn't penetrate Diane with his finger, his tongue or his penis. Even though his wife had always been ambivalent about sex, he had never been unfaithful to her. And he couldn't be, because his own father had abandoned his family when Thomas was only three years old. And Thomas didn't want to be like his father.

Diane tried to accept Thomas' explanation, but no matter how she tried, she couldn't swallow the whole thing. She couldn't help but think that Thomas really liked the power of refusal. It strongly resembled the passive might his wife held over him. It occurred to Diane that all four of them were like sexual dominoes. Thomas slept with a woman who rejected him, and rejected a woman who ached to take him inside of her body. Diane's husband craved her body, yet ignored the rest of her. And Diane, she lusted after Thomas. Go figure.

Thomas couldn't understand that Diane didn't want to take him away from anyone. She merely wanted to make love to him. To cling to him like a life preserver when life began to hurt too much. They could cling to each other to help stay afloat in this crazy world and then return to their respective families afterward, slightly more sane. Only Thomas wouldn't hear of it.

So, upon his suggestion, Thomas and Diane tried to be just friends. But it didn't work out too well. It had started out as a purely sexual relationship and only being friends was like back-pedaling. Diane told herself that she would rather have Thomas in her life, if only as a buddy, than not at all. He had opened Diane up to herself, awakened parts that she never knew existed. And she didn't want to lose that. Plus, Diane harbored a teeny-tiny, teensy-weensy hope that maybe, just maybe, Thomas would weaken and finger-fuck her with a cigar holder again.

But Thomas refused her even that. Whenever they were alone, or even in a crowd, their eyes would bore holes through each other. There was passion. There was fire. They would have to turn away or else try to ignore the electricity that sizzled between them. Thomas would start to talk facts and figures whenever his cock grew erect when he was with Diane. But even that did no good. Should they stop seeing each other? That would be too painful. But then seeing each other was painful in a different way.

Diane tried to accept Thomas' decision, but she wound up feeling remorseful, and worst of all, foolish. She couldn't help but remember all of the promises, about how they'd sneak off for a weekend in the Caribbean, how they'd make love for hours, how he'd make her climax again and again. Had they really been lies? In the curls of her cerebrum, Diane knew that Thomas longed to give Diane all of those things, but he simply couldn't. Thomas always told Diane the truth. And sometimes the truth hurt.

Did Thomas try to hurt her on purpose or did it just seem to happen that way? It hurt when he spoke of Monique, his former lover. It hurt when he spoke of how, in a rare display of passion, he convinced his wife to drip mother's milk all over his face and then lick it off. It hurt because these women had something Diane would never have—him. Diane wanted to hurt Thomas like she'd been hurt, but she couldn't. Then she realized that he was probably hurting too. She saw it in his eyes.

In her more fragile moments, Diane wondered if Thomas was using her to feel like a man because his wife had emasculated him. And it was pretty wonderful to make another woman wet, to make her squirm for you, to make her desire you, even in her sleep, wasn't it? All that, without technically committing adultery. But then again, Diane knew that Thomas was probably in love with her. Only it frightened him. And when men are frightened, they usually pull away. When women are frightened, they usually open up even more, throwing reason to the wind, like delicate flowers of flesh, poising themselves for the pain. After all, pain was better than denial. Wasn't it?

Then the holidays came around. Diane's husband was so wound up in his own sad, little world that he still didn't notice anything. Not her mood swings. Not her tears. He had hardened himself to other people's feelings a long time ago. The only thing that existed and mattered was his own irrational sorrow. That could be why Diane clung so tightly to the idea of Thomas; at least he didn't ignore her. Although Diane's husband often entered her body, he rarely ventured into her mind like Thomas did.

For Christmas, Diane bought Thomas an earring. She had had a pair of white gold crosses made up especially for them. The only two of their kind in the entire universe. She put hers through a hole she'd pierced in the cartilage of her left ear the day after Thomas' birthday. The piercing was intensely painful, yet seemed significant. Thomas wouldn't accept his earring, however. He told her to hold it for him until he was ready. That's exactly what Diane did. She waited. She had become very adept at waiting.

Then, one fateful day in February, Thomas agreed to meet Diane at a local diner. But only if his friend Kenny could come along. "That way I know nothing will happen," Thomas explained. But when Kenny went to make a phone call, Diane's foot found its way to Thomas' crotch. He held it there.

Out of the blue, Thomas asked for his earring. How did he know Diane had decided to take it with her that night? Thomas knew all sorts of things. He slipped the post through the hole in his ear. It was almost a religious experience. The two of them felt it, but Kenny had no idea. He ate his souvlaki, then finished half of Diane's grilled cheese and tomato.

It was early, and none of them wanted to go home to their respective apartments alone. Thomas' wife and baby were visiting her parents in Florida, so perhaps he felt brave. Or maybe just lonely. In any case, they headed back to Kenny's apartment. Kenny's wife was out playing cards and wouldn't be back for hours. "She's a creature of habit," Kenny began as he drove. Thomas and Diane intertwined hands while Kenny spoke. "Linguini on Monday . . . ," Diane's fingers traced Thomas' fingertips. "Chicken cutlets on Tuesday . . . ," Thomas drew a tiny circle on Diane's palm. "On Wednesday, it's . . ." Kenny went through the entire week while Diane and Thomas practically made love, barely even touching. By the time they reached Kenny's apartment, it was clear.

Yes, Thomas was especially brave that night. "Maybe, just maybe, Thomas will make love to me tonight," Diane told herself. The safety of Kenny might quell his fears of falling in too deep. Only Thomas was in too deep already. Very openly, Thomas touched Diane's perfectly up-turned ass and made certain Kenny admired it too. He had Diane show Kenny how stiff her nipples got. Sure enough, when she took off her bra, they jutted out like little pinkies. At that point, Diane would have done anything, anything for Thomas. Anything for the hope that he might make love to her. And she did anything and everything that night.

Kenny's son was away playing basketball at college. The two men led Diane into the boy's unused bedroom and laid her down on the forest green sheets. Thomas sat down on the tattered weight-lifting bench and watched while Kenny ate Diane's pussy. Kenny was in ecstasy and compared its essence to lobster. Diane was in ecstasy too. She looked at the blue-eyed man with his head nestled between her legs. Then, she looked at Thomas. The sight of Diane's pussy splayed open like a moist butterfly might compel him to make love to her. But Thomas didn't move; he sat there studying her.

Diane rubbed her swollen clit against Kenny's lips. He held back the hood that shrouded her button with his thumbs. "Look at this, Tommy," Kenny gasped. And Thomas studied the glistening nib of pleasure. Diane's clitoris stood out irreverently and boldly, throbbing with each pulse beat. Kenny pursed his lips around it and sucked. Diane looked at Thomas while she was coming, his face a blur behind her flickering eyelids. Thomas licked his lips, as if he could taste Diane from across the room.

Her orgasm empowered her. Diane felt like a comic book superheroine or a mystical oracle of sensuality. That was the moment Diane realized her own strength. She would penetrate Thomas without even touching him. She would penetrate him with her eyes and with other things. She would take him inside that way. She would use the power generated by her orgasm to pierce him.

Diane's eyes snared Thomas while she sucked Kenny's dick through a condom. Her tongue traced its way up the sheathed shaft, then her lips encircled the head. Thomas swallowed hard when Diane did this, as though he were fully aware of what she was trying to accomplish. Still, Diane continued. She kneeled and eased Kenny's prick inside her, as far as it would go. Her juices coated his balls, drenched his pubic hairs.

"How does that feel?" Thomas asked Kenny.

"So tight . . . so wet," Kenny moaned. "But why don't you fuck her?" Thomas didn't answer, but Diane already knew the reason.

That night, Diane rode Kenny like the wind as she studied Thomas' expression. He tried to avoid her gaze, but a few times he became lost in it. Diane looked directly into Thomas' eyes when his friend took her from behind. Thomas talked dirty to her. Through Kenny, Thomas gave Diane pleasure in an indirect way. Plus, he got to watch. In a sense, it was even better than *Cinema Paradiso* because it was his orchestration.

"I'm fucking you," Thomas whispered into Diane's ear while Kenny pounded against her buttocks. "That's me fucking you." But still, it wasn't the same as if he really were.

Thomas even pinched Diane's nipples and helped her climax a second time. Didn't he realize that he was contributing to her strength? This was an even stronger orgasm than the first one, it shook Diane at the very root. She trembled and screamed. Tears streamed down her cheeks as her face pressed against the cool bedsheets. "Thomas . . . ," she cried in barely a whisper. Yes, Diane uttered Thomas' name, even though Kenny was fucking her. She hoped he didn't get insulted. Kenny was a nice guy, but he surely wasn't Thomas.

In a way, it was pathetic. In another way, it was sad. But no matter how much Diane pleaded, Thomas *still* wouldn't penetrate her. She even fell down to her knees and begged. But then she remembered. She remembered about her power. Diane stood up and began to dress, thinking of that power.

Kenny and Thomas drove Diane home. They sat in the front seat and she in the back, like a child or puppy. The earring Diane had given Thomas dangled from his lobe. It caught the brightness from a passing car's headlights and shone like a star for a moment. But just for a moment. Diane touched the cross with her finger. She felt strangely courageous, even though her legs were shaking. Then she began to speak. And when she spoke, it was like a writer writing a story. It was like a story she was writing in the air instead of on paper. "He was afraid to penetrate her," Diane began. "But what he didn't realize was that she had already penetrated him. She had penetrated him with her heart and with her mind."

Thomas smiled vaguely in the darkness. "And with her eyes," he said. "Don't forget her eyes."

Cecilia Tan

〜

A True Story

You know what I love about masturbation and a creative imagination? There's always something new to try. Don't ask me what it is about my parents' house that makes me tremendously horny. Perhaps it's the lingering memory of my teen years, spent poring over teen magazines, being frustrated, spending hours on the phone with cute but unapproachable boys, more frustration, and masturbation.

I went back for a visit when I was in the area for a business trip, and one night I found myself wandering around the house alone after everyone else had gone to sleep. I was tired of the jill-off-and-zonk-out five-minute orgasm routine. It was time to work up the willpower to dominate myself again. Self-bondage has been a part of masturbation for me as far back as I can remember, and that's pretty far (age five, if you must know).

Heading back to my bedroom, I knelt on my bed, pulled my panties down to my ankles and wrapped one foot around twice, binding them tightly together. Pulling my T-shirt over my head without removing it, I exposed my breasts, shivering. Twisting my shirt between my wrists, I bound my arms behind my back, with just enough room between my hands for me to reach the interesting parts of my body if I tried hard enough. Then the Top in me

ordered me to shut off the lights—it's much more effective than
a blindfold. You can't peek. I nudged the wall switch with my
shoulder and the room went black.

I sat that way for a few minutes, resting my buttocks on my
heels and my head on my knees, letting my mind go blank. I don't
know how long I sat like that, but at some point I was surprised
to feel that one of my heels was wet. I was dripping with anticipation.

"You little bitch," I thought to myself. "You can't wait for it, can
you? Well, you're going to get it." I had the sudden inspiration to
try on a belt I had brought with me. It was made with three large
metal rings, attached by two thin strips of leather; I wondered if
there was a more creative way it could be worn than just around
the waist.

Of course, I had to find it in my suitcase in the dark. I hobbled
over on my knees, reaching backward into the bag to feel for it.
Not very hard to find, though I mistook my leather-studded dog
collar for it—that gave me another idea to try later.

I kicked the panties off my ankles and threaded one leg
through each set of leather straps, putting the center ring right
over my vagina and clitoris. I didn't have anything else to attach
the two end rings to, so I hooked them together behind my back.
I praised my Topself's cleverness—she let me turn on the light
for a moment to see how it looked. Delicious.

I danced around the room in the dark a little, feeling the
leather squeeze my thighs and the hard pressure of the ring
drawing more and more blood to my vulva. I threw myself down
on the bed and slapped myself with the dog collar. But no matter
how hard I tried, I just couldn't hit myself hard enough. Perhaps
it's like tickling yourself—can't be done. I gave up on that when
another idea for the collar came into my head.

I stood up and threaded it under the ring, so it was pressed
into the crack from my anus to my clitoris. I pranced around
some more, feeling the leather rub against my skin as I moved my
feet. I looked around the room for something the right size and
shape. Hmmm . . . I rolled a condom onto a sample bottle of
shampoo and tied a knot in the end. I took the collar out of the

ring, slid the bottle into my vagina, and put the collar back. It held the bottle in place perfectly. I moaned, then mentally gagged myself with one thought—my parents were asleep in the next room. I wasn't about to try to explain anything, so I kept quiet (oh, it was hard to do, especially near the end!).

My Top decided I was going to wait some more, though. The number of minutes past the hour would be how many times I was going to pull that collar through, from one end to the other, as slowly as possible, before I could come. It was twenty-five minutes after. That meant twenty-five long, slow, agonizing strokes— each cold, round, smooth stud on the collar grinding slowly over my clit. After about twenty strokes, though, I lost count. What was I going to do? I couldn't get away with cheating.

"You're so sensitive down there, aren't you? You couldn't count because you're thinking with your clit," I told myself. "So, count with it." I decided to count the number of studs on the collar as I pulled it through. Every time I was wrong, I would get five more very slow strokes. In that instant I became a prized slave, on display, to be sold. I would fetch a higher price for more stamina.

I counted fourteen studs on the collar, gritting my teeth and whispering the numbers to myself as each nub of metal tweaked my clit. Then I pulled the collar free and counted again with my tongue, licking the juices from it. Sixteen studs. I counted again with my fingers. Damn. That meant ten more strokes! I lay still for a full minute as punishment for my impatience. As the numbers flipped on the clock radio, I started the collar moving. I thought I would never get to ten, my clit throbbing, but I imagined veiled masters watching me from behind diaphanous curtains, bidding on my price, betting on my abilities. I finished the tenth stroke—which I made extra long and slow—and then struggled up from my back to a kneeling position.

Putting one leg through the shirt between my wrists, I got one hand in back, and one in front. Holding on to each end of the collar, I started moving it back and forth in a sawing motion across my clit. As I pumped my hips, the shampoo bottle fucked me, and I couldn't have stopped myself from coming even if I had wanted to. I collapsed forward in a wet heap (and almost fell off the bed in the dark). I never get this sweaty when someone else works me over, I thought. I slept soundly next to a small pile of damp leather and clothing, and waited until my parents had left for work to wash the shampoo bottle.

Jane Longaway

Erotoplasmic Orgasmic

Dottie leaned against the window and breathed, creating a patch of uneven fog in which she wrote the initials of her lover, SB, and her own, DM. Around both of these initials she drew a lopsided heart. She had been in love with S for over four months and being apart from him was painful. She studied the initials with mild satisfaction, then resumed her study of the paper she was to present the next evening at the Institute of Parapsychology in San Francisco.

She took the train because she found it less anxiety-provoking than flying. And it gave her nine full hours to work in relative peace with just the click-clack of the wheels to lull her into a receptive frame of mind. Her paper dealt with mediumship, or what has come to be known as trance channeling. She had been involved in a study of this phenomenon and had spent considerable time with the famous Sister George, who trance-channeled sex partners from different planes, much to the delight of her many followers in the greater Los Angeles area. There was simply no safer sex to be found, since all bodily contact was on an astral plane and participants used only their astral bodies. Apparently, even in this ectoplasmic state, people of both sexes and all persuasions had extraordinarily vital orgasmic experiences. Dottie never personally participated since she had to keep her scientific objectivity (plus she had more than her hands full with SB). However, she had witnessed participants awakening from induced trance states flushed and trembling, with dampness between their legs and languid eyes.

Now, facing a week without S, she found herself wishing Sister George was with her on this trip. Perhaps a fling with some entity from another plane would help relieve the ache she felt in both her heart and her cunt. She shifted her legs around. Her nylons rubbed together, and her suit felt just a little too tight. She unbuttoned the jacket and two blouse buttons, and kicked off her high heels. There was no one in the compartment with her, so she put the armrests up and stretched out full-length on the seat to watch the scenery whip by. It was mildly hypnotic. She rested her brilliant red hair on a tiny paper-covered pillow and attempted to read her paper from start to finish. If S had come with her, this would have been a wonderful trip. After reading two pages of graphs and statistics, she took her glasses off and laid them on the floor, then closed her eyes and allowed her mind to drift.

Sister George appeared in all her 200-plus-pound glory, with her crinkly dyed-blond hair and tiny green eyes, her red rosebud mouth pursed and ready to speak. Dottie opened her eyes and Sister George disappeared. She saw a small town whiz by the window, then closed her eyes again, trying to think about S, who was tall and slender with a blond ponytail. But the minute she closed her eyes, Sister George was there; Dottie could even smell her Opium perfume, which she used a bit too liberally. After opening and closing her eyes a few times, she gave in to the vision: Sister George, wearing a pink and yellow tent dress, opened her small cherry lips and began to speak.

"So," she said, "you're ready to try. It's about time. What good is all that research without experience? Keep your eyes closed, darling, and something fabulous will happen."

Sister George took her into a trance state by counting down, using colors, and Dottie felt herself floating. She tried to fight it at first, but Sister George was good and kept it up until the image of the large woman faded completely, and Dottie found herself floating in a silver haze. Looking around her she saw land just below, and as if by magic, the second she saw it she was on it. She stood on a flat blue rock surrounded by giant ferns and thistleberries. A stream gurgled in the background; she could hear the water dash against the rocks and smell the freshness of the air. She looked down and noticed that she was naked, but it was warm enough that the goosebumps on her flesh were more from fright than from being chilled.

There was a sound of plants being pushed aside, the flat clip-clop of horse hooves, and then suddenly she saw the black muscle of a stallion. Seated on the horse was a man dressed in red leather with a black feathered hat on his head. He was large, about six foot eight from the look of him, and his face was shaded by the huge feather that hung over it. Around his waist was a silver chain, and his thick fingers were covered with glittering jewels. Dottie was astonished to find that people on the astral plane smelled rather strongly of horse and sweat.

Not quite believing in this apparition, she didn't flee when he dismounted and tied his horse to a palmetto tree. He walked toward her slowly, as if he weren't too sure if she was real either. When he got close enough to cover one entire breast with his hand, she let out a shrill scream, and he made a noise in the base of his throat and spat on the ground. Quick as a wink, he grabbed her waist with both hands, picked her up, and shook her, trying to see what she was made of. Her hair whipped back and forth. She saw that under the hat he was a strong-featured gentleman with black eyes and white teeth.

He set Dottie back on the rock and took off his hat with a flourish. Blue-black curls tumbled around his head. He let the hat fall to the ground and quickly unfastened his garments, which were held together by intricate strings. Naked, he stood before Dottie with so much to look at that she almost fainted, like one of those old-fashioned heroines; but faint she didn't. His neck, arms and chest were huge and well-muscled, the skin fair. Hair tufted from both armpits and from his groin and spread in an eagle-shaped design across his chest. His thighs were enormous, knotted with muscle; his cock, which rose out of a mass of wiry black hair, was the size of a baby's arm.

"My, my, my," Dottie said. The man made more strange noises deep in his throat, and made a speech in a language that made no sense to her whatsoever; however, she was sure it was a language. He moved up slowly, once again took her by the waist, and gently pulled her close. She was getting used to his odor; in fact, she found it sportive and stimulating. He ran his fingers over the red hair tumbled around her shoulders and smoothed his hands over her curly pubic hair, which was as blatantly red as the hair on her head. He stuck his fat finger into her honeypot, as she grasped his dick with her hand to find out what the ectoplasm felt like.

"Well," she thought, "it feels like a big, fat, engorged cock." His finger, which was prodding her sex with great success, also seemed to find that she was no mere apparition. The man withdrew his finger and smelled it. A smile appeared on his face, and Dottie found herself smiling back. She idly continued to stroke his member as the big hairy balls swung back and forth.

The man started to moan a little. He shifted from foot to foot and tenderly held on to both her breasts, giving smart little tweaks to her nipples from time to time. Then the surprisingly smooth hands ran down her belly to her pussy, and his thumbs went to work on her clit. She began moaning with him and pulled him closer, all the while keeping a tight grip on his prick. He picked her up and carried her off the rock while her hands fluttered aimlessly, then set her down in a field where the grass was thick and dew-soft. She lay down spread-eagle and waited for him while he hovered over her.

Shaded by his huge body, she took a fleeting look at the sky, which was violet in color and lit by a silvery orb. Dottie blinked and the man went down on her. He pulled her legs over his massive shoulders and, with a tongue that felt as wide as a washcloth, he licked and teased her. She wondered where the fuck she was.

He sucked on her toes, manicured only a few days before, and licked her instep. Then, pulling her by the hips, he took her buttocks in his hands and lifted her up to drive his penis right into her. She let out a huge moan. He was so large that for a moment she thought she would pass out, and she wiggled and struggled to get comfortable. Finally it started to feel good, then damn good, then goddamn good. She wrapped her legs around his waist and caressed him with both hands. He continued to mumble and moan in his strange language. A lizard appeared and came quite close to her face, darted its tongue twice, and disappeared again. The lizard had been completely transparent; she had seen its organs, the small heart opening and closing like a tiny fist.

Then, with a quick violent thrusting, he pulled her toward him as she clawed frantically at his back. An explosion was coming, an explosion that would send both of them in a million jillion pieces into the universe, flung up like a handful of sand. He came with great heaving cries and she came seconds later, her womb and pussy fluttering and convulsing. Rivers of sticky, hot spunk ran down her legs and she fell to the ground, hitting her head softly.

She opened one eye. She had hit her head against the compartment wall. The train was rocking back and forth, going into curves. Through the window she could see the brown and green farmland repeating itself over and over. Dottie caught her breath and sat up painfully. It felt as if she had bruised her back; it felt, in fact, as if she had *fucked a giant*. She got out her purse and found her silver-plated compact. The tiny mirror showed that her make-up was rubbed off and her hair disheveled. She quickly fixed herself up and rubbed her hand over the small of her back. There were traces of scratches on her skin. She found all of this very bizarre. Still, the dream had been satisfying; the big man was so different from S. The sex had been a little rough and smelly, and so completely nonverbal. S talked all the time, like an English professor. He loved to name parts, both his and hers, and he smelled like cologne, not horseshit. Dottie found a cigarette and lit it, then curled up in a corner with her thoughts. What a very nice dream, she thought, and what an extraordinary cock the big man had; it had made her feel like her insides were all hot, pink expansiveness.

She started to nod, the cigarette dipping between her fingers. Soon the heavy lids closed over her baby blues and she saw Sister George again.

"Well, aren't we the slut!" Sister George boomed. Dottie blinked up at her, speechless. "Now I'll take you even further," Sister George said, her voice becoming softer and very persuasive as she began the countdown. Swirls of sea-green color began to flow around Dottie.

"No, no," Dottie cried out, "stop this, I don't want . . ."

She was falling, had been falling for a long time. Her body passed through colors and patterns of light, tones of music, and even different smells. Her mother's smell, the smell of baked apples, the smell of lavender, the smell of forty-weight oil, the smell of wet asphalt and the smell of chocolate mints. She fell until she thought she could fall no more, yet she kept falling. And all the while she clenched and unclenched her now transparent hands. She found that she could pass through solid rock and ice; she had no weight, and more important, no clothes. She put her hand to her breast, and it swelled to meet her grasp. Her hair fanned out around her head like an Ondine's, and like an Ondine she was falling through emerald-green water. Falling alongside her were strange creatures: a penisfish propelling itself by deflating its two huge balls; a winged creature of both sexes, with four round and pert breasts, and a smallish cock under a wide-open vagina; mermen and mermaids fucking in daisychain style; a huge mouth that seemed on second glance to be a sexual organ, the dreaded *Vagina dentata*. She drifted in this strange place until she came to rest on a plant whose silver-green protuberances embraced her and caressed her body. Two thick stamens emerged, covered with a sticky substance that worked as a lubricant as they entered her pussy and anus. She was being fucked by a *plant*, and quite nicely too. She started to moan and wiggle, helping the plant along. Amorphous figures circled her and the energetic plant, and began to flow into each other at a frantic rate. She watched them, but the plant creature was beginning to overwhelm her. Its leaves and stamens were covered with fine hairs that tickled and stimulated her to distraction. Against her better judgment she found herself responding to the plant, calling it "sweet cabbage" and "my dear little honeysuckle." It held tight to her, tentacles holding her legs slightly apart so that her clit was exposed to the delicate fronds delighting her. She wondered about getting this thing back into her world, as it would have made the perfect house plant. But then the ectoplasm, which had been dancing and merging in front of her eyes, coalesced into a huge, flower-shaped vagina and an equally huge towerlike penis. It began fucking, the flower vagina quivering like a jellyfish as the penis thrust in and out. This went on with increasing vigor until the penis-shaped ectoplasm pulled out and ejected a spray of matter which covered both her and the plant.

While the plant examined itself, she managed to free herself from its wild embrace, and ran as fast as she could in the first direction she found herself facing. Seeing something to her left, she headed for it and found herself in a forest of mirrors of all shapes. Even the ground beneath her was reflective, so she saw her image everywhere she turned her gaze. It was cut up, distorted, fractured, whole here and fragmented there. She was surrounded by images of herself from every possible angle and in every possible light. She saw her face with twenty blue eyes at once, ten lips opening and closing. For a moment she was so astonished that she just twirled around and reveled in the different views of her own naked flesh. The swell of her buttocks, her sharp little knees, her fiery red hair all captivated her. She twirled and danced until she felt unmistakably that someone or something else was watching her.

At first she shyly covered her breasts and pubis with her hands and called out, "Who's there?" No one answered, but she could feel someone just the same. The presence was unmistakable; it was as if she were inside some huge consciousness. The mirrors reflected her distress and bewilderment. Now a thousand blue eyes looked piteously back at her, and then she saw one brown pair. It was a pair of honey-brown eyes with big pupils. The eyes were languid and appraised her frankly, while she turned around in vain to find who was behind them. Then, as she grew quiet and waited, a face appeared bit by bit: the eyebrows, the nose, the lips, the chin, and so on until a stranger's beautiful face was visible. She realized with a jolt that it was the perfect face she had been looking for all her life. Whoever it was had taken on the mask of her ideal of male beauty. He continued to evolve body part by body part, slowly, as if pulling the ideal dimensions from her own imagination. There he was, but in the mirror.

She ran her hands over the cool reflection. The image was tall, well-muscled, with strong thighs, narrow waist and broad chest and shoulders. His head was molded from all her dreams: high cheekbones and patrician nose, sensuous lips and perfect teeth just a little crooked in front; his jaw was strong, and he had the hint of a black beard. She was so enchanted by this image that she pressed up close to one full-length mirror and undulated against the glass. Her movement gave her no release, although in other mirrors, if the angle was right, they appeared to be joined at the hip. Dottie was desperate to touch the man in the glass, and he seemed to be sharing her desire. His cock, which now reached his belly button, was pumped up with lust. As she kissed and licked its reflection, the illusion in another mirror was of their touching hands.

He made no noise, but his face was superbly eloquent. His bushy black eyebrows knitted together as his eyes shut in pleasure. She caressed the mirror with her backside and imagined what he could do in the flesh. If only they were on the same side of the mirror! Thinking of this, she had an inspiration, and looked around for something that would smash the glass. He was hers if only she could get him out. The image of the perfect man grimaced as she moved away from the glass, and he banged his fists in frustration. She looked around her, but everything was mirrors; it seemed impossible to move any of them. Each one reflected her lover, pleading with her to come back. She walked from the forest trying to find some rock to smash the glass, but she only saw mirrors and more mirrors. The beautiful man beckoned to her repeatedly, until she screamed and ran headlong into the nearest mirror, shattering it into a million pieces. Suddenly the man, the forest, everything disappeared and she was in a room with one open window but no doors.

The room had a huge platform bed heaped with pillows of yellow silk and draped with netting. Dottie ignored the bed and ran to the window, still aching for the mirror man with the Calvin Klein fashion body. The window looked out on a landscape that seemed tiny; she was very high up and the drop was sheer. She enjoyed the cool breeze for a moment, then sighed a little and sat on the down-filled bed. She thought she might just take a little nap, since nothing made any sense. For some reason the glass had not cut her, but she felt devastated by the loss of the perfect man. Soon she was curled up in the delicious bed with her hair spread out on the yellow silk.

She sank down into the softness of the bed, and had almost

drifted off when she heard something. It was the pad of feet. Wrapping some yellow silk around her naked body, she sat up. To her joy, it was the mirror man looking at her with nine types of desire burning in his caramel eyes.

"Oh, it's you!" she said breathlessly, touching him. Yes, she could touch him, and his skin was quite warm and real. He lifted her hair with his hands and ran his fingers through it. Dottie let the silk slip down. Her nipples were soft, rose-colored lips ready to pucker at the slightest touch. He bent down, his curly hair tickling her throat, and sucked on them.

"How did you get here?" Dottie asked.

"I didn't, you got into the mirror," he said, in a voice that sounded like he had breathed helium seconds before.

"Shhh, darling, don't speak," Dottie counseled her dream date. She put a finger over his mouth and licked his nose, then, on second thought she raised herself, rolled him over and sat on his face. This ruled out listening to him sounding like Truman Capote. They occupied themselves with licking each other until they were both drenched in juice. Then, with his prick as hard as hunger, he mounted her and they had the most profound fuck she had ever experienced. It felt like his cock was swimming in the ocean of her being, as if he was redesigning her interior. She felt the buildup of all the cum in his balls, bursting to shoot, and she felt herself building up to a similar extravaganza.

They both began to shudder and groan; the tension was more than the usual tickle, it felt dangerous. His cock seemed to penetrate not only her womb but her stomach, her lungs, even her brain. Every atom in her body was bracing itself; and then it happened. It started at her toes and worked its way quickly up. She gushed and undulated as he exploded his load deep and hot inside, a shower of stars. She screamed, she clawed his most perfect back with her fingernails. She came to the tenth power; dripping with his sweat and her juices, she was blasted right back into the train headed north.

Dottie groaned on the seat and opened her eyes to find her legs wide apart and her blouse open to the waist. She felt exhausted and tingly all over. She sat up, buttoned her blouse, tucked it into her skirt and ran her fingers through her hair—all

the while feeling like she had run a marathon and placed first.
Her notes were scattered on the floor. She quickly picked them
up, straightened them, and snapped them into her briefcase
where they could damn well stay until she gave her presentation.
She no longer gave two figs about it; it was all statistics and rhetoric as far as she was concerned. The real meat was in the experiences themselves.

S also seemed like a pale runner-up in her book; although she
thought kindly of him, he was so vulgarly alive and constrained by
the laws of this plane. Still, she would send him a postcard from
San Francisco as soon as she got settled—and after, she thought,
after she called Sister George.

Tips

Andrea stood before the mirror, arms raised. The rows of dirty in-candescent bulbs lit her like a shrine. She thought herself a sort of sarcastic virgin. A fisher of men.

She sat down on a metal folding chair. It was still slightly warm. She could never get comfortable in these; if she leaned back, she couldn't see her face, and if she leaned forward on her elbows, she couldn't do her makeup. She got up again and shifted her legs. Stilettos didn't suit women who stood still for long.

Andrea took out her eye shadows, blew softly on the applicator, and wondered whether Sunlit Burgundy or Sassy Periwinkle went better with dark green.

She put down the eye shadow. Fuck it. She walked over to the full-length mirror, turned, and bent over. She slid her hands be-neath her T-back. She just couldn't stand it when those things got twisted. She'd heard it could give you hemorrhoids.

She walked slowly through the club. It was too cold, but less smoky than it had been a couple of years ago. The pulsating lights and noise merged into the drinks. They overwhelmed the senses to an almost desperate level. But she always smiled, made eye contact. At the vaguest sign of interest, she'd stop. All it took was a raised eyebrow or a pause in conversation.

"Hi. Are you guys having fun tonight?" She hated this part. It was too boring even for money.

"Yeah—what's your name?"

"Andrea." She extended her gloved hand. She always wore long black gloves. She didn't like the men to be able to really touch her.

"No, no. Your real name." She turned her head briefly. They all thought they were smart if they showed her they knew it was a stage name.

"Madame Extravaganza. May I join you?"

"Sure."

The redhead seemed the most lively. Andrea sat down very close to him in one of the club's overstuffed chairs.

"So what do you do?"

"I work for Walmart. I'm one of the regional managers."

In the three years she had been working, she still couldn't figure out how to feign interest in Walmart managers. She propped her elbows up on the table, flung her leg over his thigh, and did her best to look fascinated.

"Oh, really?" He was studying her fishnets. Good. Maybe she could skirt the intricacies of Walmart management altogether tonight.

They sat like that for a song or two. He didn't seem to want to talk; she was grateful. His hand on her thigh felt comforting. The music was too loud, a handy excuse to avoid the banter. Perhaps she was going to get away without even knowing his name. She'd forget it anyway.

"Hotel California" came on. She turned to him. He was watching Jackie on center stage and she could see his crow's feet, too harsh in the soft light. Some stray white hairs edged in around his temple. This was about his speed.

"Do you like this song?"

"Yeah."

"Would you like me to dance for you?" It was illegal to ask that—solicitation. But some guys took too long.

She stood up. She turned and rolled her short, sheer skirt down over her undulating hips. When she had it around her thighs, she bent over and slid it down her legs. She held the pose a moment.

This would give her time to stretch. He looked at her tight hamstrings and thought about her pussy being right there, right beneath that sequined black panty thing, right in his face. He shifted in his chair.

She could see from between her legs that he was hard. Perfect. Still bent over, she reached up and let her fingers slowly slide down her ass to the backs of her knees. They loved that.

She turned at the song's line about pretty boys and dipped down. She unclasped her bra from behind with one hand and held her breasts in its cups with the other. It was a lacy emerald under-wire that created a little cleavage. The thin satin straps hung down over her shoulders and beneath her arms. All she had to do was take her hand away. Now her breasts were at his eye level. She swayed there for a bit. She had small breasts and was never sure if they liked looking at them or not. A waitress asked her to move so she could get by. The place was filling up.

She threw her leg up on a table. Her spike-heeled shoe was right beside his beer. It made him nervous and hot. Should he watch the naked woman in front of him, or the drink?

Andrea went down on her knees. She raised her head up at him. He smiled. She whipped her head around and let her hair swing across his crotch. He couldn't feel anything, of course, and that was the point.

She stood and turned away from him. She let herself drop onto his chest and belly, her back arched above his lap. He liked her breasts from this angle; they fell slightly to her sides and up. His hand wandered up her waist. It tickled. Deftly, she crossed her arms beneath her breasts and turned her hands up prettily at their sides. He'd been foiled, but couldn't help admiring the new cleavage she'd created. Tact had its rewards.

When the song ended, he folded a pristine twenty in half and slid it under her T-back at her hip. She sat down and let him order her a drink. She looked across the club. It was going to be a good night.

She had already made sixty-four dollars before it was time for her to get ready for the stage. She stood in front of the full-length mirror, admiring her efforts, searching for flaws.

She thought she looked stately. She had put her hair up; this was a breach of strip bar norms, but she couldn't resist exposing her throat. Her eyes had hovered tenderly over its contours more often than any man's had.

She was a real dancer, and she resembled the ballerinas she had trained under; her dark hair offset her fine features, and her breasts were small and round. They were the breasts of thirteen-year-old virgins or Parisian women. They didn't quite belong on a stripper; they were best suited to young tomboys or gymnasts.

Her stomach was soft and flat. It wasn't the hard sort of flat that some of the older dancers had acquired through endless sit-ups; it was the gentle flatness only youth insured. You could look at her stomach and admire it, but it didn't demand the same respect as chiseled muscularity.

Men told her that from behind she looked like a mare; her ass and upper thighs were sturdy and dense, and when she walked, you could see the muscles shifting beneath her skin. When you looked at her, you could almost feel her bones and blood and salt. Her body was a hymn to human form. If he could bring himself to it, a religious apologist could point to her body: she wouldn't be possible if not for the intention of some Being.

But to Andrea, her body was a simple asset. Although she appreciated it, it remained a commodity and a tool. She allowed herself no sentimental indulgences.

She was young, only twenty-one, but Andrea was more honest with herself than other strippers who had been in the scene longer. She had perspective. It was plain: all workers had a supply that filled a demand. Strippers peddled arousal to the lustful.

Why not exploit her body while she could? Her college degree would last longer.

She was turning over these long-familiar reflections as though they were cherished heirlooms when the DJ introduced Chloe. Andrea was next on stage.

"How's the crowd, Steve?"

"Pretty lively for a Tuesday." He pressed his middle and index fingers firmly against the top of Andrea's neck as he put in her CD. Steve was a friend, and Andrea let him touch her casually. She allowed no other male employee such license.

She closed her eyes and felt the pressure of his fingers against her muscles. He circled them slowly and purposefully to the persistent bass in Chloe's second song. One wayward glove was slouching beneath Andrea's elbow. He watched her arms; he felt disappointed unless he raised their sparse black hairs. Andrea was just beginning to fall in step with his goals when Chloe's song began to fade. Andrea smiled at her DJ, checked her teeth for lipstick, and strutted onto the stage.

Her pulse and breathing caught up with her legs in seconds. She surveyed her audience and hit the floor like oil. Her knees bent and her back arched into the long line of her outstretched arms. She drew her torso back and lifted her eyes. She had them, all right. She raised up, threw one leg out at ninety degrees, and thrust her hips forward so that her pelvis twitched provocatively.

Then she was on her feet and hopping over to a tip. The man held out the bill a little too brazenly for her sensibilities. She'd show him. She fell back onto one hand and perched the other one effortlessly onto one raised knee. Her legs were spread wide as she offered the surprised client an uncensored view up her loose silk skirt. The filmy green fabric fell further back to her waist with each contraction of her ass. She stood and then knelt down to his level. He raised his eyebrows and slipped in his dollar respectfully.

That first tip was always the toughest, but once she had demonstrated her talents to one unsuspecting voyeur, business skyrocketed. Now they were surrounding the stage.

She executed five flawless chaîné turns toward her second patron. She stood still before him a moment, making him wait. Then she knelt and rested her wrists across his shoulders. She thrust her breasts toward his face several times. Just as he began to beg her to lose the bra, she spun around on one knee, lowering her torso so that her breasts hugged the polished parquet stage, and popped her pelvis for him. His jaw slackened slightly while he peered at the curve of her pussy straining against her T-back. He wondered if the tight-fitting garment pressed against her little clit, and got an immediate hard-on. When she turned for her tip, he looked stupidly at her for a moment before remembering to slip it in.

When her second song eased out over the club, Andrea was kneeling on the stage. Her head was thrown back and her eyes closed. The pose looked beautiful and gave her a moment to collect herself.

She raised her right arm above her head, looked out sleepily at the men, and dragged her left index finger down the length of her arm before letting it skirt the curve of her right breast. Nothing legally classified as lewd conduct, but unmistakably suggestive.

In any city, just find out what you can't do, and then do everything else. If you can't touch your own damn breasts, drag your gloves over them. If you can't handle the men, then blow in their ears.

With this in mind, she let her atrociously long string of pearls dangle down between her legs. She swayed very slightly and got them to move back and forth across her upturned cunt. Guys dug that; they imagined that the little plastic baubles were dragging across her clit.

Andrea turned on one foot to find her patrons waiting. She got down to business. Her pelvis rotated, her hips swiveled, every gesture an exaggeration. She crawled around like some depraved slave girl.

She looked leisurely up at the last one. His nose was almost touching hers. He watched her. The way she breathed through her mouth, the way her eyes darted from his eyes to his lips and back, like he had just kissed her. Oh, his cock was getting very hard. So real, so real.

He flashed a fifty and whispered, "Please touch yourself a little. Rub your clit for just five seconds."

Fifty dollars. She let her fingers edge around the elastic of her T-back.

The song ended. Andrea felt relieved and a little disappointed. She accepted a ten and wondered how much she could make if she went to that man's table.

Steve was wiping off the dressing-room counters when she walked off the stage and Gabrielle took her place in the spotlight. He was a good DJ; the others tended to whine about their less glamorous duties, but Steve accepted his chores graciously. It was crazy, but he genuinely enjoyed tidying up after his dancers or getting them sodas from the bar as they preened.

He offered her a fresh towel. Andrea always worked up a good sheen.

"Were they biting?" Steve asked.

"Sure. But you know me. I lose out on a lot of money 'cause I take too long on each client. I only got a few dollars."

"You may not take in much on the stages, Andrea, but every man who tips you is floored. You do your songs and you stay busy. Don't bitch about those little tips to me. I know how much you put out. Man, you probably aren't even giving me ten percent."

Steve had her. If she made three hundred and fifty dollars, she'd give him twenty-five. Most nights she topped three hundred, but he had never seen more than thirty from her, and only that much on the night she had made four hundred and sixty-seven dollars. All the dancers were supposed to tip the DJs at least a tithe. Few did.

She changed the subject. "Steve. Are you gonna finish rubbing me, or what?" She felt a twinge of guilt at exploiting this nice young man's weakness, but, God, his fingers were strong.

"Uh-huh. You just meet me in Staten's office after your sets on the runway."

Andrea walked back to the dressing room after her final set. She wiped off again, touched up her makeup, and straightened her stockings. She chucked her bills into her locker and slammed it. She didn't bother putting her skirt and bra back on.

Steve was waiting for her in the manager's office just as he had promised. "Who's taking care of Eden's music?" she asked.

"I had Staten replace me for a little while. I told him that one of my dancers had gotten a nasty cramp and I was obligated." He grinned and cut his eyes sideways. Yes, yes. Get rid of the manager. Very good.

Andrea draped herself all over Staten's old soft couch. Its familiar contours whispered of all the bodies it had held; Staten upheld one inviolable policy in his club: tired dancers were always welcome to come and snooze on his sofa. He even kept a worn down comforter and a little pillow handy for them. Best of all, he really let them sleep.

Steve knelt on the floor behind her and resumed his massage. Andrea closed her eyes and concentrated on his nimble fingers. He manipulated her trapezius muscles persistently, waiting for them to soften and spread under his touch.

"You're so tight," he whispered. Oh my, she had a live one on her hands tonight. He had placed his mouth very close to her ear on purpose. When she realized that Steve wasn't going to politely draw back, she closed her eyes. He continued to breathe nonchalantly onto her neck, and she creamed right through her T-back.

He knew he had gotten to her. Dancers weren't a simple matter; they tended to develop callouses. Money wouldn't work, and God knew compliments were a waste. You had to shock them just a little. Jar them.

He stood up and knelt down on the sofa in front of her, between her legs. She reluctantly opened her eyes and looked over her catch. He was an object of beauty. A bit roughened. Steve had to be charming because he was a devious little thing at heart. He had a slightly malicious streak and she saw it.

"What do you want, Andrea? Hmm?" he mocked cautiously. He thought she might be the sort who bit back. God, he hoped so. But she wasn't going to answer him. He bit his lower lip. He looked down and saw that she had wet herself. "Andrea," he drawled in feigned surprise. "You're making a mess."

What a bastard. He took her breasts in his hands and twisted her nipples softly. It humiliated her a little, to be handled like this by a co-worker, but he was relentless. She moaned.

"Andrea, Andrea. You like having your nipples pinched, don't you? Don't you?" He was merely stating the obvious, but this senseless reiteration of her pleasure intensified it. She had a verbal fixation. She'd read so many dirty books when she was little. Words got to her and few men knew how to use them.

"Where would you like for me to touch you? Do you want me to rub your neck?"

He slipped his hand under her T-back. "Is your neck still bothering you, Andrea? You know, I can massage it for you some more if you like."

He had her clit captured lightly between his thumb and his index finger. He looked at her with exaggerated doubt. "Your neck feels better now, doesn't it?"

This one wasn't going to stop until she played. Her clit was engorged and trembling. His touch was very light. Andrea drew in a breath. "My neck is fine, Steve. Thank you. You are terribly considerate."

He increased the pressure of his fingers and she shuddered.

"Good. I want you to feel relaxed when you go back into the club. Staten would be angry with me if I had taken time off for nothing. You are beginning to feel a little better, aren't you?"

"Yes. Steve. I feel . . . You're really turning me on."

"I am?" His fingers were dripping as he withdrew them from the T-back. "Oh, look at this," he said, holding up his hand. He licked off his fingers. "Yum."

Andrea snatched the opportunity. "How hard am I getting your cock, Steve? Let me see," she sneered sweetly. She pressed her hand between his legs and retaliated.

He grabbed her wrists hard. "No."

"Why not, Steve? Are you about to come in your jeans? Can't take what you give?"

He glared at her. "Think I ought to get back to work, Andrea? The work you dancers are paying me for?"

She briefly considered her options. "No."

His venom rushed out as soon as she answered. "No? You mean you want me to stay here a bit longer?"

Before she could respond, he was slipping her T-back down over her hips. He smiled at her and looped it around his long mousy hair, making a haphazard ponytail. He was getting too confident. Cocky even. Arrogant men were Andrea's favorite vice.

Steve peered studiously at her trimmed pussy. He didn't take his eyes off it as he meticulously explored its every fold and crevice. She was soaking and open. Her clit had swollen. She felt self-conscious, being examined so impersonally. Completely absorbed in his probing, he ignored her.

He looked back up at her face after a few excruciating minutes. "You're blushing, Andrea. You shouldn't. Your cunt is absolutely exquisite. It is just as beautiful as your face or your ass. I just love it. You don't mind if I pay it a little bit of attention, do you?"

"No." She was almost panting now. He worked three fingers of his left hand up her and had his pinky wriggling in her ass. He could feel the muscles in her pussy envelop his prying hand, clenching and relaxing and clenching again. She was very strong. He felt grateful that his cock wasn't in her; with a cunt this wet and demanding, he would have come long ago.

His right hand kept on playing with her clit persistently. He would tease, circling her clit mercilessly without really touching it, then flicking over it gingerly until he had her whimpering out loud. Now he got her clit between his second and middle fingers and massaged steadily. She couldn't stop him.

"You're gonna make me come, Steve." This time he offered no reply.

He leaned forward and traced his tongue over her lips. He looked at her face. He loved seeing a woman aroused, half out of her mind. He played with her lips and tongue cautiously. It was about time he kissed her.

She came so violently it startled him. She went over the edge suddenly and viciously. Her body absolutely writhed against his hands. He stood his ground, though. He had her screaming for nearly two minutes before she had finished with him. When he withdrew his hand she virtually flooded the sofa.

"Thanks."

"Oh, you're more than welcome, Andrea. It was my pleasure."

Andrea didn't get back out onto the floor until 11:45 and most of the men who had tipped her had gone home. She made only a hundred ninety-eight dollars that night, but when she left, she tipped Steve forty.

China Parmalee

Local Foods

Oh my darling, I see you so rarely now, my dearest love. These lonely letters from my room are really not enough. Why tonight, I don't know, but I have been thinking of you and missing you. Do you remember the last time we were together? It was here, five feet from where I sit. You, your smell and your skin and your warmth filled the room so suddenly. Have I ever told you how much I love the way you just appear with no warning, how when I leave you in the morning I never know if you will be there when I come home? I never know how long you'll stay. You remind me so much of a cat. Not just your eyes and your little mouth and the slow way you move, but other things, harder to describe. Your transiency, I think. You come and go and I have no control; I can only pet you and make you purr and hope you will stay with me a little longer. And yet I know you love me too and that you'll always come back, if I just hold out my hand and sit still long enough. Lately I have seen you much less than is usual even for us, but when I do I remember why I love you so much.

Yes, I think I came home and you were just here. There are times when I cannot sit next to you and breathe the perfume you put on without wanting to hold you, stroke you, scratch your white, white neck. And this time we were doing homework and it got late and we turned out the light and we talked like always.

And then too soon of course, goodnight, goodnight. It starts as always. You tickling my back gently with your nails and sometimes harder and I squirm and writhe a little, not too much yet. There is the delicious feeling of waiting, knowing that we have all the time in the world, that we can take it slow. And then you move around to my front, take off my shirt which is, I suppose, a joke to begin with. And you are so good, my dear, and not always gentle like one would fear, no, you know how to bite and scratch and fight too. You are as strong as I am, then stronger and you push me down and I breathe harder, a little hoarse now and you whisper to me, "You're so beautiful, I love you, I love you, so beautiful," and I believe you. I will believe anything you say and do anything you ask and you kiss me, your sweetest mouth so soft, mine feels large, bruising, but you move down my neck and shoulders. The funny buzzing begins, it feels a little serious; your lovely, tiny, pink mouth finds my breast and sucks and nibbles. You've made perfect soft bites from my belly, my sides, a hand tracing down and resting on the inner thighs. Now is the time to moan a little, please sweet, yes, please, you are so close but not there. I remember quite suddenly, awake from the daze, that I have my period and reluctantly I tell you, but you are not afraid and you reach down and tickle and tease, and what is there to be scared of anyway? Your hand locks on my womb, my clitoris, the games are over. I buck and sweat and move with your hand back and forth so fast, little hummingbird speaking now, don't know what I am saying, little sighs, louder ones, warmth is building your heavy breasts against me, I'm feverish, I'm floating, I'm buzzing all over the final movements. You don't stop and yes, now, yes, throw my arm around you, hold you against my heart and you hold me and wait for me to stop shuddering and you kiss me and tell me you love me, how much you love me, and I can only whisper a small assent.

We laugh and we pet and we sigh while I recover, we tangle our legs up and giggle and then I want to kiss you again, feel you under me, and the same dance begins again and you move so much, you moan so loudly. But I am not embarrassed, I am proud, of you and of myself and of the terrible racket we are making with no thought of the radio to drown out our own music. I love the way you arch when I touch you lightly, I love the large creaminess of your breasts, I love the way their nipples feel tiny and firm in my mouth, how they roll between my lips. I love the way your back marks so easily and your body flushes so readily; I love your body more than my own, its every softness and wet-ness, I feel beautiful to be with you, to create this glowing in you.

Now it is my turn to taste at your stomach, and yes, your thighs and the pudgy backs of your knees and your soft feet and back; a bite at the tendon of the thigh, a long sigh from you, a question perhaps. I ate a fresh tomato earlier today and this is what it was like. You lift your hips, an offering, and I stick a shy tongue into the dampness that marks you. Your own sweet smell is magnified all around me and I lick around trying to find the core. I slip a finger in and you are waiting, you gasp. More in earnest now I find the center, the pit, the hard little seed caught in such softness and I suck on it, circle it, play with it, try to nibble it and you are moving wildly and breathing loudly. I press another finger into you. I love the feeling of you encasing my fingers with pure heat. I know that despite soap your smell will remain on them all day, and I work my mouth, kissing and fondling you. I continue as long as I can, as long as you can stand it, and it becomes difficult to keep up with your movements, and finally you say stop, "I can't take anymore," and I rise and I kiss you and your juice, dear to-mato, is spread on our mouths as we lie together panting.

Ruby Ray Leonard

Story for a Man Who Will Never Write a Story for Me: An Unfolding

There is domestic violence under our very noses. Every night, I listen to her screams. He is no cultural event. I see him in the incinerator room, removing yesterday's papers. She's the magistrate: fur-robed, bedecked in high ideals. One night, I hear the unmistakable sound of a beating behind their locked door. The muffled whimperings of a man as a larger woman methodically punches him. Were it a woman's sobs, I would immediately notify the authorities. I do not report this spousal abuse. I mock myself: Afraid of being laughed at by a policeman?

Not likely. I am only choosing to live vicariously.

You and I meet for soda and argue philosophies of evil. Discuss the past briefly, ungraphically. I am married now, so things can go no further. At home, later, I am without reason. I masturbate next to a sleeping husband, imagining you blindfolded. Better still, blind. I squat nearby and feed you wet fingers. I cannot decide whether I've already tied your hands or if you've voluntarily complied with their passivity. I squat closer to your face, examining your teeth and gums. Every child molester in my past wears your face. You know, the ones that get you when you're too young to scream. Through terror and disgust, they make your body betray you. Forever after, the repellent act leaps to mind just as you come. It's not so different with you, my friend. Here, next to a dreaming husband, the body betrays better judgment. It's only a fantasy, I tell myself. Breathe into the fear.

Last night, I reread the book of poems you penned at twenty. Such an addiction to women, even then, and such contempt! Stuck in the flyleaf is a poem you wrote when your daughter was born. In blue ink you've written: "Never published—or submitted (anagrams don't do well these days)." By then you were thirty, a cynic's eye deeply embedded in your skull. I spent the next eight years waiting to meet you.

I fly to Miami with my husband. I imagine you in every waking moment: lapping the cunts of adolescent coeds, paying boys from dysfunctional families to bend over. I see you diddling old ladies in wheelchairs and laughing as fat men with small penises grovel at some harridan's feet. I picture you, me, and the buxom, black stewardess in a room in Paris. You are milking her teats. You spy me, hair short as a boy, and order me to fuck her. I strap on a dildo and do it until she passes out. We dine on rabbit stew and later dump her body in the closest river. You have a moment of conscience, but I whisper: No one will miss her. Let's go dancing tonight.

The second night, I have a dream. We couple, and I tell you my husband will kill us if he finds out. When we leave the bedroom, he is waiting with his henchmen. "I am going to kill you both," he states unequivocally. He does. My murder wakes me up.

The next morning, I wait for women to vacate the hotel steamroom, so that I can relieve myself. Never enough privacy. Finally, I do it in the spa shower. Not pretty, no pornographic ballet. I lie down in the stall, sprawled on wet tiles, rubbing furiously. I imagine us, spooned on the bed—you between my legs, my nipples pressed against your back. I close my hand over yours and guide these hands to your cock. Lap at your ear like a dog and whisper: show me how you do it. Our biceps grow strong with movement as I pour stories into your head. During a job interview, an old man made me tie a scarf around my crotch and rub the fabric in to test it for stain resistance. I was thirteen and he claimed to be a bathing suit designer. Even then, I wasn't so naive. I was just anxious to test my tolerance for fear. Parading in high heels, silk against pubescent down. Eyes searing me like a brand. Oh baby, he said, sit on my face, let me put my tongue up your ass. And I did.

But the story doesn't end here, I whisper, my skin against your back becoming wet plaster. Some months later the old man arranged a meeting between myself and another thirteen-year-old girl. Maria was Mediterranean, sloe-eyed. I sat stiffly behind a desk in the old man's office. She sat on the desk, her dark legs bare and dangling. She was the kind of girl destined to star in a Times Square flick opposite a German shepherd: this is all I can say. The man directed us toward a back room with a makeshift cot. Her tongue flicked the very back of my soft palate; this was the nicest part, her broad tongue in my mouth. I felt I'd seen the cot before. An epic film with scores of Civil War soldiers laid end to end; a sea of dead and dying. Her saliva was thin and sweet. The ceiling had exposed water pipes. A good place to swing a noose. She moved down between my legs. It was a quiet room. Her small, soft hands were deceptively strong as she pushed my upper thighs apart and fixed them there, like splayed butterfly wings on an entomologist's glass slide. Her tongue wiped me back and forth; she placed two fingers at the very rim of my cunt, holding me open like a speculum. I didn't want to come. I fought my body. She insisted, pushing her entire brown face into me, humming against my clitoris. I was terrified of having to reciprocate. But I'd always been polite. I don't remember if I came, or only pretended. I moved between her legs in a blur. Roused not by pleasure, but by the need to please. Mommy, am I doing it right? Am I a good girl? Will you love me? Between her legs the air was heavy and sour. Her fingers grabbed my hair; she humped my face like a small, furry mammal. She came much more quickly than I. Or pretended to. Her labia glistened—a dark, red ruby in the fluorescent lights. I felt the old man's eyes on my back, but I never heard him breathe.

I am finally sated. Head near the drain, just like the shower scene in *Psycho*. At night, I watch every seedy street whore and picture your billfold on her bedside table. Perhaps I give you too much credit, painting you a lover of all women. In truth, the only other women that I ever saw you with were perfect, thin blondes, younger than you by a decade or two. They always seemed rather cranky and worn out. I wondered if they had been that way when you met them, or if you had just sucked the hospitality right out of them. A rapist with a rapier mind can exhaust even the most vital of girls.

I am astounded that you recall our first meeting. I am, in fact, consumed with guilt. I remember nearly nothing said at any time during our meetings, just these three conversational fragments:

1. You told me that you once came close to smashing a woman's skull with a lamp.
2. At a party, I mustered all my haughtiness and said to you (after you'd again used a word or reference unfamiliar to me): "You speak beautifully, but you know, the point of language is to *communicate* with other people, so what good is all your beautiful speech?" So many words that the harangue lost its sharpness.
3. In bed, when I bemoaned my subservient proclivities, you told me that to be a good masochist, one must know a great deal about sadism. Insinuating that you held the power to reverse all trends.

The things you've forced me to do! Now I'm being driven to poetry. I'm not even a writer, much less a poet. But I do write a poem, attempting to elevate lust to intellect. What I am really trying is an exorcism: if I expel these thoughts, they will cease to exist. I write the poem. For the next two weeks, I repeat its lines over and over in my head, as if I can turn sexual heat into something rote and unpleasant. If I can hear my own pathetic voice

droning, I might tire and be done with it. Folly. Finally I decide
to show the poem to someone else. Wisdom whispers that a secret
shared abdicates its power. I show the poem to an English professor who believes that I have stories to tell. How about that: I
show a crunchy poem about an English professor who writes poetry to an English professor who writes poetry. Sitting in his office discussing it, I suddenly don't know where to put my legs and
arms. I am wearing daisy-patterned socks and a serious expression, but my extremities are twisting in an imitation palsy. My
mouth opens wide around my sentences. I am ungainly; my feet
and hands are too far from my trunk. I fight that old in-utero
need to collapse on myself and suck a finger or toe. I am not a
nail biter, but now that my locks are shorn, I'm a hair player. Not
pulling it, never that. I splay my fingers wide and drag them
backwards on my head from the temporal lobe to the nape,
screeching to a halt by my adam's apple. Then I start over again.
This poem about a poet is based on a true experience, I assure
the poet. Things feel horribly incestuous. Are there secret
meetings where all English professors meet to discuss the birth of
the sonnet? Will my name come up? Will I end up a phone
number on the English Department john wall? "Hello, so-and-so,
who wrote 'A Cold Wind Blows and Other Poems,' gave me your
number and I thought . . ." "I'm sorry, I've read that collection
and it really sucked. Anyway, I've moved on to nonfiction now."
My tricks have worked. I am so thoroughly disgusted with myself
that I plan, suddenly, to discard the poem. I'll just bury it, like
bones.

You're the superior poet, anyway. You've never written a poem
about me. Over lunch you offered that your next book (a treatise
on beauty) would be about me, although I wouldn't be mentioned
by name. A master stroke and a good idea; after all, if my husband
ever finds the poem I've written about you, I will say that it's
about him. Luckily, the best writing is open to interpretation.

I tell the professor that I've run into an old lover (I am using
you, I snarl in my head. Can't you see that you are party to the
exorcism?). The *best* lover, I say, lest he think that I turn squishy

and moist without provocation. Here's the conflict, I outline,
switching to the third person. A married women has lunch with
an old, best lover and is terrified because she is still attracted to
him. She's got this husband, of course, so she absolutely cannot
sleep with the old lover. The professor points out that if she can't
sleep with him, it's not scary at all. Only if she entertains the notion that she *can* sleep with him does the thought assume night-
marish proportions. The poem is full of dread when she realizes
not just how far she might go, but how far she *will* go! My head
is full of wind chimes and my knees open and close like a bel-
lows. I see how terribly right he is. Smugly unveiling his sticky
little facts. Testing. I parry, telling him that I'm writing a story
about you also, a very pornographic story. I mean to sound self-
possessed, but I am just a high-heeled adolescent in a scarf, dying
of exposure. (The scene is not without its small amusements,
however. At work, I unravel rapists, killers, thieves and thugs. In
real life, English professors apparently unravel me. They are so
right, on two counts. The pen *is* mightier than the sword. Paper
cuts hurt the most.)

On the way to work, I remember the first time that I masturbated. Seven years old? Eight? Older maybe—I was reading
Fanny Hill. I hadn't gone to the bathroom in a long time. My
bladder was full, belly distended. I became increasingly aroused
as I read. When I could not stand the pressure between my legs
any longer, I went to the toilet and urinated. I thought I'd had an
orgasm. I arrive at work and during the long elevator ride, I
sneeze. Bladder full of morning coffee, the tiniest trickle of urine
escapes when I sneeze. All day long, my wet panties will remind
me that I still cannot control my body.

I go to lunch at noon. Wishing you were here, watching me eat.
Shoving greasy chicken into my mouth, lipstick smears like a
lashmark across my cheek. "Fix your lipstick," you'd insist, a di-
rective more intimate than an invitation to undress. My husband
hates the way I eat. Says I'm not "dainty," I look like an animal.
You and I know that is when I look the best. But it's no joke in
everyday affairs. My mouth is too big and gapes too wide. The

dentist is amazed, says he can practically see my larynx. When I'm with you, I think of the mouth only as a repository. A broad bin for whatever you wish to store.

Reflectionless, intransigent, you thought yourself a vampire. You loved the taste of blood. But you were not the one to teach me that. Had I ever told you that the first lover who kissed me between the legs did so when I was menstruating? Or did you guess it? I bled the way that only young girls do, my body a geyser in endless hemorrhage. The blood was everywhere, slippery and warm. We looked as if we had sacrificed animals or feasted on children. Every time I read of a sex slaying, I saw my bloodied palm print on that bedroom wall. I spied the boy twenty years later, pushing a rack of dresses in the garment district, wearing one of those jumpsuits with the company logo emblazoned on the breast pocket. I thought: life is so unfair to the precocious child. He was brave and sophisticated at the age of fifteen. Now, at thirty-five, he is someone's servant. Life itself is bloodsport.

I study myself sideways, poised like a question mark in the full-length mirror. Opalescent skin, blood-red hair, swelling hip, meaty thigh. The doubling hides more than it reveals. A slight, ribbed torso craning forward. My nipples still rosy and upturned. A stiff reminder: I just can't seem to make babies. The glass reflects one half, an unscarred back. I am as ugly as a gull. I let saliva dribble from the sides of my mouth. You know, I always drool when I come; my husband's neck gets slick with spit. He says I belong in a barnyard, or a home for the developmentally disabled. I turn my back to him, facing you. You, of course, feel that drool adds the proper note to my debasement. At work, I examine the backs of incarcerated felons for signs of childhood abuse. Their backs all scream a story. Burns and whipmarks and slashes from electrical wire. When I discuss my work with you, you interrupt, say, "I think a beating is the best form of discipline. Don't you agree?"

I am again confounded, tongue-tied. I might as well be twelve, or nine. Or four, three, two or one. (That's how much I lose my mental faculties in your presence.) I will wear plastic pants and diapers and lie on the changing table, face down. Fingers snake inside the band of tight elastic. The smell of cross-stitched, quilted vinyl; pushing cotton cloth aside. Duck print wallpaper and gold belt buckle in the corners of my eyes. You rub hard with the washcloth, for my own good. Terrycloth scours skin. When I cry, you stroke my back, beneath the undershirt. My tiny vulva is clean, as it should be. Your shoulder is wet with my spit.

My husband watches, poised above us like a guillotine blade. Over these winding years, I've loved him more than I can say. I was thirteen years old when I came under his spell. Much younger than when I first drew your breath into my throat. They say the genius of the rapist-murderer is in choosing the appropriate victim. The girl-woman who moves toward, rather than away; the prey who is unaware of the hunter's motives and thus accommodates his lust for power and control. She is a mere gosling imprinted on the largest moving object, following the daddy-thing to her death. But *I* am the conniving architect of my own martyrdom. I stalk: jaw slack, body loose. I drew him upstairs to the roof and offered a tasting. I was heroin, sure of my addictive powers. Years later, I wedged an insistent thigh between yours on a dance floor. You were older than he, more cunning and quick-witted. You knew these games. He acquiesced quickly and quietly. I had the swift movement of the cat snapping the mouse's neckbone. You were older, more clever. Your voice, like an ooze down my spine, spoke of bad girls and spankings. I smelled you both. I ferreted you out. He fell in love, a function of youth. You fell only a few short inches onto a bed. During your respective falls, I performed a deft transfer of power. An insidious Dr. Frankenstein, switching the brains of anesthetized charges. I let my own self ebb away, leaving dank, hollow pits. I became nothing beyond breath. I waited to be rewritten. The line between hunter and hunted blurred in a quick spiral dance of tongues.

A few weeks later, a draft of this story is stolen from the English professor's mailbox. I am awed and mortified to imagine a strange, thieving creep running his hands over my private thoughts. The professor says: Why are you so distraught over someone reading this, I mean, except for the content. Huh? (Why were *you* so upset when mom discovered you masturbating?) Caught. Again. Like the time that my husband discovered the hundred-dollar phone bill from the phone sex line. The prerecorded kind, offering a menu of sexual perversions (if you were lucky enough to have touch-tone service; those with rotary dial heard, "Hang on and we'll choose for you"). I was one of the lucky ones. I always requested "Annie (she likes it in the back door)" or "Candy (and her little friend Susie)." The messages were so short that I'd have to call back ten or fifteen times. My husband, cold as ice, dropped the bill in my lap and said, "Take care of this." He has grown into manhood, become a collector of old debts, a settler of scores. I called the telephone company and pretended to be the mother of an errant teenage boy. The (male) operator said, "Don't be too hard on him, ma'am, he's just a kid." My husband received full refund in the next month's mail.

Magazines will tell you that women fancy men outside the marital bed because their husbands do not tell them that they are beautiful or buy them enough flowers. Ho-hum, and such a lie. Clearly, I need something darker. Every nasty part spread-eagle on the operator's table: each fold examined, opened back upon itself. A close inspection, humiliating exposure as someone probes and describes. Not just this—I wish to be both voyeur and viewed. To have someone to ask, finally, what the others are like. How does this one smell and that one taste? How silky is the fair one's hair and did the dark one moan into your mouth? Which virgin's bravado was eclipsed by your bulk? Whose ass invited a reckoning? Do you like it hairy or smooth, red or pink, yielding and pliant or requiring forced entry? But more than this, I need to see what I could not see in the mirror. If I bend over, grasping my ankles, what will be your view? How far can I be opened? How does it look with your whole hand inside and what is the sound when I whimper? Dilating me until I know that I exist. Whispering stories that confirm my invisibility.

And what have you become? Across the table, clutching restaurant coupons. Telling me of books that you will translate from the original German. Fifty-three now. Unsettled. But still. . . . Your hand runs over the old pictures I've brought, almost a caress. You say: "I remember this girl." Letting the width of both palms cover my mouth in the glossy photo. "I remember the night we met. You danced like a whore."

You know, I lied before. I didn't wait to get home before masturbating. No, I didn't do it in the diner restroom as you might have hoped. I am, after all, a sensible girl. Dressing to meet you, I was unconcerned with my appearance. I only wanted to feel open, vulnerable and sticky. I fingered myself until I was wet, but didn't come. Sat opposite you in the restaurant. Parting my knees beneath the table, as you discussed a strumpet's dance. I wore no panties. If I were free, I thought, I would telephone. I'm coming over. No, you'd say, I have a plan for the weekend. Well, think of me while you're fucking her. I hang up. You call back, your plans canceled. I come over. (I'd never been to your apartment in the old days. I was afraid that it might smell like menstruating women in there.) I wear a tight, white structured thing. (My husband hates me in white panties, a sanitary napkin pressed between my legs. Says I look like Baby Huey.) Lie on the bed, I tell you, face down. You are tentative, momentarily unmasked. Hey, this isn't what . . . Shut up. A growl. Just *do* it. (My father was omnipresent with his camera.) I pull down your pants. Spread your cheeks. (The old man put his whole tongue in my ass.) *SMILE.* Introduce my finger to your sphincter. You grip my finger like a newborn. Now, tell me what you want. (I nursed at Maria's clit.) Tell me. Pushing deeper, even as your muscle clenches. I want . . . *TELL ME.* I push my finger deep into your ass, knuckle by knuckle. (When I was seven, I had my tonsils out. They used a pre-op anesthetic which was administered rectally. A rubber finger coated with a gel-like tranquilizer.) Ask me, ask me nicely. Now, my whole finger rotates inside you. *THIS WON'T HURT.* (I was only seven; I think I wet the bed.) Tell me. I lean closer, whisper: Can you take two? Sarcastic. *ASK ME.* (Did I only imagine us with that small Arab boy? He was handcuffed. I cradled his head in my lap while you fucked him.) Yes, you say, but only *sotto voce. YES, WHAT?* I make you beg to be fucked, until you are hoarse.

(Someone is screaming.) Now you know what it feels like. (I have that recurring dream about the stabbing. As I plunge a hatchet into the body, I feel its blade wedge between my own shoulders.) To be a good sadist, one must know a great deal about masochism.

I suppose that I will never cheat on my husband. Some things get harder as you get older. Learning to drive, dumping bodies in lakes, being a traitor to those you love. When the story is finished, I'll stop thinking about you. I'll go shopping, for books on feminism or collections of holocaust cartoons. When I buy clothes, I will occasionally imagine you in the dressing room. Watching me change, saying nothing. Your eye contact methodical, deliberate. I'll have to turn away before I become transfixed by my own reflection. If I should beat you to death, who could blame me?

I'll see that couple from down the hall, looking slightly sheepish. Not to worry, I'll tell them, everyone's secrets are safe with me.

Lydia Swartz

❦

Laundromat

Sun slanted through the east windows of the laundromat and scorched Syl's back. Wiping her neck, she wished she had something clean besides the torn tank top that was stuck to her nipples and the too-tight cutoffs riding up her butt. July was not Syl's favorite month. She shoved her two bulging baskets toward the washers and began to load.

Besides Syl, there were only men in the laundromat. A stocky, bearded guy wearing a T-shirt with a faded zebra advertising a zoo. A wiry kid who had a sparse ponytail, baggy shorts and heavy boots. One emaciated old man slowly pulling smelly socks out of a blue box decorated with silver stars. And a hairy-legged guy wearing a bicycle helmet.

The Jehovah's Witnesses came in while Syl was overloading the second washer. The man spoke: "My wife and I want [squealing noises from a malfunctioning dryer] for the world. My wife and I would like to give you [sound of dropping coins at the change machine]." Silent and neatly coiffed, the woman stood just the right distance from the man's shoulder. Syl slammed coins into all her machines as they leafleted everybody else. As they approached, she glared at them and fingered the pentagram tattooed on her shoulder. She was ready for them and they knew it.

The woman glanced toward Syl, then took her husband's arm,

quickening his pace toward the door. Syl smiled triumphantly and dropped herself into the least broken chair on the south wall. Coffee does this to me, Syl thought. Heat does this to me. It's easier than hurting.

The bearded guy sat down right next to Syl and smiled shyly. Syl looked directly at him for a minute from behind her sunglasses. Then she turned and gave the old man a slow, lascivious grin. He dropped a sock. The bearded guy cleared his throat and fumbled in his pocket for a cigarette.

All of the men in the laundromat were pointedly not looking at Syl now. This left her free to examine them.

Maybe this would be a good time for an affair with some guy, Syl thought. Maybe fucking wouldn't hurt now that my herpes is better. Maybe somebody who doesn't know me so well would treat me like a lover. Maybe if somebody else did, Elsa wouldn't have to. Maybe she'll have an affair first if I don't.

Syl remembered how little boys had seemed when she was a little girl: loud, sweaty, full of fruitless locomotion. She recalled the possessive energy siphons they'd turned into when she was a young straight girl in estrus. And she thought about how the sons of her friends seemed now: fragile, tender, fearful. How did those appealingly vulnerable little guys turn into the men she saw now—pitiful as individuals and dangerous in packs?

Maybe this would be a good time to become celibate. Live on organic fruits and vegetables. Roots and berries. Drink quarts of pure artesian water. Exercise. Light candles and do rituals. God, I'm full of shit.

Well then, maybe this would be a good time to try to have casual sex with girls. The other dykes I know can do it. The dyke sex magazines are filled with stories about it. I certainly can imagine it when I'm checking out the girls at the Wildrose. Maybe there's something wrong with me. Maybe I'm not completely out yet. Maybe I'm not really lesbian. Or bisexual. Or whatever I am.

Syl considered the possibilities. Jan's lover was in Holland and Jan hadn't had sex for at least six months; what harm could a friendly roll in the hay do? Or how about Dena—Dena'd done just about everybody else, why not Syl? And of course, there was always that nineteen-year-old who'd been hanging out at the women's center for two months, hinting less and less subtly that Syl should be her first.

Or why not just invite them all over for a naked solstice party! Right, Syl. Get a grip. Remember the last time you were going to have a brief, passionate fling with a girl? That was two years ago. Elsa came to play for the weekend and she's still there. Only now she doesn't play, of course. Now she's got other uses for that wicked, hard flame in her gut.

Everybody in the laundromat was now staring at Syl. Oh shit, Syl thought. I've been rubbing my fingers up and down the inside of my thigh all this time. Great. Now everybody here has a hard-on.

There's the ticket! Exactly why she'd fucked so many men before she came out. It was pre-holocaust, and they'd known their way around casual sex. No respect, no repercussions. Just whip it out, do the thing, light a cigarette. If only Syl could get hard, get laid, get the hell out. How simple. All Syl needed, she realized, was a dick and a time machine.

With a clunk and a groan, one of Syl's washers went into imbalance and stopped. Syl sighed noisily and hauled herself over to look inside. One pair of jeans had wrapped its legs around the agitator and was hanging on so tight the agitator couldn't move. Syl pulled and poked and pushed and stirred until everything looked okay, then dropped the lid. She leaped onto the lid and crossed her legs, waiting to see whether the load would tangle again.

With a vintage 1973 dick, Syl thought, I could get what I want without risking my heart. Just in and out, gone before things get sloppy. Any hole will do. That guy over there, for instance. The one with the little ponytail. I bet he'd bend over and I wouldn't have to ask him twice.

The guy had a heart-shaped face, stubble over pale, soft-skinned cheeks. Young and innocent-looking, but also away from home and looking for some notches on his belt.

Syl could see it. She'd walk over to him and ask him to come outside to look at her shirt. *Still see a stain on this?* He'd lean over to get a closer look and she'd put her hand on his crotch. He'd wiggle. She'd tell him, a little roughly, to pull his pants

down. He'd look a little scared, a little pleased, and do it. He'd
turn away from her and incline forward.

She'd pull out a condom and roll it on, then rub lube rudely in
the guy's asshole. And she'd stick the dick up him. When she
went in, he'd start slamming his butt against her pelvis as she
banged into him. In a couple of minutes, she'd come, then pull
her deflating cock out. After she threw the condom in the planter,
she'd tell him to take off his shirt and use it to wipe the cum off
her dick. He'd do it. She'd zip up, they'd go back inside and finish their laundry. Never ask each other's names, probably never
see each other again. Even if they did, just smile and nod slightly.
No hello.

Yes! That was it. If Syl had a dick, she could just fuck Jan. And
since she was a boy, it wouldn't count. Well, maybe not Jan. But
definitely Dena. Dena would be up for it. Dena would be hot for
it, as a matter of fact. Syl would call up Dena and say, "Dena,
guess what? I've got a 1973 dick." And Dena'd be waiting for her.

She'd get to Dena's and find the door ajar. Inside, it would be
all dark except for a trail of little candles leading to Dena's bed.
Dena would be wearing a merry widow and crotchless panties (a
typical Dena outfit). Her pussy would already be rosy and feverish (Dena'd started without her). Dena would be lying back on
satin pillows (typical Dena decor) with her legs apart. "Where is
it?" Dena would rasp (Dena was a heavy smoker). "Let me see it."

And Syl would. Syl would slowly open the buttons on her 501s
and let the dick flop out, all long and hard and ready. "Come
here," Syl would say, and Dena would scoot down on the bed.
(Neither of them would make gynecologist jokes.) Syl would stick
it in a little at a time, moving it in small strokes at first. Dena
would demand more. Syl would be stern. She'd give it to her little by little, make Dena squirm. Syl would finally be fucking
Dena hard, leaning her whole weight against Dena's upthrust
thighs, Dena gripping the bedposts and pushing back. Syl would
feel Dena coming, gripping her dick as it shot cum.

Syl would collapse against Dena. They'd both sleep for a few
minutes. Then Syl would pull her softened dick out of Dena's
wetness, wipe it on the bedspread a little and stuff it back into
her jeans. She'd lick Dena's buttocks and thighs, then stand and

walk out of the apartment, closing the door softly behind her. Dena and Syl would never mention it.

The washer had stopped, Syl realized. Another imbalance? She hopped down and looked. But no, the washers were done. Time to load everything into the dryers.

She threw wet jeans viciously into the chapped lips of the dryer. Three of Elsa's impossibly tiny panties and one of Syl's tank tops flew in, clumped together. Their shared "Dykes to Watch Out For" T-shirt. Two pairs of boot socks. A hot pink bath towel. Well, at least Syl didn't have to carefully pick out her black bustier so the underwire wouldn't get twisted. Syl hadn't worn that in a while.

She mused. Wonder what it would do to that nineteen-year-old—what's her name? Debbie or Susie or something?—if I shut her in the library at the center and stripped off denim and leather until I was down to black lace, garters, and silk. See if she knew what to do. See if she'd follow my directions.

"Wonder if she'd be squeamish?" Syl thought. "Wonder if she's really a virgin?" Bet she'd go for my tits first, just brush them with her hands to start, then go after 'em with her lips and tongue. Easy, easy. Then I'd guide her hand to my wet pubes, let her get the feel of that. She'd be breathing pretty hard, scared of what was going to come next, scared she wouldn't be able to do it, scared she would. All the time sliding her fingers up and down, circling my clit. Feeling how it's different, feeling how it's the same as hers. *That's good,* I'd tell her. *A little harder. On top. Now around . . . like . . . thaaaaaaaaattt . . .*

Before I came, I'd pull her hand away. She'd look hurt, confused. Was she doing it wrong? Hurting me? Then I'd lift her hand up to her own mouth and stick her fingers between her own lips. *Like that taste?* Her eyes would be all round and dark. Before she could answer, I'd lean back on that couch, the one that smells like it's been used for the same thing a thousand times before. *Taste me,* I'd tell her. *Lick it, come on.* I wouldn't smile. I'd make myself sound harsh. She'd look pale. I know what she's been thinking all these weeks; I've seen her watching me. She's been checking out all the sex books at the center, one by one. And here it would be. Her first wet cunt, her first pair of hungry thighs.

She'd get on her knees awkwardly, put her hands on my ass too gently. Put her tongue on me tentatively. Goddess yes. That little shy thing, just thinking about her . . . she wouldn't know what it's doing to me, she'd be too nervous and afraid of making a mistake. She'd lick me slowly, tasting, trying to swallow, until I got her face and chin so wet she knew it didn't matter. I'd push myself against her until she got the idea to push back. She'd find my clit with her tongue and fumble with the hood until I was about to fly off that couch. *Yes yes yes,* I'd yell at her. *Yes right there, like that, yes!* And she'd have her first woman climaxing all around her. She'd let go of me when I bounced.

Syl would make sure she landed in the neighborhood of that sweet little mouth. *Do you know what you did to me?* She'd flush with victory. She'd go for it again, an eager student.

Syl continued her fantasy. I'd tell her to put her fingers inside me. I'd be open and wet and soft by now. I'd move and make it easy for her to find the right hole, no matter how excited she'd become. She'd go slow, just careful, not knowing that it drives me crazy. Well, I guess she'd figure that out pretty soon. And then I'd be begging her to go faster, harder, to fuck me. She'd be confused at first. I mean, we're lesbians, aren't we? We don't fuck, do we? But I bet when she felt the way my cunt grabbed her hand, she'd catch on. She'd fuck me and lick me until that couch was a soggy mess.

And then, I'd push her hand, her face away; I'd roll her over and strip her. I'd move my hot, wet body above her. Gently suck her hard little nipples. Tease her wet cunt until she was moaning and pressing against me. Get a scream out of her with my fingers first, then go down on her. Grab her soft young hips and smash her sweet virgin bush into my face. And eat it slowly, eat it fast, eat it with my fingers in her, stick my tongue in her while my fingers gently tortured her clit.

By the time I got done with her, she'd be soaked, I'd be soaked, we'd both be too exhausted to move and the room would reek in the best way any room can reek . . .

"You finished with this washer?" It was the hairy-legged guy.

"Oh, er, yeah. I'll just get the rest of this out of the way. Sorry."

Syl threw the rest of the wet laundry indiscriminately into the last two free dryers. With that much in them, it'll take an hour for it all to get dry, Syl thought. But the alternative was standing around like a playground monitor, ready to jump on the next open machine.

Hell and damn, Syl thought. I hate laundromats. I hate heat. I hate July. I hate goddamn Elsa. Lets me wash her goddamn clothes but never lets me help her get them goddamn dirty.

The cigarette smoke in the laundromat's stagnant air was making Syl a little bit sick, and a little bit sorry she didn't smoke any more. She scowled at the rotating wash. Five minutes went by. She stared sourly at the back of the old man, who was ever so slowly loading a dryer. One sock. Pause. One shirt. Pause. Another sock.

With a decisiveness startling even to Syl, she turned and strode to the bearded guy's chair. She stopped and looked down at him. He looked alarmed.

"Can you spare a cigarette?" Syl growled, finally.

"S-sure," he stuttered, scrabbling desperately in his pocket. With shaking fingers, he lit the slightly sweaty cigarette for her.

"Thanks," Syl spat at him. She walked out to smoke in the parking lot. The guy smoked menthols, wouldn't you know. Ugh. Syl took small puffs and blew them out quickly.

Goddamn menthols heat laundry July bearded guys Elsa old men tight sweaty goddamn clothes to hell. *Maybe if I had some ice cream . . .*

The cigarette was burning close to the filter when a familiar car turned into the parking lot. There are lots of rusty blue Datsuns on the road, but Syl knew of only one with a silver "E" nailed onto the door.

Elsa pulled up the Datsun right in front of Syl. It squeaked loudly when it stopped. Elsa had her hair slicked back in a ponytail or something. Syl couldn't see the usual brown flood flowing over her face and shoulders. In fact, Syl couldn't see anything on Elsa at all.

Elsa got out of the car, all five feet and one inch of her, pale

and lean and determined Elsa, looking greedy and feral in a black
bandeau top, doeskin short-shorts, and a pair of stiletto-heeled
sandals.

Syl could smell the filter starting to burn in her fingers but discovered she couldn't move to stub it out. Elsa slunk toward her,
almost smiling. She took the smoldering filter from Syl's fingers
and crushed it beneath her heel.

"I thought you were painting this morning," Syl gurgled. Something had happened to her voice. With a sudden panicky feeling,
she wondered if this were really Elsa—Elsa the distracted, Elsa
the absent, Elsa the frantic or stone-tired.

This Elsa had brushed her hair shiny; it spilled down her back,
lighter brown strands shattering sunlight. She cocked one hip toward Syl in a way Syl dimly remembered from their first days together, two years ago. This Elsa was pouring power out of her
tiny body.

"What are you doing here?" Syl asked in a small voice. "I didn't
realize you'd heard me leave."

"I was waiting for you to leave," Elsa said in her deep voice. "I
wanted to surprise you." She spoke softly enough so Syl had to
lean forward to hear her. And then Elsa darted one hand around
Syl's head and forced it forward. She engaged Syl's lips, then her
tongue, then all of her mouth, before Syl could get a word out.
Syl would have said something about the boys just inside the windows who would be watching, but after ten seconds it didn't
matter.

After ten seconds, Syl had her hand inside Elsa's shorts, cupped around a buttock. And Elsa had her hand inside Syl's tank
top, squeezing a nipple. Then Elsa found the wet seam on Syl's
jeans. Syl whimpered. Elsa laughed into Syl's tongue.

Syl had half-leaned, half-collapsed into the laundromat's window, and now it creaked in its frame. Syl got a millimeter of air
between her and Elsa and whispered, "Not here, for godsake."

Elsa grabbed Syl's wrists roughly and dragged her larger, limp
body toward the Datsun. Elsa yanked open the back door and
shoved Syl backward onto the seat. While Syl was trying to get
her balance, Elsa nimbly unzipped the cutoffs. Syl lurched forward to stop Elsa, bringing her ass off the seat just long enough

for Elsa to yank the cutoffs down to her knees. From there, Elsa planted her feet and tugged until, with a little backward stumble, Elsa peeled them off onto the ground outside the car, underpants coiled inside.

Elsa didn't bother to pull her shorts off, but climbed on top of Syl and began riding Syl's thigh while rubbing Syl's crotch with her hip. Syl could hear another car pull up nearby; she reached up to push Elsa away. She missed, and found her hands full of Elsa's breasts.

Elsa's wetness was coating Syl's leg, even through the shorts.

Syl dimly heard a child's voice through the ringing in her ears and the waves threatening to crash outward from her groin. "Mommy," a high-pitched voice lisped outside the car, "you dropped my shirt." There were more words, but Syl couldn't identify them.

Veins were standing out on Elsa's neck and she was making the soft yelps that Syl knew preceded full-force howls. She was slamming herself up and down on Syl, rocking the car, which was squeaking louder than a cheap motel bed. Brown-gold hair thrashed around Elsa's face; Elsa's deep brown eyes held Syl's hazel eyes, daring her to look away, to break the bond . . .

Syl knew she was going to lose it. She was losing it. Those yelps, those intense brown eyes always made her cunt flutter and her vulva turn inside out. Elsa began to keen, and let her whole weight down on Syl, and rocked. Rocked hard.

Syl lost it. She still had her hands full of Elsa's tits; her fingers sprang out straight and sounds she didn't recognize as her own scraped her throat. She was vaguely aware that somebody might be standing at her feet, watching, but that just made her come harder. There were voices.

Syl's waves and Elsa's were bouncing off one another and building the momentum of both. It went on. It went on some more. The car's squeaks were quick and anxious now. Finally, it was too much—for Elsa, for Syl, for the rusty Datsun. With one huge groan, they all lifted up for a long throbbing minute, then settled in, sated and sweaty.

Syl and Elsa, busy kissing and licking sweat off one another, did not notice anything else for a while. Then Elsa rolled to Syl's side a little, and Syl could see out the car door.

The old man was crumpled against the cab of the pickup parked beside them. His red, shriveled dick was just visible inside his open fly, and there was a wet cum stain on his pants. The man was breathing with his mouth open, his head back. He was pale and damp. His hand, still resting near his organ, was trembling slightly.

Elsa turned around to see what Syl was staring at. She waited until the old man moved his head forward a little bit.

"Would you mind handing us those cutoffs and that pair of panties?" Elsa asked politely.

The old man looked at her, at them. He moved his mouth for a while before he managed to produce any sounds. When he did, they were garbled. Mumbling, he bent down and groped for the cutoffs without taking his eyes off the two women.

Elsa took the proffered clothing from him and said, "Thank you." He replied, "You're welcome," in an almost normal tone of voice. He just stood for a moment, looking sweet and grandfatherly, then tottered away, zipping his fly with still-trembling hands.

Syl tenderly pulled strands of gold hair off Elsa's sweaty forehead and smiled. "Well," she cooed, "are you going to help me fold the laundry?"

Elsa smiled in a familiar way, a diabolical way. "Of course I am," she drawled. "What do you think I came here for?"

Emily Alward

〜

Nicolodeon

When I walked back into my office he was leaning against my desk, unhurriedly waiting for someone. A tingle of pleasure warmed my cheeks. He was a real hunk, and nobody else used this office, so he *must* be seeking me. Then territoriality and caution took over. My office was not public space but was snuggled cozily within the walls of my lakeside house. I froze in place. I took a deep breath and tried to sound both friendly and firm.

"Oh, sir. Excuse me, but are you sure you're in the right house?"

"Nemel," he said.

"What?" I asked. The man was making no sense at all.

"Nemel. Isn't that the proper form of address for a gentleman? In the world you're writing about," he added, as he saw my frown of confusion.

"Uh . . ." My thoughts floundered. He could have read some of my stories, I guessed. Was he one of those obsessed fans who harass celebrities? Not that I was much of a celebrity; those stories had only been published in a few obscure magazines. Unlikely but possible, I concluded regretfully. I couldn't think of any other explanation. If I could just unobtrusively open the top left-hand drawer and find the letter opener I'd have a weapon. I fumbled in the clutter. At the same time I fixed him with my prized truth-raking stare. He stared back. Instead of flinching, a trace of annoyance clouded the good humor in his storm-gray eyes.

"Nemel," he repeated. "Nemel Ryenn, to be exact. First name's Nicol." He held out a hand.

Alarms clanged all over my head. He'd given the name of a character in one of my stories. *A story that hadn't been published yet.* The greeting was being proffered at a slightly different angle from a normal American handshake, too. Very much like the Cionese gesture of homage, *and I'd never described that gesture in print.* Things were definitely getting strange.

I reached out and clasped his hand. It felt nice and strong and competent, just as my story's heroine had found when she first met him. *STOP IT,* my sense of logic screamed at me. *CHARACTERS DON'T WALK OUT OF YOUR WRITING AND INTO YOUR LIFE.*

Oh don't they? I screamed back silently. *Then how do you explain this?*

My logic-monitor had no answer.

"Well, Nemel Ryenn, what can I help you with?" I sighed.

"We need to negotiate about my life. You didn't give me much of one in that last story." The merest hint of amusement edged his voice: almost the exact same tone he'd used on my heroine the last time she'd spoken to him.

"Oh, uh, I'm sorry about that. You see, the story is really about Lirriane and that baby she adopts, and finding time for her writing . . ." I floundered.

"Yes, I know. You didn't even bother to let me start in my new job. How did you suppose I was going to support myself?"

"Now wait a minute! That's unfair. I *did* say that you'd started work, and were doing wonders organizing the House's accounts. Except the editor asked me to cut that part out."

"Literary women! They're all the same," he said disgustedly. He dropped his hold on my hand. I jumped back, with the strangest flutter of regret at losing physical contact with him. "On any world. You're only interested in getting one thing from me."

"And what is that?" I asked coolly.

He didn't answer. He just stood there, watching me, appraisal and little-boy vulnerability mixed together on his marvelous face.

Hmm, I thought, *he's right. I never even sensed this clash of emotions in him. I just used him as a foil for Lirriane's mid-life restlessness.* My cheeks tingled again, this time with shame. It was a very uncomfortable feeling. I wondered fleetingly how he had traveled here, and if I could find a time-space gate to send him back, so I wouldn't have to deal with these complaints.

"The part you can't bring yourself to write about," he said finally.

The last of my composure skittered away. How had he managed to see into my mind so clearly? For while I was deploring his complaints I had also been admiring his physique, and wondering if it would be possible to further enjoy his body without promising to give him his own story or novel. I gulped, took a deep breath, and reminded myself that he was, after all, only a fictional creation. It calmed me, slightly.

"Look, I can see why you might feel that way. But try to see it from my point of view," I implored. "If I wrote at length about all your management innovations, nobody'd want to read it. Then we'd *both* be out of a job. . . . You're a very attractive man, you know." I smiled shakily at him.

He smiled back, but his eyes were fixed on my left hand. "Do you suppose you might put that weapon down? Makes it hard to concentrate on what you are saying."

Suddenly, I realized I'd been clutching the letter opener the entire time we'd talked. If he was truly who he claimed to be, no wonder he was edgy. The Cionese had legends of empresses who dispatched their favorites to the Nextworld before the men could trade on the lady's pleasure for power. The usual instrument was a ceremonial dagger.

"Oh." I dropped the letter opener. "Sorry. I didn't mean to threaten you, Nicol . . ." I watched for his reaction to the shift to familiar usage, but he didn't flinch. "It's true; we do need to talk. If you can tell me more about what you want out of life, possibly we can give you a terrific future. Are you here on a tight time schedule, or can you get back whenever you want to?"

"No. The only time I can go back is when Koii and Clarit are both full and riding on the hundred-and-tenth demarker, which brings them into alignment with your moon. It should happen halfway through your night, this evening."

COME ON NOW! The internal skeptic screamed at me again. *SURELY YOU DON'T BELIEVE YOUR LITTLE INVENTED SATELLITES, PRETTY AS THEY ARE, CAN REACH OUT AND TRANSPORT PEOPLE ACROSS THE GALAXY? THE CIONESE DON'T EVEN HAVE A VERY ADVANCED ASTRONOMY.*

I said as much.

Nicol Ryenn gave me a hurt look.

"You're letting Lirriane's nephew develop a whole system of biology. What makes you so sure we couldn't do the same with astronomy?"

Logic-monitor subsided, muttering incoherently. This whole happening was impossible anyhow; why worry about a few more inconsistencies? I checked my watch. The afternoon was almost over. There was an obligatory party scheduled at my cousin's house tonight. I looked at Nicol Ryenn appreciatively, and inspiration hit. It would be nice to show up with a handsome escort, and let people speculate how he'd come into my life. My cousin Sheila always serves a sumptuous buffet—surely even a man from a far-off world could find something there to eat. We could talk about his personalized life plan during any awkward lapses in the conversation.

And, I told myself, it would also provide a valuable reality check. If nobody else at the party could see or hear my visitor, I'd turn myself in to the local psychiatric clinic.

That didn't happen. Nicol was a big hit at the party. Nobody had trouble seeing or hearing him. Some of the women perceived him far too intensely for my liking, in fact. I had to pull him away from three bright-eyed flirts and one New Age touchy-feely type. Women in his world are extremely possessive of "their" men so fortunately he didn't mind these proprietary actions. Somehow he managed to pick up enough of our culture—maybe gleaned from mind-reading me—not to make a fool of himself in conversation. When computer glitches or Elvis-sightings came up he just listened; he was perfectly able to join in the "big issues" discussions on war and peace and conservatives versus liberals.

Sheila pulled me aside at one point and said, "Jeannie, he's charming! And so knowledgeable. What's he do for a living?"

"Uh, he's sort of an accountant, I think."

"He sure doesn't *look* like an accountant." She eyed him appraisingly. "He's European, isn't he?"

"He's Cionese."

"Huh? Is that how he identifies himself? I know the Soviets and the Yugoslavs are breaking apart because of ethnic differences, but the *Italians?*"

I shrugged. If Sheila thought Nicol the heir of a proud Italian family, it would avoid a lot of unanswerable questions.

Actually, from his appearance, the European identity was a good guess. His soft suede boots and subtly tailored wool pants fit right into the image. The open-collared white shirt looked eclectic—and great—against his tan, but was pure American, salvaged from some clothes left by my ex-husband, because his intricately embroidered Cionese tunic would have caused too many comments. He'd needed help with the unfamiliar shirt buttons, so that had given me an excuse to touch him again, which was very pleasant.

Watching him now from across the room, I clutched the warm memory close. A clock chimed eleven times. I fiddled with the cat's-eye pendant I was wearing, and worried about carrying out my part of the bargain. Everyone seemed to be having a grand time at the party, Nicol included. Maybe he'd forget that he had come here to hassle me about neglecting his life. Should I feel guilty if he did?

Nah! the answer came quickly. *Just enjoy him, the way a Cionese woman would.*

Somebody turned on the TV. A crowd clustered around it, and Nicol joined them.

The next thing I knew, he had turned away from the set, color draining from his face, looking like he was going to throw up. He staggered toward me. Sheila and I eased him toward the bathroom, but he shook his head, so we found a secluded corner out of the line-of-sight of the TV and the group.

Could electromagnetic pulses affect him so strongly? It was entirely possible; an author doesn't always realize everything she's

put into her world. There was much I didn't know about his people's physiology, despite the fact that they look just like us. His
next words interrupted my chain of thought.

"I'll be all right. Sorry to alarm you. Those flickering lines gave
me a headache, that's all. Can't imagine why you people want to
torture yourselves with them."

"Yes. Well . . ." There was no way to bridge *this* culture gap.
The Cionese representations of human figures were always three
dimensional: statues, amulets, drama, even visions of the holy
women resemble holographic projections. Having never seen television before, he truly could not sort the two dimensional signals
into a coherent pattern.

I reached out to touch his cheek in reassurance. He put his
hand over mine as we stood there silently, exchanging the empathy we dared not talk about.

Meanwhile, Sheila had disappeared, sparing me the problem of
explaining why a sophisticated Italian businessman couldn't comprehend TV. Nicol and I found a window seat with a nice view
into Sheila's moonlit garden. He put his arm around me. I nuzzled close to him. He began to talk about his hopes and dreams.

He had grown up on a back-country farm but always knew his
future lay elsewhere. Ambition and curiosity led him to the capital city in his youth. After a stint of studying at a respectable col-
legium, he knocked around the world a while, working and
lodging wherever the enthusiasm of the season led him. He'd
even spent a year chasing pirates around the Sea of Themeny.

"Ahh!" I murmured. "Wonderful! We can get some good adventure tales out of *that* year."

He groaned. "Just put them in a flashback, will you? I don't
want so much excitement anymore."

"Very well," I conceded reluctantly. "What *do* you want?"

He wanted to try some new techniques for staff and inventory
management, he said, without the constant built-in hassles that
plagued him in his previous jobs in the mercantile cooperatives.
The chance to do so was one reason he took up Lirriane's offer.
He added, almost embarrassed: "I need some security. A place
where I belong. I want some time to raise flowers and read
poems and figure out why we're here at all."

I longed to enfold him in my arms and heart. What he wanted was so reasonable, so in accord with his own world's values of civility and self-fulfillment. It was no usual event, either, to find a man who'd admit to such an inner agenda, although of course Cionese men are more aware of their emotional needs than most American men are.

But Lirriane had a different agenda for him. Kind and honorable she might be, but she shared the Cionese female attitude that men basically exist to make women happy. I had my own agenda too. Writing low-key stories about mid-life crises was not going to further my career in the action-oriented field of science fiction.

Nevertheless, I had a certain responsibility toward this Nicol Ryenn, didn't I? I sighed—the darned man was evoking an inordinate number of sighs from me—and reached out for his hand.

"I think I can give you what you want. But I'll have to make you suffer, too."

A wash of moonlight spilled down on the shore path we followed home, putting me in a romantic mood. Nicol seemed equally mellow; he ambled along like a man who had just set down a heavy burden. We didn't need to talk much. When a frog jumped onto the path, or a duck swam alongside, he stopped and watched delightedly. I was glad he felt free to enjoy these small glimpses of an alien world.

The first awkward moments back in my house were broken when he fumbled with his cuff buttons. I rushed to help. After we'd unfastened them, the shirt came off. I leaned against his bare chest. His hand cupped my head. The other hand turned my face toward his. He traced my profile tenderly with a finger.

It was all so tentative, so different from the precipitate sexuality I'd written into his world, that I had no idea how to make matters proceed. And how I wanted them to! Any doubt that Nicol was a real flesh-and-blood man had vanished. I could feel the slight nubs of beard when my hand touched his cheek, and breathe in the faint smoky essence of male from his skin. He was altogether one of the most desirable men I'd ever met.

Nicol himself didn't help or move things along at all. He just stood there, radiating virility, and gazing at me like a connoisseur admiring a work of art. *Why doesn't he kiss me?* I raged, baffled. The next moment I realized why. In concentrating on the consummation of various romances, I had always skipped past the kissing stage in those stories. I would have to show him how.

My lips found his. Going slowly, sampling the delicious texture and taste of him, parting in delight as he responded with a gentle abrasion that ended in the welcome invasion of his tongue. Anticipation burst into a flame of seeking. Our mouths and hands and neurons reached out to bridge the barriers of self. The rest of our clothes began to slip off.

We spiraled slowly into passion. It was a slow, deliberate slide with the promise of ecstasy to come. The dynamics of our coming together seemed foreordained. I unbuckled his belt and reached to stroke him; he was caressing my hips. All at once he turned away and said, "I can't." His voice shook.

My senses shrieked from the sudden jolt. My ego shrieked too. I floundered for the balm of some reasonable explanation. "I know I don't shimmer in heat like the women of your world do. Maybe I'm not attractive to you?" I ventured fearfully.

"That's not a problem."

From the usual signs I hadn't thought it was, but what other explanation could there be?

"Is it Lirriane?" I asked.

"No," he whispered.

A mauve streak of light fell on him. I could see warring emotions reflected on his face.

"Believe me, I want to," he told me.

I stayed silent, churning with hopes and fears.

"You're—you're my creator," he said finally. "It would be sacrilege."

Oh gods! What a tangled web I'd woven with my words! Neither of us deserved these torments. I still quivered with desire, achingly aware of all the places I wanted him to fill.

"Don't you know each ruling House of Cion started when someone made love with a deity?"

"My ambitions don't go as high as progeniting a new House," he said, but he was smiling.

I did not mention the unlikelihood of fertility in transspecies union.

He held out his arms and I went into them, noticing happily that his erection had not faded. It teased me with small seeking pulses as I pressed tight against him. My clit replied with flutters of desire. My hands struggled frantically with the unfamiliar clasps of his trousers. I felt his fingertips caressing the line below my buttocks, and then a glissade of pleasure at the delicate queries he traced between my legs. My wraparound skirt had dropped easily at the first of these gentle explorations, but not until his touches played me into a jangle of longing did I manage to unwrap *him*.

He was worth the wait. In our mental meetings I had always seen Nicol clothed, the taut curve of muscle and glint of little golden hairs on his skin mere hints of the man beneath the clothing. Now my arms held, and my cells reached out to, a male who met all my fantasies, and more. I pulled back, slightly out of his embrace. Seeing him in the duskiness of night shadow, I absorbed the lines and angles and swirls of his body; felt the beat of his blood and the crest of its surging in his cock.

Very tentatively I knelt and licked the little drop of moisture off the tip. It tasted like semen should taste, but it was also like heather and life and the sun-mist of a faraway planet. I lifted my face up to look at his and caught the expression of bliss as my tongue wrote tickle-phrases around the shaft.

"I'm glad there's something you want from me too," he said.

"Um," I agreed, thinking of how women in his world focus more directly on their own needs.

Then I did too, as he lifted me up and we fell in a joyous tangle on the bed. Caresses by hands and lips and nose and phallus covered me. My nipples, tingling, rubbed against his chest. Our bodies pressed against each other with raw delight. Dizzy with the flickering anticipation in my cunt, I wriggled to demand him just as he pushed in.

"Welcome to my world," I whispered.

Thrusting slowly but tentatively at first, then faster, then surprising me with exquisite circular motions, he blurred my world with bliss. I matched him as our rhythms and perceptions meshed. We careened and plunged along a brink of rapture, sometimes dipping in. Finally, almost ready for a break, I tried to simply lie there and let him do what he was so expert at doing.

But then he eased me around, so that his hands cupped my breasts and his thrusts caressed my magic spot. I stayed very quiet, waiting for the pleasure to surge back.

Instead of building up in small increments mixed with tension, I exploded. I fell through stars . . .

. . . and stars . . .

. . . and more stars. Half a galaxy must have whirled through my dazzled consciousness.

When I could talk again, I murmured, "We must do this again sometime."

"Of course," he said, and held me closer.

In a little while he fell asleep. I stirred in my cocoon of contentment and raised my head. A streak of light still poured across the floor. I eased out of Nicol's arms and walked over to look out the window.

There were two moons.

Even when I fled back and pulled the covers over my head, mauve Koii and pearly Clarit still burned behind my eyelids.

The last thought I had before falling into a restless sleep was of Spinrad's novel where jumps through hyperspace are propelled by the female orgasm. Somehow, even when you write science fiction, you don't expect somebody else's wild idea to reach out and slam you across the universe.

The next thing I knew, morning noises were battering my ears. Carts creaked along the street. Shuttlegulls squawked on the windowsill. Someone was pounding on the door.

"DON'T YOU WANT TO GET UP AND SEE THE WORLD YOU BUILT?"

"No!" I moaned, burrowing deeper into the pillows. Across a zillion miles of space, that damned logic-monitor had still managed to follow me!

Nicol got up to answer the door. I could hear his voice, husky but calm, countering a woman's excited questions.

Then firm steps clipped across the floor. I pulled a quilt around me and looked up into hazel eyes darkened with fury.

"Hai, at least you have good taste, Nicol Ryenn. She looks a lot like me, even. Is there any other possible extenuating factor?"

Several excuses flashed briefly through my mind. *He hasn't signed his contract yet?* Or, *He's my dream man; I have special rights?* Nicol looked really uneasy, as distressed at my embarrassment as at her anger. I hoped he wasn't going to explain that I was a goddess. It would be easier to deal with his outraged lady than with one more twist in the reality continuum.

Clutching the quilt tighter, I held up my hand, stalling for time. What could I ever say to make things right? I liked Lirriane. At least I did before this unfortunate clash of property rights occurred. I liked her so well I'd sent Nicol into her life, to give her sexual delights and honest management practices and loyalty and love. She too was looking for the flowers and poems that make responsibilities bearable. But Lirriane was a proud woman. She might well send her new companion away because of what I'd done.

I looked at her again. There was as much hurt as anger in her eyes.

I made the only possible excuse.

"My deepest apologies, Nemelyya. He didn't do anything to dishonor your trust. It was entirely my fault. I seduced Nicol Ryenn. He couldn't help himself." True, or at least universally believed in her world. "Here, I will gladly pay the fine for unauthorized access to this man of yours." This brought me up short; I suddenly remembered I had no money with me. And even if I had, American money wouldn't work here, where they used semiprecious jewels for currency.

The cat's eye pendant still dangled between my breasts. I'd put it on for the party last night because it was striking and festive, and I had been in a mood for adventure. I pulled it off and held it out to Lirriane.

She nodded formally. She took it, and started to turn away. Then she asked, "Was he as good as he looks?"

I smiled at her. "Better."

Nicol walked with her into the other room. Amid their murmured conversation I heard her tell him to be in her office by suncrossing.

"Do what she says," I told him when he returned to me. "You need each other. I won't make you suffer any more than absolutely necessary."

"And you?" he asked. I think by now he had forgotten I was a deity at all.

"I'll be all right," I said, and meant it. Not that I was trying to be noble or anything. But I'd had a lovemaking that would keep me glowing for a month, and I wanted Nicol to get on with his life. Besides, I had to figure out how to get home before I complicated any more story lines.

Michelle Handelman

⟱

Blood Past

The blood passed slowly through his lips like fire on a lake, simultaneously caressing and drowning the fever of excitement that passed through the audience. He was Juris, the great glass-chewer of Haiti who devoured shards of glass like a lover sucking the sweet juice of his woman's vagina. Slowly, he rolled the glass between his teeth and tongue and a great spray of saliva shot forth, covering the audience in a moist shroud of love. This was the art he was most practiced in, having been trained in his youth to carry on the tradition of his father. Though he was wise he was still not a master, as sometimes the blood would escape from his heart. But the audience did not care. They were there to be entertained, not enlightened, and when the blood came, they would rise to the occasion, human torture being the greatest entertainment of all.

I stood in the back of the crowd. There was a circle around him on this sweltering Spanish night and bodies pressed hot together, simultaneously arching forward to gain a better view of the show. When Juris took an old bottle of perfumed water and broke it beneath his foot, I felt a shiver run through my body like the slight release just before orgasm. The audience moved closer, I felt the breath of one hundred steamy bodies down my neck. The scent of roses and lust filled the air. He picked up a piece of the bottle

and placed it on his tongue, and as his teeth met the glass I felt
another orgasmic surge. The combination of the movement of his
lips and the sweltering bodies being pushed against me made me
dizzy; the sound of Spanish guitars played the strings of my sex.
I wanted to be that bottle. Yet, as he chewed I realized that it was
not only the intoxication of this magical act that was touching me,
but the actual presence of a hand from the crowd which was
gently searching beneath my skirt. I didn't dare turn around. The
introduction was already made.

I felt this foreign hand rub itself tenderly along my thighs. The
fingers were warm and smooth. At once I recognized the hand to
be that of a masseuse or one who often wore gloves. I could not
tell whether it belonged to a man or a woman and I did not care.
My nerve endings were tingling, and as Juris put another piece of
glass between his lips, my body shook as two fingers separated
the lips of my vagina. They pushed in and out of my cunt, slowly
at first, gradually building up speed until I couldn't hold back.
Heat poured forth from my swollen cunt and I coated the hand
in a large spray of juice. Outwardly, I had to control my body so
no one would catch on to this public display, yet the fingers
pushed deeper every time I stood more rigid. I arched my buttocks to allow deeper penetration and offer the tip of my clitoris.
His hand . . . her hand . . . that mysterious hand that belonged to
the entire audience grabbed my clit just as Juris was at the climax
of his act. In perfect synchronicity, Juris chewed the glass, the audience gasped and I orgasmed. The hand moved faster and slid in
and out of my vagina several times before it came around to grab
my clit again. The two fingers left my gasping pussy. Throbbing.
Pulsating. They pinched my clitoris and remained there for several moments as the pressure built in my cunt for the pleasure of
several orgasms. The blood appeared on the lips of Juris and my
cunt shot forth a river of ecstasy. The performance was over, the
crowd was satisfied and my stranger disappeared.

I walked back to my hotel room languorous and fulfilled. It was
the act of glass-chewing that amazed me more than the act of sex.
I had seen it with African fire walkers and snakesitters—the ability to leave your body and mind at will for a higher state of spiritual existence. The body was left to work as a finely tuned

machine trained to avoid all points of pain while concentrating on that space between emotion and thought. The blood pressure was lowered, the breathing deep, and the heightened nerve endings . . . numb. One could endure death without fear. Pleasure through pain. I planned to return the following day.

The next evening, as I turned down the road heading into town, I was taken by a surge of the scent of magnolias and salty sea air. My nose lifted like a child to her mother's nipple—I wanted to consume the flavors of life until I was full and plump. A wind flirted with my skirt and I felt the pale hairs on my labia ruffled gently by the gods. Upon entering the center of town I noticed the crowd was larger this evening and there were several more children chasing each other through the adults' legs. My attention was directed toward Juris as he introduced another performer: a beautiful woman with golden hair piled high atop her head; she was dressed in a corset of polished steel. Strapped to her hip were three exquisitely carved daggers. This was Alia, a sword swallower and Amazon whose mere presence pushed the audience to the precipice of enchantment. She swallowed swords like liquid, and the men in the audience couldn't help but feel a great bulge rise between their legs as Alia opened her larynx and consumed twenty-two inches of cold steel. She was a true feat of nature. I felt so small watching this remarkable example of human concentration—a woman able to chase her ghosts away with the flick of a tongue and capable of satisfying any man.

After Alia's act, Juris took the stage while she softly sang octaves to soothe her throat. Juris pulled from his robe a shimmering crystal phallus, about five inches high; it had a vein of blue running through the center. When light struck the crystal, rays of color pierced the whole audience, and as he held up the hypnotic phallus, Juris told a story of the Haitian voodoo priest and his queens.

"In every kingdom, the head priest chose his favorite concubine for sacrifice on the holiest of days. She was prepared in the finest silks and bathed for hours in olive oil and coconut milk. At dusk, the voodoo priest would meet her for a long walk by the river, then they would retire to the royal chambers to make love until sunset. As night fell, the priest would recite a spell while still inside the sacrificial whore, and pass a poisoned capsule from his lips to hers—she would bite down and die instantly. A bit of blood was extracted from her body and placed inside a crystal phallus, which the priest then used to satisfy his other whores. You see, the blood is blue," Juris said as he held the phallus higher, "because it has never had a taste of oxygen. The more blue crystals the priest attained, the higher his status within the sect. This is where we get the term 'blue blood.' "

The audience didn't know where his talk was leading. It didn't matter. Juris had such a seductive way of speaking and gesturing to the audience that no one could move in his presence.

Juris continued: "And so there was a great priest from an unknown town who I met in the market one day. He told me he could no longer live in his land because he had sacrificed a sacred goat to feed the townspeople after a severe drought. The people refused to eat the goat and banished him from the land. He was on his way west with one last possession to release.

"He gave me the crystal you see before us. This was the blood of his last concubine during his final days as the high voodoo priest. Yesterday, when Alia came to meet me here, she spoke to me of this great holy man's death. His town received his body with flowers and feasts because after the death of that goat all their crops began to grow. Tonight I shall consume the blood of his life force. But I need a woman from the audience to assist me. Is there anyone here strong enough to join me?"

It was a moment when I could choose to take the leap onto the other side or remain forever an observer left to watch someone else fulfill my dreams. It was the magic of Spain. It was hot, and as the sweat poured down my thighs, I stood, a stranger surrounded by the magic awaiting me. I stepped forward and Juris took my hand to help me out of the crowd. His power electrified me. I felt the heat pass through my fingers, up my arm to the crook of my shoulders, through my breasts and straight down my belly to nestle hot in my sex box. A truly virile man. He placed the phallus in my hand, and as he bent his head back he told me to slide the crystal in and out of his mouth. My juices were already flowing. In front of all these people, Juris and I were performing the act of fellatio with a holy relic of his motherland. A relic containing the blood of a whore and the scent of a thousand lovers.

I slid the strong rock into his mouth. His lips enveloped the instrument until there was no space between the phallus and his mouth. I pulled it out and pushed it in. I pulled it out and pushed it in again; each time it shimmered in the evening light, covered with the saliva of Juris and getting wetter and juicier every time it entered his mouth. And it was all too much for me to take. My legs were trembling and I could feel an orgasm coming on. My nipples hardened beneath my blouse and my breasts heaved with each stroke of Juris's tongue. I caught a glimpse of Alia on the side of the ring, completely immersed in the sharpening of her blade, and then my attention returned to Juris and the ever-moving phallus. I pushed it into his mouth deeper than before, and my pussy quivered with the power of seduction in a public arena. All eyes were upon me, a hundred or so tourists, locals and lovers; their gaze made the event all the more eroticized. I slid it in one more time. Then, under the power of the setting sun reflecting in the eyes of the audience, Juris bit down on the crystal phallus and the blue blood poured forth . . . down his chin, mixing with oxygen for the very first time and turning bright red as it reached his neck. Then Juris did what he was trained to do: he chewed the glass for the women, men and children as he did every night, bringing magic and illusion to the curious travelers and hospitable locals in the south of Spain.

Like new initiates into a secret service, the crowd broke off into little groups, huddling and whispering. The essence of the evening, the sharing of this holy experience, created a bond among the members of the audience which would forever connect them. And when they crossed paths again, their mutual nods would acknowledge this bond. As the crowd slowly disbanded, Juris asked me where I was from.

"I come from Chicago, but I'm on my way to Africa to teach English. I'll be there in two weeks. I came here last night and admired your show very much, which is why I returned tonight. I have always been fascinated with sword swallowers, and I would like it very much if you would introduce me to Alia."

Juris told me to wait a moment. He walked over to the van

where Alia was packing their belongings. After a brief exchange, Alia came toward me and Juris continued the loading. She extended her hand, which was just as strong as Juris's, introduced herself, and spoke English with some difficulty.

"I have been swallowing swords for thirteen years now," she said. "It is a beautiful tradition and I am proud to continue its life force. I trained with the bravest man in all of Cuba. He watched his mother die by the sword of a soldier, and felt driven to defeat the strength of the sword himself. If you like, come with us to have a glass of wine and I will tell you of my training."

I followed her to the van and the three of us drove south. We drove to a cove on the beach where Alia and Juris had set up camp. Their dog was there, along with a stove and two hammocks slung in the trees. Juris went to greet the dog and give him a run on the beach as Alia and I brought out the wine and a few glasses. We made ourselves comfortable on a large, smooth rock. Now she was more candid with me, and with a throaty laugh she began talking of her early years: "The first time I performed in public, I was so nervous that I gagged on the sword. I had to concentrate, I had to imagine that I was sucking on my lover's cock, which grew larger and larger with the depth of our love. And my throat loosened only with that idea—that I could consume all the love being given to me by the man I loved most."

"So sword swallowing is an act of love?" I asked, upon which Juris jumped into the conversation.

"Don't let her fool you. It's all about sex, completely about sex."

Alia jumped on him and the two of them wrestled around in the sand, poking each other and throwing teasing remarks. We drank and laughed for hours, and Juris began caressing my neck. Before I knew it, we had our tongues in each others' mouths. Alia whispered something to the two of us and then whistled to the dog; the two of them walked down the beach. Juris's tongue probed every inch of my mouth. The tip of it ran back and forth across my gums. He flicked the inside of my upper lip while sucking my bottom one—it felt like being sucked by the tides of the sea. With long smooth strokes, his tongue searched and retreated. Each time I was dizzier with passion. He moved down to my breasts and began rolling each nipple in his mouth like the glass between his teeth. All the attention and skill he used with his glass chewing were brought to his lovemaking. He sucked harder on my nipples, surrounding them with soft little bites; the harder he sucked the deeper my cunt swelled. His hands lightly brushed over my throbbing vagina and he grabbed hold of my knees with all the power of Haiti. He spread my legs open and just looked at my dripping cunt, glistening and palpitating like a moist creature from the sea. He just sat there and looked. The power of his gaze sent my muscles into a frenzy. To have my cunt fully exposed to the sea and the air . . . his breath on my breath . . . his eyes on my sex . . . I couldn't stand it.

I begged Juris to have me right there. The tension was building, and already my cunt started shivering in orgasm. Juris took a vial of blue glass from his pocket and slid it right up my cunt while I moaned in relief. The glass was cold and smooth, and as he pushed it in and out of my pussy the difference in temperature created a fine vapor that mingled with the sea air. Then he placed the glass back in his pants, removed his trousers, and deeply thrust his cock all the way up my pussy to what felt like the bottom of my belly. He fucked me and fucked me and each time he entered I felt my insides tremble, and the tip of his penis seemed to fill my body until there was nowhere left to go.

When I regained some composure and looked up, I saw Alia behind Juris's back, fingering herself. When our eyes met she took one of the daggers from her hip and began touching the tip of her clit with it, all the while keeping eye contact with me. The blade just barely touched the clitoris and every time it brushed her swollen cunt her eyes rolled back in her head and her knees collapsed a little. She was driving me crazy and there was no stopping her. Then, when I could actually see the juice pouring from her pussy, she slid the blade of the dagger about four inches into her cunt and remained very still. The juice flowed over the blade and her hand, leaving a small puddle of this dangerous love in the sand beneath her.

Juris turned around, sweetly laid her down in the sand and began lapping up all the juice of her cunt like a cat cleaning his sister. He slowly licked her clit over and over, until she was screaming with orgasm for the second time around. Then, as I watched Alia dig her hands into the sand, Juris pulled the blue vial from his pocket, placed it in his mouth, and bit down, shattering the whole thing into tiny pieces. He chewed. The great Juris chewed the glass more vigorously than he ever did in public. He no longer possessed his mind or his body, only his mouth. And then, with a mouth full of glistening shards of blue glass, Juris started licking Alia, sucking and spitting the glass into her vagina . . . ecstatic and sublime. Alia was now in an orgiastic trance, their magic being transferred from orifice to orifice. I watched with honor, and was reminded of all mortality. For as Juris chewed, small drops of blood fell from his mouth like flaming rose petals to the sand and the sea . . . burning the sand with the blood of these modern mystics.

Blake C. Aarens

Table for One

Damn! Three hours before I'm supposed to meet her for dinner and then be her dessert, Joanne calls to cancel. Again. I know she said she likes to build up anticipation, but this is ridiculous! That woman's been stringing me along for three months now.

I refuse to believe that my being in this wheelchair has anything to do with her canceling. She asked me to dance at Keisha's birthday party, and sat on my lap while we watched the video of Sweet Honey in the Rock. But you know me, I still had to check out that possibility.

I don't know whether to laugh, cry, or roll around my apartment cussing and moaning. I went out and bought a new bottle of musk oil, spent forty-five minutes trying to iron my clothes; I even trimmed my pubic hair! And I can tell you it was hell getting those little curlicues out of the bottom of my seat. I did all that just to hear her tell me, "Something came up." I was polite to her on the phone, but right now, I'm angry. And so horny.

I go into my office to check my book and see when we'll be able to reschedule. Next weekend is out; I have plans every night from Thursday to Sunday. Then I notice that tonight is the full moon. I smile, finally understanding why I am so tense and aroused.

I go into the kitchen and open my back door. Sure enough,

there she is, glowing full and round up in the sky. I check to make sure Mrs. Lopez isn't outside singing to her birds. I can't smell cigarette smoke from Nona upstairs, so I slyly open my robe and let Her light shine on my body. The cold night air makes my nipples stiffen and I close my eyes and arch into the breeze. I slide my hands down my neck and over my breasts. I draw circles on my belly. And though I can't really feel the pressure, I stroke my thighs and delight in the sight of my hands on my skin. I feel as if I'm rubbing the moon's very glow into me.

"Uhnnnh, girl. You sitting out here turning yourself on." I laugh out loud and go back inside, shutting the door.

"What I need," I say to my tortoiseshell cat Sonja, perched on the back of the couch, "is to meditate, do some kind of ritual to mark the moon's changes and the ones Joanne Taylor is putting me through." In response, she throws me a cat kiss—a long, slow blink—and then settles her head on top of her tucked-in paws. I take that to be a sign of approval.

I want to be undisturbed for at least the next hour, so I put Sonja's dinner out, turn the ringer off on the phone and the volume down on the answering machine, and put out all the lights. I sit in the dark for a while, listening intently to my own breathing and the rhythmic sound of Sonja's purr. Then I begin to prepare my bedroom for the ritual.

I light four candles on my altar: a black one for identity, a white one for purity, a purple one for gaiety, and a dark cherry-red one for, well, you know, lust. The room is glowing, but not brightly enough. I grab my yard stick from behind the door and open the top curtains on my bedroom window. That way the only being who can peer in is the moon Herself. And She does, her cool, strong glow falling down the center of my bed. She knows what I have in mind. My attendant helped me put fresh sheets on the bed this morning, and I can't wait to slide under the warm cotton flannel.

I light one stick of patchouli and one of sandalwood incense. The room smells like a temple and is ablaze like one too. I inhale deeply and am dizzy with the heady scent. I bend over the smoke, letting it pour over my nipples and seep between my fingers. I even hold my dreads over the incense burner until my entire body smells like a church. With my bracelet of bells wrapped around both wrists, I clasp my hands as if in prayer and shake them, cleansing the air with the high, clear sound of the bells.

I touch my chakras with the heart-shaped amethyst crystal that my ex-lover gave me for Valentine's Day two years ago. After sticking my finger in the glass of wine on my altar, I suck it dry, filling my mouth with the bittersweet taste.

"Mawu," I say, bowing my head, "Goddess of the Earth, the One who gave me birth and continues to sustain me. Be with me. Mawu is here." I tilt my head to look up at the moon.

"Yemaya, Goddess of the moon, who changes monthly in Her circled orb. Show me by your example how to likewise flow through my changes. Be with me. Yemaya is here." I pivot in my chair to call forth the Goddesses of the remaining four directions.

"Maat, Goddess of the west, where the sun sets, the teacher, the feeling self. Be with me. Maat is here. Aphrodite, Goddess of the south, where the light comes from, the healer, the emotional self. Be with me. Aphrodite is here. Amaterasu, Goddess of the east, where the sun rises, the visionary and the child, the spiritual and intuitive self. Be with me. Amaterasu is here. Skaadi, Goddess of the north, where the cold comes from, the warrior, the communicating self. Be with me. Skaadi is here. The circle is cast and I am between the worlds. What is between the worlds is of no concern of the worlds and affects the worlds. Aché."

After a silent three minute meditation, I open the top drawer of my bedside table and survey the contents. I take out my bottle of Probe, a jar of jasmine massage cream, a handful of silk scarves, and my bright red, five-and-one-half-inch battery-operated vibrator. I've never turned the thing on, but with the batteries inside it, it's nice and heavy. My lap, too, is heavy with the implements of my ritual.

I put on a CD of African drumming, and wheel myself over to my bed. After turning down the covers, I slip my arms out of my robe and sit for a moment with my eyes closed. I cup my hands over my mound and rock to the drumbeats. I take the things out of my lap and put them onto the pillow. Then, I lock the back brakes on my wheelchair, grab the chin-up bar rigged overhead, and hoist myself up into bed.

The sheets are warm and my body still retains the heat from my bath. I drape the scarves over the bar above me, so that whenever I move they graze my skin. The sensuous caress of silk sends an impulse throughout me: the tops of my ears grow hot, my throat constricts, my nipples stick out from my body, and the lips of my sex begin to swell and moisten.

With the jasmine-scented cream I give a loving massage to every inch of my body that I can reach, paying extra attention to those parts I don't much care for. My belly's not flat, but then again, the Earth herself has hills and valleys.

The aroma of jasmine mingles with that of the burning incense. I close my eyes and imagine myself in a dense forest, the sound of running water close at hand. Seeking out pleasure in unexpected places, I cup the rough skin of my elbows, knead the hollow of my throat, and probe into my belly button. The massage completed, I lie on my bed with my hands at my sides, my breathing slow and concentrated, coming from deep in my belly. My body resonates with the vibrations of the drums and the pleasure of my own tender touch.

With delicate strokes from the tips of my fingers, and the brief slips of silk against my chest, I turn myself on in stages. My fingers feel like feathers on my naked skin. I feel the flow of blood through my veins, the throbbing of my pulse in my throat, the sensation of tingling in my fingers, and the expectant clenching of the muscles of my cunt.

I am ready. I slide my hands under my hips and lift my legs one at a time until I have spread them wide open. My fingers move through the coarse bush of my pubic hair, my thumbs and forefingers outlining the V of my mound. I tap my clit lightly and feel it draw away from the sharp contact. I press and pull on my oily inner lips, enjoying their softness, their fullness, opening them up like the petals of a flower. And then I am within the moist temple of me, pressing at the walls and gripping around the fingers I wedge deep inside.

Exploring different strokes, touches, and pressures, I run my finger around the outside of my mouth and then suck it inside. I drag my wrists across my swollen nipples, gently pull my pubic hair, make increasingly smaller circles around my clitoris, slowly plunge four fingers into the luscious wet of me and then yank them out, stimulating myself to just before the point of no return.

I stop touching myself then and inhale deeply, holding the pleasure in. My left hand is at my side and with my right hand I trace a path from my cunt to the center of my chest, drawing the fire of arousal into my heart. The pounding of my heart is strong and sure, and I am shaken by the power within me. With relief I exhale and let the energy I have built up spread to the rest of my body.

I repeat this process eight times. For that is the number of the Infinite. At first it is exquisite torture, but by the eighth time, my ritual has transformed genital arousal into whole-body ecstasy.

I am lightness. Floating. My energy expands beyond the boundaries of my body. I could swear I feel the weight of my thighs on the bed, a slight bend in my knees, tingling in my toes. And when I spread myself open with the tip of the red vibrator, it is all that I can do to keep from coming. Then I realize that I no longer need to keep from coming.

Pinching my clit between my thumb and forefinger, I nudge myself toward orgasm. When it comes, I moan loudly, invoking all the names of the Goddess my mind can recall, including my own. I plant kisses of benediction on Her full, heavy breasts, lap at the holy water between Her thighs, writhe in ecstatic agony on my bed.

And then I am spent. My breathing slows to normal and my vision clears. The clenching of my cunt has expelled the vibrator from my body. I cup both hands over my mound and sigh.

It is then that I hear the clicking of the answering machine on my bedside table. On instinct, I reach over and turn up the volume to screen the call.

"Amani? Are you there?" Joanne's voice asks. She waits to see if I'll pick up and then continues on when I don't. "Sorry I had to cut you off earlier. Minor crisis with one of my clients; I think she'll be okay now. I guess you decided to go out on your own—"

I pick up the phone. "Hey girlfriend. Naw, I didn't go out, just decided to call it an early night. I'm already in bed."

"Oh, you are?" she says, her voice flirtatious. She clears her throat. "Do you think I could come join you?"

"I'm ready and waiting. You know the address."

"Ten minutes," she says.

I hang up the phone and await her arrival.

Genevieve Smith

Academic Assets

Dr. Catherine Andrews
Director of Graduate Studies
Department of Political Science
Plymouth University, VA

Dear Professor Andrews,

I am writing this recommendation on behalf of Kyle William Harper, who is applying for a graduate fellowship to your political science program. I have had the pleasure of knowing Kyle since his freshman year at Kent, when he was enrolled in my Introduction to Western Civilization course, and he was most recently a member of my senior honors seminar on The Politics of the French Revolution. In both courses he distinguished himself. His work is thorough, insightful and original, and his aggressive yet respectful classroom personality indicates his strength of character and ability to both assist and learn from his fellow students. He never hesitated, as many less ambitious students do, to take advantage of special departmental workshops, colloquia, or my own office hours. We are quite sorry that Kyle has not chosen to pursue his graduate degree here at Kent. Our loss in this case will certainly be your gain. I cannot recommend Kyle highly enough, and should you accept him he will surely be an asset to your program.

Yours sincerely,
Emily E. Jackson

She proofread the printout one final time and sighed. It was a good letter, and along with Kyle's record, it should do the job. She fished a clean sheet of department letterhead from the tray next to her office computer, then returned it restlessly to the stack.

She just wasn't satisfied.

Because it didn't say what she really wanted to say.

She checked the clock—another hour until her current "significant other" got out of his meeting in the Philosophy department. They had exchanged angry words before he left, and the scene had sent her straight to some work she had been putting off. Initially a chore, now Kyle's letter provided a needed distraction.

Pouring herself a fresh cup of coffee, she started a new document file.

Dr. Catherine Andrews
Director of Graduate Studies
Department of Political Science
Plymouth University, VA

Dear Professor Andrews,

You're only human, right? Well, so am I, so I hope you'll excuse me when I say that you really should give Kyle Harper a graduate fellowship to your department because he has the world's most perfect ass. Honestly. It's stunning. If you asked for pictures with student applications instead of GRE scores you'd know exactly what I mean. But maybe not—I think you have to see him in the (firm,

rippling) flesh to really appreciate him. My first sight
was four years ago when he was a freshman in a standard
Western Civ course. My first thought: "Promising. Very promising." He would have stood out even if he hadn't been
practically the only black student at a school nicknamed
"Wonder Bread U." But eighteen-year-olds always look pretty
green to me (do you find that too?), so I honestly didn't
much notice him. I gave him his grade (a respectable
A− or something like that) and he went the way of hun-
dreds of other freshmen.

But then he reappeared in my senior honors seminar this
fall. At first I didn't realize that this was the young man
I'd seen almost four years ago. Suddenly (or it seemed
sudden to me) he was six feet tall, with a body that just
shouldn't be legal—perfect proportions, gorgeous brown
skin. And that ass. I wonder if the other students noticed
me watching him every day as he made his way to the
same spot: back seat, middle row (he knows he has a perfect
ass—he took that stroll every day on purpose just to torture
me). Maybe the men who weren't looking at him themselves noticed; anyway, most of the women were straining their peripheral vision to watch Kyle and his glorious
ass.

It was bad enough to watch him in my classroom and
not be able to touch. Then he started showing up during
my office hours. Orifice hours, I began to think of them,
because those were the most attentive parts of my body
when he sat down and scooted his chair up close to
mine. He was always the proper, respectful student, but
most of the time his questions were pretty lame; I really
think he just wanted attention, and like most beautiful people,
couldn't resist watching the impact he had on me. I
would try very hard to maintain my polite-but-firm pro-
fessorial classroom persona, but Christ! All I could think
about was lunging for the door, locking it behind us, and
dropping him to the carpet for an afternoon of sweaty
sex, starting with the best blowjob he'd ever had (which
reminds me—why don't we have a nice word for oral sex

that doesn't sound like work? Or pasta? If you can think
of one, let me know). I've since added a big overstuffed
chair to my office furniture, and if I had had it then,
the temptation to dive onto it with him might have been
too much. But I'm not completely amoral; I lusted after
Kyle, but I lusted, alas, in silence.

Is this getting too graphic? Sorry—I did warn you
that I'm only human.

Emily glanced at the clock. Ten more minutes until Nick
showed up. Better hurry. Nick was always so prompt. Especially
when he was cranky.

I suppose that I should say something about Kyle's academic
status. He is a good student; not spectacular, but very good.
And he is definitely serious about his career plans. His
best quality is his determination and ... but what am
I saying?! Sure he's smart, but his best quality is still his
ass. Bar none. Would that I could have gotten my hands
on it. If you do accept him into your program (and you
honestly should), be prepared to suffer pangs of lascivious torment. At least until he graduates in two or three
years.

Then he's fair game—for a game I suspect he's up to.

Very Truly Yours,
Emily E. Jackson

She leaned back on her swivel chair and surveyed the glowing
screen with satisfaction. "Now that," she thought, "is more like
it."

Her reverie was cut short by three quick taps on her office
door. Ordinarily he would have just walked in, but their heated
exchange had clearly left Nick uncertain about his welcome.

She stood up and stretched, taking her time to let him in.
When she did, he entered slowly and stood by her desk, shifting
from foot to foot. She remained silent while he gazed around her

office, searching for a neutral conversation opener. Finally he noticed the overstuffed chair.

"That's new, isn't it?" he said with a cautious smile.

"Yes, it is." She took him by the hand, led him in front of it, then pushed him down onto the cushions.

"Are you still angry with me? Because I'm really sorry that I—"

She put her finger over his lips, then began unbuckling his belt. Too shocked to move at first, he soon began to help her, and in no time his pants were around his ankles and she was savoring his warm flesh. She stroked his smooth shaft with her tongue, wetting him with her saliva, teasing the head of his penis with her closed, moistened lips. When he finally began to shift uncomfortably from the prolonged anticipation, she plunged his entire cock into her warm mouth. She was rewarded by his heavy groan, and the satisfying sensation of fullness that sucking him always gave her.

The unexpectedness of her assault and the novelty of sex in her office were too much for him. He came quickly, and hard. She swallowed his semen with pleasure, drawing on him until he moaned in half pleasure, half pain. From her seat on the carpet she rested her head on his lap, twining her arms back around his waist and up to his shoulders. He played with her hair gently.

"Does this mean you forgive me?" he asked quietly, after a comfortable silence had elapsed.

"Could be." She smiled as he began to knead her shoulders and neck. "Why don't we go to my apartment, where we don't have to worry about being caught by the custodians, and see if we can settle the rest of our differences? I've got some wine coolers and pop tarts." She stood and brushed off her knees, checked her hose for runs, then began gathering her things.

"Sounds good to me. But give me just a minute, will you? I'm feeling a little drained." Nick opened one eye just enough to gauge her reaction.

"Lame, very lame," she chuckled, turning off the computer.

"Then why are you laughing? Hey, wait!" He leaned forward, suddenly finding some energy. "You didn't save that file!"

This time she laughed outright. "Oh, don't worry about that," she reassured him. "It was a letter for a student. I'm not so sure I had the tone quite right anyway. Now hurry up and let's go, you big faker. You have a back rub to earn!"

Debbie Cohen

∽

Look What the Cat Dragged In

It was a crisp and sun-dappled Sunday morning. As I stretched my leg and poked my toes out of the covers to test the air, Barnacle promptly pounced on them. Wiggling toes have been a weakness of his ever since he was a kitten. Tahiti was lounging on the pillow next to mine, quick to capitalize on the still-warm place my lover grudgingly left as he stumbled about, dressing for basketball. She casually placed her paw on my face and gently stretched her claws into my cheek. Though the day was mine to sleep away, my cats had an agenda of their own; they had decided it was time for me to get moving.

I lay in bed just long enough to prove to Barnacle and Tahiti that they had not won, then crawled out of bed and into my bathrobe. As I put on coffee, the cats chased each other around the apartment. Coffee meant Sunday and Sunday meant they would be adorned with collars and admitted to the outdoor world of scent and adventure. They sat on my newspaper, pounced on the drawstring of my robe, and stuck their noses in my juice until I opened the sliding glass door and let them roam free. Barnacle led the way and I watched as they disappeared around the bend of the deck, where they bounded down the steps onto the busy sidewalk and immediately sprang back up, their tails twitching caution and ears alerted to receive and translate every sound.

Such was our Sunday routine. With my lover gone for a few hours, I would spread out, scatter books and papers and lounge in my mess, treating myself to an occasional glance at the joyously romping cats.

I settled into the couch, swathed in my down comforter, and deposited three potentially interesting books in front of me. I had just tearfully parted with ten characters at the close of a World War II novel and was hesitant to re-engage in the realm of emotional devastation. So I selected my favorite, well-thumbed (and fingered) collection of erotic short stories written by women.

Slowly I read, pausing often to reach into my warm cocoon to cradle my breasts, circle my nipples, stroke at the firm wet muscles between my outspread legs. I invited the characters under the covers with me to play out their brief, potent scenes. I allowed curious tongues to travel my thighs, golden curved cocks to plunge into me as I cowered helplessly in a corner. I invited women's expert fingers to rummage through my insides and tickle me into convulsions. I saw myself, dildo in hand, bearing down on a trembling woman. I was tied to a bed and sucked raw. I was tenderly bathed and carried to bed. I groped and I pressed, I grappled and I lunged. I was swimming in a sea of honey and sinking sweetly.

As I came for the fifth time, a harsh background noise came sharply into focus. It was coming from the house next door, which was being reconstructed. I identified the noise as a jackhammer and wondered if the workmen had deliberately returned on Sunday just to aggravate me.

Time to collect the cats. Both of them are remarkably lacking in any survival skills; they stick their noses into flame, they crawl into the cavity of the sofa-bed as it's being folded up, they love running under heavy moving objects. I imagined Barnacle running up to the jackhammer to give it his ritual proprietary sniff. I'm not fond of this image, so when the workers come out, the cats come in.

I pulled on my robe and stepped onto the deck to start my search. I almost tripped over Tahiti, who was cowering behind a potted plant. Barnacle was nowhere to be found. I checked the stairs, a nook in the side of the house where he likes to nap, and then headed down to the street to peek under cars—another favorite hangout.

Finally, cold and cursing under my breath, I approached one workman who was taking a break. As I asked about Barnacle, I could just imagine the track playing in his brain: "Neurotic bitch over-concerned about her cats." He feigned sympathy and smilingly agreed to keep his eye out for Barnacle. Instead of slapping the smile off his face, I thanked him and returned to my book and quilt.

I was disappointed but not surprised to find that the stories which had me writhing minutes before could not penetrate my concern for Barnacle and the grating noise of construction. I abandoned the couch for the shower, where I hoped to at least drown out the noise. I let the water run over my face, my hair, my breasts, and then opened my legs and shuddered at the full, warm lick of water I received. Slowly I soaped my body, giving special attention to the tender cavities between my toes and the hollow where my neck and collar bones meet. I admired my long fingers as they stroked the soft flesh of my inner thighs. You are beautiful, whispered the steamy women circling me. You are just right.

There was a polite knock at the bathroom door—a knock my lover knows is expected of him before entering. This small gesture has eliminated a great deal of fright on my part, as it prevents me from being unexpectedly shaken from my steamy shower dream world.

"What happened, did the game end early?" I shouted above the water, as he is usually gone three hours at least. There was no reply.

"Honey, are you okay? Why are you back so soon?" Still no reply. I wiped the soap from my eyes and leaned out of the shower.

There stood the amused construction worker holding a sooty and confused Barnacle. As he lowered Barnacle to the floor, the cat took great interest in the man's jeans, and sniffed contentedly at a dark stain on his right leg. I, too, took interest in the man's jeans, as a bulge was steadily forming under my gaze. "Thank you," I managed to whisper, and stood riveted.

His look of amusement fell as his eyes traveled my body. I watched him appreciate my taut nipples, my round belly, my dripping hair. He reached out his hand as if to touch and then withdrew it. The shower rained confusion on me, pelting me with rage, fear and desire. I began to mumble something resembling "Get out of my house" when he spoke.

"Show me," he pleaded hoarsely.

"Show you what?" I replied, feeling very naked. What did he want to see that he wasn't already seeing?

"Show me. Show me what you were doing on the couch."

My jaw dropped. On the couch. When? Today? How could he have seen that? A flush began in my face and flowered throughout my body. He had watched.

"Okay, but I'll need some help" came out quicker than my intended demand that he leave the bathroom.

The jeans and T-shirt quickly came off. While he struggled with his boots, his eyes remained riveted on me as if I would be sucked down the drain any minute if he didn't keep a close watch. I turned the water off, but remained dripping in the tub. I showed him my ass, held up my breasts for his hungry examination and teased him with moans and thrusts until he was finally free of the boots. Then he came to me.

I was standing with my legs spread wide, and as he stepped into the tub he offered me his thigh: "You might be more comfortable resting on this." I was. Reaching for my hands, he took them from me. He gently kneaded my palms while telling my breasts what he intended to do with them. I began sliding myself up and down the thigh that held me. I pressed it tight between my legs, like a huge cock, and rode it until my clit was swollen solid.

He kept his promise to my breasts and cradled them as carefully as I had earlier. He teased them with the tip of his tongue until the nipples strained as if they would burst. Just as my yearning to have them surrounded became almost unbearable, he took one breast at a time into the warmth of his mouth while squeezing the other swollen nipple. As he lifted the second breast in consideration, a shooting fire ran from my asshole up my spine and I came in long, shuddering spasms against that rock hard thigh.

He sat me down on the edge of the tub, rubbed his erect cock gently against each of my flushed cheeks and said, "Now, show me." After pushing my knees open with his, he stood back and waited, holding his cock firmly and slowly rubbing up and down. He looked at me as if it were me he was stroking and I pretended he was. I mirrored his movements, parting my lips and stroking the soft inner flesh. I squeezed my bulging clit and spread my legs wide, wide open. Three fingers slid easily in, and they took up their familiar rhythm, pumping slowly and teasingly. I flicked my clit and my nipples alternately and waves of pained pleasure flowed over me. I withdrew my fingers when my ears started ringing, and a dam fell on the ripples rising to wash over me. Not yet.

As I writhed with the agony of postponed pleasure, he dove for my legs and pushed them open wider, spreading my lips back into a wide smile with his thumbs. With one generous sweep of his tongue against my clenched and straining clit, my body flew from me in powerful heaving convulsions. He held me against his chest until my body was mine again.

"Now I have something to show you," he said, producing his pulsing, hard cock for examination.

"Thank you, but we've already been acquainted," I responded, turning away, feigning disinterest.

He took the opportunity of a back view to spread the cheeks of my ass wide open. He whispered into my twitching hole, "How would you like to get reacquainted?" A rhetorical question, of course.

As the introductions were being made, I climbed out of the tub, got on my hands and knees and wiggled an imaginary tail. He sat there, interested, but did not move. Tail snapping the tile wall, I stalked him, nuzzled his shoulder and then took a fleshy bite which I rapidly followed with long, slow licks. His breathing thickened as he grasped my thigh and made a long scratch up my leg with his fingernails and followed the trail with his tongue. Taking me by the waist, he got up on his knees and entered my ass. He reached around and with three fingers fucked me from the front. "Just how you like it," he cooed in my ear; he got an incoherent gurgle as a response. With his other hand he tweaked at my clit and I spread wider and wider, surrounded, full. The rhythm of our bodies swelled up in me like music; I fragmented into sharp pieces of piercing pleasure.

As I lay entangled in his arms and legs on the bathroom floor, I became aware of the cold tile pressing into me. "Follow me," I told the nape of his neck, as I struggled to my feet and slowly made my way to the bedroom. He headed for the living room, where I assumed he would scoot out the front door. Instead, he returned with the comforter I had left on the couch and ballooned it over me as I lay curled in bed. He looked at me tenderly, and held my face in his hands for a moment. Again he briskly left me for the living room. This time he returned with Barnacle under one arm, Tahiti under the other. He gently deposited them against my belly, where they immediately took up grooming each other.

The last thing I remember was the low rumble in Barnacle's throat as Tahiti dug her mouth deep into the pelt of fur at his neck, and the sound of my front door softly closing.

Linda Niemann

Blue Letter

Your denials will do you no good, and your hands will be useless in keeping me from unfolding your secrets one by one, at my pleasure, once I have you in this place. Time will stand still, the hours growing fat and sluggish, the light reddening and swelling outside the dirty windows facing the street.

You will meet me here, even though you can't yet imagine you will, because you want to be spread under my hands, splayed out on the sofa, the sun from the window hot on your cunt. Sweat will form in the hollows of your thighs and the ropes will pull tight as your body reaches for my tongue or the whip, whichever I choose to caress you with next.

I have bound your breasts with rope so that they resemble cocks or obscene balloons, the nipples swelling with blood. They love the whip that merely stings and leaves faint traces like a cat's claw. I suck on them to bring your cunt forward into my hand.

You are so easy; the merest brush with my nail on the hood of your clitoris and my hands would fill with your come, but I won't allow you this yet. Instead I whip you for giving in to me so fast.

I force your belly down so that your ass straddles my knee. I can feel the heat, like putting my hand into a hot oven, a slick glove on the edge of a burn. I want to see your ass redden under my belt, feel it pull away from the ropes holding you open. I have a dildo in your cunt which I can slowly engorge with air as you take the strokes of my whip. When I am satisfied that it has stretched you enough, I turn my attention to that other opening you are trying to protect from me.

For that I think I will find some strangers, the ones with their hands on their cocks and their ears glued to the walls of their rooms. All I have to do is invite them in. I hear their footsteps outside my door now.

There are two of them, one young and slight, a worker fresh from the fields. The other is heavy and unshaven. I give the young one the pleasure of your ass, but only while his is being used in the same fashion. I tell them not to be too quick with you, because your mouth will be mine. I want to taste each penetration there, under my tongue, in your gasping cries.

When they have gone you will be untied and held in my arms, your body washed and rubbed with almond oil. With my long blonde hair I will kneel and dry your feet, and if you wish it, tell you stories until the moon falls off the edge of the world.

Susan St. Aubin

Hope

When my husband and I got married we agreed to share our fantasies and our lovers.

"Did you ever think of making it with two people at once? A man and a woman? Or two other women?" he sometimes asks just before he enters me.

He wants me to join him in his favorite fantasy, but I have a better one of my own, a memory of a girl named Linda Hope I met just once when I was five and she was twelve.

One Saturday, I went with my father to a farm where he often bought produce.

"Nothing like eggs warm from the hen," he said, his hands tapping the steering wheel while I bounced on the gray plush seat beside him.

"And corn and tomatoes off the vine—you can't get anything like that in the store." He turned off the highway onto a long gravel driveway that went uphill to a gray house. A woman in blue jeans and a big girl wearing shorts and a T-shirt sat on the front porch railing, watching the chickens that scratched and pecked at the gravel.

"That's Irene and her daughter," my father told me as we got out of the car.

Irene smiled and waved as we crunched our way across the driveway.

"Linda Hope," she said to the girl, "why don't you show Patty the barn?"

"Linda Hope," I whispered. I could almost taste the sound of it, round like a chocolate egg.

My father and Irene went inside the house. "Any tomatoes yet?" I heard him ask.

Linda Hope tossed her long braid of brown hair over one shoulder and trotted across a field of dry grass. At the barn, she turned and said, "My name's Lin. That's L-I-N, if you can spell yet. Do you like horses? They're all out in the pasture today. We could go see them if you want."

"I don't know," I answered. I was afraid because I'd never seen one up close before.

Lin shrugged. "Well, there's some kittens up in the loft, if you want to see them."

Inside the dim, mud-smelling barn, I followed Lin to a ladder. Her bottom hung out of her white shorts in half-moons an inch from my eyes as I climbed behind her. In the loft above us were bundles of hay. Our climb seemed to go on forever, with Linda Hope's skin nearly touching my face and the sweet smell of her filling my nose. The palms of my hands were sweaty and I was breathing heavily.

This is what I think of when I make love with my husband, climbing and climbing. Whenever he tells me about one of his lovers, or one of his fantasies, I see the barn and Linda Hope bending over in her too-tight shorts calling, "Kitty, Kitty, Kitty," while scuffling the loose hay with her hands. I don't want to share her.

I could meet someone else to share, but it's a question of opportunity; he's a professor, so it's part of his job to talk to lots of attractive young people anxious to please him. I'm an administrative assistant in the registrar's office, where I stay eight hours a day and never see anyone unless they have a problem I'm supposed to solve.

My husband's lovers don't appeal to me. He displays them at

dinner parties like potential desserts, but they're usually too tall, too small, too stupid, or too phony. His women are thin and remind me of tropical birds with their green and purple eye shadow. His men aren't much more inspiring. One of them (too short) talks incessantly about his thesis on the bisexual nature of twentieth-century British literature.

"Consider Bloomsbury," he says. (Too stupid! Too phony!)

I remember Linda Hope's long braid and long full legs, and think I might prefer a woman as a lover, if I could find the right one.

In my office I write his lovers' names on scraps of paper and rip them into tiny pieces. It's a magic charm that sometimes works.

The short man's bisexuality thesis is rejected by his adviser. Another lover, a girl with long red hair who once wrote a paper on the comedies of "Shakesphere," but was forgiven because of that hair, drives her car off the road and into a tree. She only breaks an ankle (fate, too, can be forgiving), but heeds the warning and moves to New York.

My husband decides that older women (by older he means those in their early thirties, still five years younger than he is) make the most stable lovers. I write their names on scraps of paper and they disappear one by one.

I can't complain. If I want, he meets his lovers only when I'm at work, or out of town, and he tells me I'm the only one he enters without a condom. We're together every night. Sometimes I wear silk teddies and garter belts; I have a whip I made of braided strips of silk, and long peacock feathers I use to caress his shoulders and the back of his neck. We're just ordinary people, though. I don't wear spike heels or boots with spurs or anything like that. I have a silk slip the color of ripe peaches, slit up one thigh. It's too good to wear all day, so I only put it on at night, for him.

"I could eat you in peach," he says, and does.

Then he begins leaving me alone in my peach silk to spend his evenings at the library—not the university library but the public library downtown. This happens at first once, then two or three times a week. For an article he's writing, he says, involving city documents. One of the librarians is particularly helpful.

"I'd like to have her over for dinner," he says, as he always does when he finds a new lover. "Her name is Hope. You'll like her."

My heart catches in my ribs as an image of Linda Hope in the barn comes back to me.

"Want to see something?" she asked. She sat beside me on a bale of hay and slowly pulled off her T-shirt. Right in front of my nose were two bumps of flesh the size and color of small peaches. They even had a sweet peach smell to them. I pulled back.

She laughed. "They're breasts," she said, pronouncing the word so that each letter sounded distinct. "Breasts like our mothers have, only smaller. You can touch them if you want."

Carefully, I reached out my fingers. Her breasts were hard, like not quite ripe fruit, and covered with a light, invisible down that tickled my fingertips. I took my hand away and sat on it. My eyes filled with tears.

She pulled her shirt back over her head and smiled at me. "You don't have anything like that yet, do you?"

I stood up and said, "Of course not. Who'd want them, anyway?" I climbed down the loft ladder, then ran across the barn into the sun.

For the first time I'm curious about one of my husband's lovers, so one day after work I take the bus to the library downtown to have a look.

At a long counter by the front door are two librarians—or perhaps they're clerks—neither of them his type. The man's blond hair looks bleached, and is cut in bangs over his forehead. The woman has frizzy hair and wears heavy black eyeliner in a style popular twenty years back, though she can't be more than twenty herself.

The woman sitting at the reference desk has long blond hair and looks like she's barely out of high school. An older woman approaches her, a woman of perhaps fifty with shoulder-length white hair curled under in a way that seems natural. She's not short or tall, not fat or thin, but has the kind of build my father used to call healthy. Her face is tanned and her long gold earrings have some kind of purple stone inlay that glints through her hair. Her skirt is purple too, and her lavender sweater scoops low enough to reveal the tanned skin of her full breasts, where a gold medallion, one of those Mexican ornaments like a primitive sun with rays stabbing in all directions, hangs from a gold chain around her neck.

"Hope?" asks the blond woman at the desk, her voice rising with her question, and they murmur together.

The name is a coincidence. Linda Hope was just seven years older than I, which would make her forty-two now. Still, this Hope is one of the most attractive women I've ever seen, and I stand transfixed as she puts one arm around the woman's shoulder and bends over the desk, revealing more of her breasts. They study a stack of yellow cards, and both look up as I approach.

Hope's eyes, a clear, dark brown, seem to tunnel straight through me. Close up, I can see her hair is only white on top; underneath, it's black as a shadow. For the first time I salute my husband's taste.

When I ask her for a book on Mexican art, Hope leads me to the card catalogue. She smells like lemon. I can't take my eyes from her breasts.

"That's a lovely pendant," I say. "Pre-Columbian, right?"

"Yes," she answers in her soft voice, "but just a copy. I bought it in Mexico last summer."

We talk of travel. She's been all over Mexico and plans a long trip to Peru next year. She finds me three books, one with color plates, and walks me to the door, still talking of boats and flights and donkey guides to Machu Picchu. I'm sure she has no idea who I am.

When I come out the library door, I see my husband parking our car down the street. I step behind the bushes and watch him stroll into the library, his full briefcase knocking against his leg, then I go to the car, unlock it, and leave my books on the front seat.

Back in the library, the clerks behind the circulation desk talk to three teenage boys who seem to be arguing about a book one of them holds behind his back. The blond woman's head is still bent over her stack of yellow cards. The nameplate on the desk where she works says Hope Caputo, but Hope isn't anywhere in sight, and neither is my husband.

I walk past the reference desk to the bookshelves, and past the bookshelves to a door that leads to a corridor with books lining both walls. I'm not sure this area is open to the public, but there's no one to stop me. I walk until I reach another corridor, and walk down that one to another. Here books aren't just on shelves, but are piled on the floor as well. I hear a man's voice, answered by a low pitched woman's laugh. I turn another corner and flatten myself behind a stack of books. I see my husband's back and, over his shoulder, Hope's face, eyes open, looking to see where the sound of my footsteps is coming from. He lifts her sweater and reaches his hands inside to feel her breasts; she strokes and kisses his face. His hands reach lower, to her skirt, which he lifts to her waist. Her thighs are heavier than he usually prefers, and her garter belt is stark white against her tanned skin; my breath catches when I see that she doesn't wear underpants. His hand slides back and forth between her legs, while her hand massages the bulge beneath the left thigh of his gray tweed pants.

I squat behind the books, reach inside my underpants, and slide my own fingers back and forth. At last I'm making love with my husband and one of his lovers, but he has no idea.

She's breathing faster, saying, "Oh, for once I'm glad we're understaffed," until she falls against him and they stagger, like a two-headed creature, knocking over a pile of books.

Startled by the noise, I take my hand away and scrunch lower behind the books, trying to hold my breath. My heart seems to wobble in my chest.

Hope's sweater and skirt drop to their proper positions and she begins to pick up the books. The blond woman comes pattering down the hall from the other direction.

"What happened?" she asks. "We heard a crash."

"Nothing, Julie," Hope calls, singing her words in three tones. "I'm just looking for a book I thought was back here."

My husband stands to one side while they restack the books.

"There." Hope dusts her hands against her skirt. "I'm sorry I couldn't find it for you, but if you check with the university library, I'm sure they'll have it."

"Thank you for everything," he says, and follows Julie down the hall.

In a minute, Hope goes after them, and I follow her on tip-toe down a short corridor that leads straight to the reference desk.

"Julie," Hope says, "tomorrow I'd like you to . . ."

The phone rings. Julie picks it up, while Hope turns to the shelves behind the reference desk and begins rearranging books. At the circulation desk, the clerks attend to a line of twelve people, all carrying piles of books. Hope turns around when an elderly man approaches her desk.

My husband isn't there. When I leave the library, the car and my books are gone, so I take a bus home, where I discover my books on the dining room table.

"Were you at the library downtown?" he asks. His eyebrows come together the way they do when he's anxious.

"I had some shopping to do," I say. "That's why I put my books in your car when I saw it."

He doesn't ask me why I have no packages.

At work I write Hope's name on a Post-it note, but I don't tear it up. I write my husband's name on another Post-it note and lay them side by side, then stick them together. I write my name on a third note, stick it to the other two, and fold all three into my purse.

One Friday night my husband invites Hope to dinner. Though I've thought of her constantly, I haven't seen her in the month since I went to the library. She shakes my hand with no sign of recognition when my husband introduces us.

"I'm glad to meet you, Pat," she says. She wears gray slacks and a gray cotton knit turtleneck, tight around her breasts. Her lips and cheeks are rouged deep pink, and her silver hair glistens in the candlelight. Behind her hair I glimpse the shine of her silver earrings.

At dinner, she drinks rosé from a glass that looks as silvery as her hair, and tells us she's had a lucky month: she found an antique rocking chair at a garage sale for twenty dollars; a lump she had removed from her breast turned out to be benign; and the city decided to allow a new librarian to be hired to replace one who'd left two years ago. I'm glad my power seems as great for the names I don't tear up as it does for those I do.

My husband looks at me with raised eyebrows. I smile and massage his foot under the table—at least I think it's his foot, though suddenly I'm unsure. I imagine corridors and stacks of books, and feel a warm glow that seems to travel upwards from the base of my spine to the top of my head.

I clear the table while Hope and my husband sit in the living room. I have simultaneous urges to join them, and to walk out the back door. I'm in the loft again, aroused and frightened all at once.

I'm wearing a black lace bra that shows the pink skin of my breasts. I could take off my blouse and join them, bringing coffee on a tray. My husband has never seen this bra, which I know he'll love. I look into the living room, where he's lit a fire.

Because I don't have the courage of my fantasies, I bring in the coffee with my rose silk blouse buttoned all the way up the neck.

"It's warm in here," says Hope, plucking at her shirt.

"Take it off," says my husband, raising his eyebrows at me again. "That's why I made this fire."

She looks at me. I sit beside them and pour coffee; I feel my cheeks flush as I unbutton the top button of my blouse.

My husband reaches over and unbuttons the rest of the blouse while Hope watches, catching her breath.

I let the blouse slither off.

"Oh," says Hope.

He touches my breast through its tracery of lace. Hope's cheeks and lips are a much darker pink than they were earlier; she watches my husband's hand on my breast. Then, in a sudden motion, she lifts her arms and pulls her turtleneck over her head, shaking out her hair, and flings the shirt onto the coffee table beside the tray holding our cups.

She's wearing the very same bra I have on, though her breasts are fuller and her skin darker. We look at each other and laugh.

My husband touches Hope's breast with his free hand and asks, "What's the joke?"

"It's not done," says Hope, "for two women to wear the same outfit to an affair."

We both laugh harder.

"One of us will have to volunteer to change." Hope fiddles with the clasp between her breasts and unfastens the black lace, which pulls apart, loosening her full breasts. I'm surprised by how little they need the support of a brassiere. There's a small red scar near her left nipple, which must be where she had the lump removed. She shrugs the black lace off her shoulders and throws it on top of her sweater.

I haven't looked so closely at another woman's breasts since I touched Linda Hope's hard peaches in the loft of the barn. I never saw her again after that day when I ran all the way to the horse pasture beyond the barn, where she caught up with me, her young breasts hidden behind her T-shirt. She told me the names of all the horses, then leaped onto the bare back of one of them and rode in widening circles, gradually moving farther away from me.

Now I reach out my fingers to Hope's soft fullness, feeling the same tingle in my fingertips that I remember from long ago. I move my hands slowly to her nipples, dark as miniature figs, and jump when I touch my husband's fingers. For a second I'd forgotten him.

Her hands reach for my breasts, unclasping the brassiere that holds them, and together we touch and look. I gently trace the red scar.

"They tell me it'll fade to nothing in a year," she says. "Careful. It's still a bit tender."

"Hey," says my husband, who doesn't want to be forgotten now that he's finally got his wife and a lover together. He strips off his jeans and shirt and stands before us, his penis erect at the level of our eyes as we sit on the couch fondling each other. With a united sigh we turn to him. Businesslike, Hope takes his cock in her mouth, neatly as she stacked the fallen books in the library, while I stand to kiss his mouth and stroke his ass.

What do three people do at the crucial moment; crucial, that is, for a man?

"I wish I had two penises," he pants.

Hope pulls her mouth away. "Sorry," she mocks. "No time to grow another one now."

We look at each other and manage not to laugh. I push him toward her like a gift. I see myself crouched behind that stack of books in the library, and remember how much I liked watching them.

Hope pulls him to the floor in front of the fire. He slides her out of her slacks, then lies on his back while she massages a condom onto his cock. She sits astride him while I hide behind a chair, pretending they don't know I'm there, until she falls forward and they're both still. Then I take my jeans off, too, and stretch out on the floor near them, feeling the warmth of the fire on my back.

His breathing is deep and regular with an occasional snore.

Hope smiles. "He's probably the only man in the world to fall asleep on *two* women," she says as she moves closer to me, then whispers, "You know, I saw you that night in the stacks," and kisses me on the lips. "I guessed who you were," she says, kissing my cheeks and my chin.

She kisses my forehead and the line where my hair begins and says, "I knew you were his wife the minute you walked into the library because he described you so perfectly, down to the last detail—the way you walk, the way you twist your hair around one finger when you get nervous. I could see you were nervous because you suspected who I was."

My husband moans in his sleep and mutters something like "move" or "more" as he rolls closer to Hope, who lies beside me, stroking my shoulders and kissing my breasts.

"I've wanted to meet you ever since I first heard about you," she says, "and knowing you were there that night, watching us, oh!"

Her kisses move down my stomach and across my light brown fur to my clit, which she licks and sucks until I glow and flash all over. We lie in each other's arms stroking and kissing and watching the fire while my husband's snores become slow and steady as rain.

I close my eyes to the feather strokes of her fingertips across my shoulders, and wake to rain tapping on the light gray of the

windows. My husband still snores beside me. By the window,
Hope pulls her gray sweater over her head and shakes her hair,
running her fingers through it. The fire is out and the room is
cold. I wrap an afghan around myself and throw a rug over my
husband, who groans and rolls over on his side, pulling the cover
around him.

"Ssssh," Hope whispers. "Don't wake him. I've got to go, it's
nearly six and I've got to be at work by nine. It's my turn for Saturday."

At the door she puts her hands on my shoulders and kisses me,
her tongue lingering in my mouth to caress the insides of my
cheeks and lips.

"I'd like to see you again," she whispers.

"Both of us?"

She shakes her head. "You."

"What'll I tell him?"

She shrugs. "That you're working late. Let's make it Thursday.
I'm off at five-thirty that night."

On Thursday I wait for her in Mario's Trattoria with a glass of
red wine sitting before me on the black and white checked formica table. It's a new place with walls of glass and an open
kitchen, where the cooks and waiters shout at each other in what
sounds like Italian, though I entertain myself by thinking it could
be Romanian or Bengali. This is not the setting for an intimate
dinner, but Hope has told me the food is wonderful.

The library isn't far away, and at a quarter to six she strolls in,
a large bag of books and papers hanging from her shoulder. Today
she's in brown—brown and white striped shirt and brown wool
skirt and sweater, with copper coins hanging from her ears.

We kiss quickly, like the old friends we're not, before she sits
down and waves to the waiter, a thin, dark, balding man in a red
apron, who brings her a glass of red wine and a menu for each of
us. While the kitchen staff chatters, Hope smiles and says, "My
family all spoke Italian when I was growing up. I was the youn-
gest child, so I never learned to speak it properly myself, though
I understand it. Half my sisters were born in Italy, and half here.

That's nine of us, all girls. I'm used to a lot of noise. I find it very restful, which must be why I love this place."

She recommends the tortellini, the eggplant parmesan, the baked lasagna. My head already spins from the wine. The steam rises from the kitchen, blurring the darkening windows. We decide on pasta pescatore, with shrimp and calamari and chunks of unidentifiable, salty fish in a sauce of garlic and tomatoes. Her foot feels for mine under the table; she has her shoe off and slides mine off too, and our nylon clad toes slip over each other. Coins clink into a juke box and Italian opera swallows the kitchen noise. We have more wine and, for dessert, a dense vanilla ice cream with small, light cookies that taste like they're made of ground hazelnuts.

"Biscotti," she says, crunching into one.

She tells me about her ex-husband, who also spoke Italian and was an accountant. She tells me about their son, now an artist living in New York. We don't mention my husband.

People leave the restaurant—it's eight o'clock, then eight-thirty, and I realize we're stalling. The kitchen is quiet and the glass walls are black. I feel like I did in the hayloft with Linda Hope: I can stay, or I can run. This time I stay. We have coffee and more biscotti. I tear the cover off a book of matches and tear half of it into tiny pieces, which I leave in the ashtray. When she asks, "Would you like to go back to my house?" I nod.

Only then does the waiter bring our check, which she pays.

"My treat," she says. "I invited you and we're only here because I'm too lazy to cook."

She excuses herself to go to the bathroom. The waiter returns the tray with her change and a receipt. I take out a pen and write my husband's name on the remaining half of the matchbook cover, then shred it, showering the pieces into the ashtray.

Hope comes back and picks up her receipt, leaving the change. We smile at our waiter as we walk to the door.

"*Buona notte,*" he murmurs, and we go through the double glass doors into the night.

Calla Conova

Just the Garden and I

The white-noise whir of an electric fan covers the rattling of the neighbor's dishes. Cool from the shower, wearing a cotton kimono, I wind my way through the dark house and unbolt the door. My garden yawns a cricket song. Desert-dry air sweeps across my bare feet, billows up the undulating space between legs and foreign fabric. I cross the threshold and the garden unfolds like a secret lover. Kimono ties loosen as a cat rouses to prowl elsewhere.

Now I can begin to dance in rhythm with the murmur of patient moon-washed leaves. I am a cobra, cajoling my light garment to shed and slide its comfortable personality to the surprised lawn. The monotonous fan hums inside the house—it murmurs with the TV and says, "Cover up, come back in, don't leave me alone."

But I am free now, the floozy entertainer for a million rapt grass blades, who gaze up between my swaying legs. They transmit encouragement via alpha waves, sensitizing every inch of my pioneering body. I offer a dandelion a better view; my conspiring fingers unveil my night-blooming bud.

Bend, squat, lift leg—a dog in heat couldn't do better. Fingers, spit-wet, range to various erogenous zones, re-wet and stroke for the sake of the camellia bushes who spent themselves several moons ago in their own wild display. "Look! This is how it's done in July," I say.

Above, filtering the stars, the jacaranda tree with its swollen purple clusters notices my warm night openings. Unabashed pink four o'clocks drop a shiny seed or two in applause for my quivering thigh. I rival the perfumes of the night garden. The jasmine and I understand the satori of creating musk.

My song rises, breathy, sweet and raw. I press against the smooth sycamore tree. The back of my neck surrenders to its possessive love bite. The garden knows me. Knows how much is enough. Knows when to leave an ebbing echo in my ears. We swap sex stories. We laugh at age-old pollination jokes. I have shown this leafy audience the most private and shocking parts of me. They reply that they have always done so for me—and in broad daylight to boot!

I apologize for thinking that I was the first to make love alone, under the stars. But that doesn't diminish my sorority with the flowers. Lusty communion complete, I take back the kimono, forget to say thank you, and return, like an errant puppy, to the comfortable hum of the TV and fan.

༄

Something Special

Jean called me on a Thursday night. "Will you please be an angel and come take care of Missy until Saturday? She won't eat if I put her in a kennel. I have to fly up to Seattle and get the Brent contracts signed." She had barely paused for breath.

We're identical twins, but she's a big-city businesswoman while I'm a desert-dwelling artist. Before she can go on I say, "Okay. Okay. Don't panic. I'll catch the seven a.m. flight out of Phoenix and I'll be there before noon." *There* being her tiny gem of a house on Russian Hill in San Francisco. "When's your flight?"

"Six-thirty. I'll leave the key in the usual place. I should be home Saturday afternoon. And I promise you something special to say thanks. I feel like my brain has turned to scrambled eggs. I hate these last-minute deals."

"Stop worrying. Calm down. Good luck. I'll see you Saturday. Bye."

The sky is a cloudless blue and the air soft as silk the next morning as I get out of the cab in front of Jean's house. The key is in a pot of geraniums on the small porch. As soon as I open the door, Jean's poodle, Missy, greets me with frenzied joy. Hunger sends me into the kitchen. While I eat I keep up a one-sided conversation with Missy. We spend the afternoon lazing in the back yard, and take a long, brisk walk before dinner. After eating we retire to the living room to watch television. By ten I am ready for a shower and bed; I let Missy out once more. When she comes back in, she curls up in her basket and promptly falls asleep.

As I am about to undress in Jean's bedroom, I notice a snapshot tucked in the corner of her dresser mirror. It is a middle-aged man with silvery hair and a nice smile. It must be Nathan; Jean has written me about him.

They are not yet lovers, and probably never will be. She'd said he was fifty-three, a widower and an engineer who apparently grew up on a cattle ranch in northeastern Wyoming. His father died recently and left him the ranch. Nathan was in San Francisco visiting his married daughter when he met Jean. They both happened to be at an exhibition of nineteenth-century western painters. That was less than a month ago, and I recall that Jean said Nathan was going back to Wyoming very soon. She couldn't understand why he wanted to give up a successful career in Casper and go back to being a cowboy. Loving the outdoors as much as I do, I understand completely.

Jean keeps her relationships lighthearted and brief. I've told her she's like a butterfly flitting from man to man, sampling their nectar then moving on. I imagine she is feeling mild regret that she has not sampled Nathan, but in a week or a month she'll have someone new.

Jean and I tend to like the same type of man—strong but gentle, intelligent, with a keen sense of humor and a very healthy appetite for sex. We have both been married and divorced. I am between relationships, and my hormones are raging.

I kick off my shoes, and slip out of my slacks, silk blouse and bra. Even at forty-four my breasts are still firm and full. I push my panties down, exposing the soft nest of my pubic hair. After hanging my slacks and shirt in the closet I go into the bathroom, turn on the shower and step in. No need for a shower cap, as I keep my honey-hued tresses cut short and softly curled. Jean wears hers shoulder length.

With eyes closed, I turn my face up to the gentle spray, feeling all the fatigue of the day drain away. When I open my eyes I almost have a heart attack. On the other side of the clear glass shower door is a man, wearing nothing but a big smile. Just as I draw breath to scream, I realize the man is Nathan. I had no idea he and Jean were on shower-sharing terms.

He opens the shower door and steps in. "I'm leaving tomorrow instead of next week, and I couldn't resist giving you one last chance to have your wicked way with me."

"How did you get in?" I gasp.

"I went 'round to the back when you didn't answer the bell. The window was open and here I am."

"Yes, here you are," I gulp, realizing there is an absurd humor in the situation.

"You've cut your hair! I like it." Our different hair styles are the only way most people can tell us apart. Is it possible that Jean hadn't told him she has a twin? A dozen other questions flash through my mind, but before I can voice them or simply say, "I'm not Jean, I'm Joan," he draws me into his strong arms and kisses me. My hands come up to push him away, then, as his insistent tongue slips between my suddenly yielding lips, my arms wind around his neck and I lose myself in the moment.

His hungry lips slide down my throat and close over one nipple, sucking it into a hard pink bud. My hand eagerly seeks and finds his erection. I am delighted to find him generously endowed. I gasp when his fingers deftly make their way between my pliant thighs and expertly tease my tingling clitoris. "Oh, God, that feels so good," I sigh.

"I can't wait to eat your hot pussy, then I'm going to fuck it," he murmurs huskily. It sounds good to me. Wrapped in towels, we move into the bedroom. I sit on the end of the bed, my legs slightly parted. He drops to his knees on the rug and kisses the inside of my thighs until I let myself fall backward onto the bed. Then he buries his head between my legs and pleasures me with his tongue. When I come he keeps licking and sucking until I come again and again, feeling as if I'm melting. Only then does he lie beside me.

"I love what you just did," I manage to gasp. He kisses me and I taste myself on his lips.

"I loved doing it," he says, his blue eyes glowing. "I'm really

glad I came here tonight; I hope you are too. You might have
kicked me out. I like a woman with a sense of adventure." I keep
silent, afraid of giving myself away. And in any case, it's a time for
action, not words. Impulsively, I roll over and straddle his thighs,
all eagerness and heat as I lower myself onto his enticing, rigid
cock. His warm hands clasp my waist to support me as his pulsing
erection penetrates my moist, receptive pussy. Smiling down at
him I sit on his rod, rocking gently.

His eyes glaze with passion as I clamp my cunt muscles tight
around his shaft. Voluptuously I rise and fall, savoring the delicious sensations that bring soft sighs from my parted lips at each
descent. I come with a convulsive shudder. He rolls me over and
rests quietly inside me. When my breathing finally slows he begins to thrust, slowly, deeply, his cock submerged in the liquid
core of my lust. Nathan gradually accelerates his movements until
I'm on the edge again. Sensing it, Nathan pauses, tantalizing me
by lightly licking my lips. My hands roam over his muscular
shoulders and arms, coming to rest on his tight buttocks. My entire body begins to tremble as he moves resolutely within me. I
feel the muscles in his ass tighten with each forceful stroke. Almost without warning, a blinding, breathtaking climax shoots
through me. I hear my strangled cry as if from far, far away. Only
then does he allow himself to come, his passion-contorted face
glistening with sweat. Clasped in the circle of his arm, my cheek
pressed against his chest, I listen to the muted drumming of his
heart until sleep overtakes us.

It is past two when I wake. Nathan is sprawled in sleep, utterly
relaxed. His face, below the mop of silvery hair, shows strength,
in the strong jaw, and sensitivity, in the full sensual curve of his
lips. His hands are shapely, with blunt cut nails. Stealthily I pull
down the sheet. At the bottom of his taut belly his pale penis lies
soft and small in a thatch of dark hair.

Just looking at him rekindles my passion. I take his penis entirely into my mouth, swirling my tongue around the velvety tip,
sucking gently, thrilling as I feel it wake, thicken, grow long and
stiff. His hands rest on my hair, and his gasps of pleasure make
me want to fuck him again. Before he can come, I sit up.

"You can wake me up like that anytime," he laughs.

"Come down to the carpet with me," I order, getting off the bed. He raises an eyebrow but obeys. I get on all fours and tilt my ass up. "I want you to do it to me this way, cowboy." Just imagining him fucking me like that makes me wild and wet. When he puts his hands on my hips, I shiver.

He kisses and nibbles his way down my back to my ass. Then he presses against me and rubs his hard cock back and forth over my clit. I squirm and jerk, almost ready to come again.

When he mounts me, his hard cock slips easily into my creamed cunt. I see our reflection in the mirrored closet doors; the sight is wonderfully lascivious. Nathan's hands move to hold me by the shoulders as he humps into me. His penis, slippery with my juices, enters deep and slow, then pulls almost all the way out. Hearing our gasping moans makes me even hotter. Nathan's eyes meet and hold mine in the mirror. The cords in his strong neck stand out, his breathing sounds ragged. My cunt makes deliciously obscene sounds with each stroke of his cock. His body arches sharply over mine and his tempo quickens to short, hard thrusts. His sweat drips onto my back and ass. I see the room through a red haze; my heart pounds furiously, my muscles quiver, straining to hold me up. Weakly I let my head droop, oblivious to everything but the pleasure of my rapidly approaching orgasm. I have no sense of time; minutes or hours might have passed, but only our bodies matter.

At the very moment of our coming, split seconds apart, I can't tell where my body ends and Nathan's begins. Still connected, we collapse sideways onto the soft carpet, totally exhausted, breathless, drenched with sweat, his cock and my cunt slick with cum, and, at last, sated.

Eventually we find the strength to crawl into bed. We sleep, limbs languidly entwined. When I wake Nathan is gone. On the bedside table is a note scrawled in a masculine hand:

"Darling, You were incredible! Please come to Wyoming. I can promise you lots of good 'riding.' Yours, Nathan."

On Jean's return I tell her about Nathan's unexpected visit, my face blushing crimson. "He was just so adorable, and I was so hungry for sex I couldn't resist." I look at her anxiously. "You have every right to be mad as hell."

She smiles. "Don't be silly. Even though I didn't have Nathan in mind, indirectly I did give you something special."

❦

Best Friends

I've known the day of Richard Nixon's birthday as long as I've known anything. Erin McCormick told me. She said Joan Baez and Richard Nixon were both born on January 9th. "How could anyone know that," she asked, "and still believe in astrology?"

We were fifteen years old and she was peeling onions for potato salad. I was spooning yellow stuff onto slick cooked whites of eggs. We were getting ready for the school band trip. Erin played the French horn. I was percussion.

"If you can't believe in astrology," she said, scratching an old mosquito bite on the back of her leg, "what's left? Events spin out of control, no plan or reason."

I stood there, crunched on a sweet pickle and thought for a minute. It had been a rough year for me. The rest of the girls were preoccupied with boys. Pressure to fit in was tremendous. I was afraid that I wasn't like anyone else on earth.

"What about God?" I started to say, then remembered a rainy day discussion on Nietzsche weeks before. Was everything in the universe random, then? Was there really no plan? Erin's back was to me. The cold water was running in the sink. She was waiting for an answer. I shrugged and said, "No control sounds exciting to me."

She turned and faced me. "Does it?" she said. Her green eyes were glazed from the onions, a spray of moist freckles glistened on her nose and cheeks.

Later I remembered that day. I see her standing in my mother's kitchen, her eyes watery, commenting on irony and the universe. I remember the way she sniffed and wiped her eyes on her madras shirt tail as I told her my theory that life was like a slot machine—you got what you got, and the only way to keep it from spinning was to not put your quarter in. I remember how beautiful she looked. The other girls were obsessed with boys. I was obsessed with Erin. I wanted her more than anything in the world. I told her all I knew about life. Tried to impress her. I was fifteen and I knew everything.

I broke my ankle doing a stupid stunt on my bicycle that evening after we made the food. I never got to go on the band trip. Later I heard the potato salad was thrown out. Hardly anyone in the band liked onions.

Then on the late-night trip home, in the bright yellow school bus, Erin was somehow impregnated by Vernon Pratt.

Vernon, sometimes a substitute triangle player, though usually on the pom-pom squad, didn't merit band trips, but was playing the bass drum in my absence.

Talk about ironies. Talk about the spinning wheels of fate. Okay, okay. It wasn't the first time they'd "done it." But Erin had said she'd quit.

For years, every time I heard Joan Baez I felt a twinge. Sometime later when Richard Nixon was in all the papers, I thought about Erin over my morning coffee and chocolate doughnut. Still wanting her, I couldn't figure how Vernon and the kids fit in.

Erin and I had grown up together. We had been best girlfriends since fourth grade when her father, who owned a fourteen-lane bowling alley, had let Erin have slumber parties there. A group of five or six girls would spend the night, then have milk shakes and hamburgers for breakfast. I learned to play a mean game of pool there when I was ten years old, a skill that served me in later years. When Erin's father had his first heart attack, she and Vernon took over the management of the bowling alley. The place became the young couple's life. They had three babies by the time I finished four years of college. Vernon's hairline had started to recede and his former flat stomach hung over his belt buckle. Erin had perpetual dark circles under her green eyes.

I had my coffee and doughnuts in the bowling alley on Saturday mornings one summer. I was getting ready to start grad school. Erin worked the early shift on weekends because of Vernon's part-time job at a filling station. When business was slow, she'd draw a cup of coffee, light a filtered cigarette and slide into the booth across from me. One morning in July she finally said it.

"I hear you like girls."

I looked at her over the rim of my coffee cup. I thought she'd known. I guess I figured everyone did. I sat the cup down slowly and nodded.

"Is there someone special?" she asked.

"Not right now," I answered. "In my junior year there was someone for a while. A pre-law student." I shrugged. "It didn't work out."

We were quiet for some time. Sun filtered through the Venetian blinds. Cigarette smoke swirled around her red hair like a halo. Striped shadows fell across her ruffled uniform, and her freckled face. She stubbed out a cigarette. "Were you always like that?" she asked.

"I suppose."

"Did you ever think about me?" It was almost a whisper.

Our eyes met. I nodded.

She fidgeted with her lighter.

I waited.

"Do you still?" she said at last.

I sighed, "Sometimes."

"Vernon and I do three-ways," she said quickly. "I really like the part with women."

The last bite of my doughnut slipped from my fingers and splashed into my lukewarm coffee. I watched it float then sink into the murky blackness. I looked at her again. My eyes were round. "You do three-ways," I said at last. It wasn't really a question.

She nodded. "Would you like to join us?"

"You and Vernon?"

"Sure."

It was too much. I mumbled "No thanks" and got the hell out of there.

I would like to say I never thought about it again.

I actually thought about it a lot. I wanted her. But every time the fantasy got to the part where Vernon unbuckled his belt, I stopped. Erin sent me a Christmas card at school that year with a chatty letter and a picture of the kids. In February, at my mother's funeral, she sat next to me and held my hand. Vernon sat in the back with a baby on each knee. When everyone went away and I was left to wander through the empty rooms of my mother's home, Erin tapped at the front door.

I looked at her standing in the yellow porch light, gentle snow flakes falling behind her, a bottle of rum clutched in a fuzzy red knitted mitten.

"I think we really need to get drunk," she said.

I opened the door wider and let her pass into the dim over-heated living room.

"Have you had supper?" she asked, throwing her coat across my mother's rocker.

"Ham," I said. "Everyone brought ham. I've been serving and eating it for days. I'm sick of the stuff." I was looking at her coat across the chair. "I'll probably never eat ham again."

"Here," she said from behind me.

I turned.

She was holding a glass up.

"Drink this. It'll make you feel better."

I took it obediently. "Doesn't Vern have to work tonight? Where are the kids?"

"I got a sitter."

"Just to come over here?" I picked up her coat and headed for the closet.

"How about we order a pizza?" she followed me. "Or I could cook a pot of chili?"

We ordered a large pizza with everything and got roaring drunk. Sometime around midnight, we ritualistically dumped twenty pounds of ham over the back fence to the neighbor's grateful dog. We rested our arms on the chest-high cyclone mesh that separated the back lots and watched the huge mutt eat.

The night was cold and clear. Patches of snow dotted the lawn. I could see her frosty breath. Erin touched my arm, her red mitten looked bright and warm against my navy pea coat. For the first time in days, I started to cry.

She pulled me into her arms and held me. I saw the nearly full moon over her shoulder. My tears caused the moonlight to waver and glow. There were just the sounds of the dog munching and growling and my icy sobs in the night air.

I woke late the next morning to the smells of bacon and coffee. My stomach lurched. I moved my head and felt a tremendous pain. I opened my eyes. Erin stood framed in my bedroom doorway. Her yellow sweater was rumpled. Her faded jeans were muddy around the belled bottoms. She held two glasses of tomato juice.

"You have a choice," she said. "Bacon and eggs or cold pizza."

I moaned and pulled the covers over my head.

I felt her sit on the edge of the bed and tug at the blanket. "Come on. If I can move this morning, so can you."

I lowered the blanket, "I'm going to puke."

"Drink this. It'll help." She stuck the tomato juice under my nose.

I pushed it away. "As I recall, those are the words that started this. Did we really feed the neighbor's dog twenty pounds of ham last night?"

She nodded. "He probably doesn't feel much better than we do this morning."

I sipped the tomato juice. "Coffee," I said. "I need coffee."

To this day I have trouble believing that I downed a half pound of bacon and four fried eggs swimming in grease that morning. I have more trouble believing that Erin asked me about sex again. And I turned her down again. But it happened.

"If you're not interested in a three-way," she had said refilling my coffee cup as we lingered at the kitchen table, "then what about just me?"

I looked at her. Her complexion was strikingly pale, due to the hangover. She'd pulled her hair back and held it with a green rubberband at her neck. Her eyes were puffy. And I wanted her. "I'm in a relationship," I said. "It's a committed relationship. I've promised not to sleep with others." I hesitated a second then added, "You're married. But if we're ever single at the same time, you've got a date."

She nodded, set the coffee pot down and said, "Okay."

Of course I was single a month later. I discovered that Letha slept with everyone while I kept my promise. The morning I was saying no to Erin, Letha was waking up under the flannel sheets of the woman who would be her next lover.

After the last fight with Letha, I called Erin in tears. It was Easter Sunday. I hadn't gone home because I didn't want to deal with the empty house or my extended family, who felt obligated to include me. It occurred to me much later that things came to a head because Letha had planned on my departure over the spring break. By staying at school I had messed up my lover's love life. We had a fight that started at breakfast and ended with Letha throwing her underwear and vibrator in a paper sack and slamming the trailer door so hard that she bent the lock.

I could hear Erin's children laughing in the background. I had my period and a bad case of cramps. I guess I'd taken too much Mydol because I couldn't stop crying and I knew that if I slept with Erin the pain would go away. Cramps and all.

"You don't sound good," Erin said. "Are you all right?"

"Letha and I broke up," I sniffed. "She's been fucking everybody."

"I'm sorry." Erin's voice softened. "I know infidelity is bad for a romance."

"What?" I blew my nose. Had I heard right?

"Well, Vernon and I have decided that monogamy is the best way."

I was sure she knew why I'd called. That this was the answer. "You're not doing three-ways anymore?"

"We only did a couple," she said. "Vern couldn't deal with it, even though it was his idea. He would mope around for days. Then he found out I saw someone else on my own and he suggested, after a two-day drinking and crying jag, that we close our open relationship. We both agreed to settle down. I think it's the best way. Don't you?"

"Yeah," I stammered. "Sure." I thought it was shit right at that moment. I heard one of the kids squeal in the background. Then Vernon's voice.

"Why don't you drive up for dinner?" Erin asked. "It will be just us. You'll feel better being with friends."

"It's two hours," I said. "Besides, I have plans." I was going to the bar. Shoot some pool. Find a woman.

"You sure?"

"Yeah. Thanks anyway."

"Look," she said firmly, "you're someone real special. You just haven't found the right one yet. You deserve the best there is."

"Sure. Right."

Then she said, "I love you."

"Huh?"

"You're the best friend a girl ever had," she said quickly. "And I love you."

"Erin . . ."

"Why don't you come to dinner?"

"No. I really can't."

When I hung up I stared out the window for a long time. Letha and I had shared a tiny trailer. I'd have to move or find another roommate. I couldn't afford the place alone.

I played *Diamonds and Rust* on the stereo all afternoon. I sat in my bathrobe and stared out the window. For Easter dinner I ate a one-pound solid milk chocolate chicken and several marshmallow eggs. I regretted not going to Erin's. I wondered if they were having ham.

I left school early that spring. I was so far behind in everything it was a nightmare. I couldn't live in my mother's home alone and, though I regretted it later, I sold the place and bought a condo. I got a counseling job at a battered women's shelter. The pay was low, but I found the work rewarding. The women's problems made my pissy depression seem inane. If they could laugh and go on, I could too. No one cared that I was a philosophy major who had dropped out when real life got too hard. Once I was clowning around and mentioned Nietzsche in a staff meeting. The night shift counselor said, "Fuck him! He hated women too. He was just more eloquent about it than the bastards we have to deal with here."

I babysat for Erin's kids and helped her celebrate when Vernon was finally made manager of the filling station where he'd worked part time for years.

I met Elsbeth, a round, earth-mother type, who ran a print shop. Her fondness for tribadism and dildos enthralled me. We dated. She moved in. We gradually settled into a routine. There were always plants and sleeping cats in our windows, pans left from the night before soaking in the kitchen sink and smells of patchouli and baking bread in the air. It was a good life.

I was stunned when Vernon died suddenly. Everyone was. Oh, he was a prime candidate for a heart attack—a chain smoker, a heavy drinker and overweight. For the last several years he'd worked ten hours a day, six days a week at that filling station and helped Erin out at the bowling alley on weekends. One Sunday morning he simply slept in. It was the most graceful thing he'd done in his life.

I held Erin's hand during the funeral. Her children, three young adults, sat on either side of us. We all wept together. I have to say that even I was pretty broken up. I looked from the casket to Erin's profile. Not too bad for a substitute triangle player, I thought. He'd spent his life loving the most beautiful woman I knew. In a way, we both had.

A few days later I took a fifth of rum over to Erin's double-wide trailer. The kids were with their grandfather getting through the weekend at the bowling alley.

I poured her a strong drink and slid it across the kitchen table. "We need to get really drunk," I told her.

I watched her swallow the searing liquid. Her green eyes glazed with tears. I remembered when we were children—the band trip, the onions. I laid my hand across hers. "It'll be all right. You're going to be fine."

She sniffed. "My life is over. I'm forty years old. I haven't even finished high school!"

"Erin, don't . . ."

"I can't help it." Her shoulders shook with sobs. "I don't know how to be alone. I'm not a young girl anymore. I'm thirty pounds overweight, my hair is going gray and I'm scared."

"Erin, listen to me," I said. "You're someone real special. You deserve the best there is. You're going to be fine."

"Sure," she sniffed. "Right."

Then I said, "I love you."

She looked at me. A stream of clear snot trickled down her upper lip. "Would you hold me?" she said. "Would you make love to me?"

My head was spinning. What about Elsbeth? What about all the reasons I shouldn't do it that had nothing to do with my lover of ten years?

I pulled her close and hugged her. "Erin, I can't."

"I understand," she said into my shoulder.

I squeezed her hard and kissed her moist neck. There was a faint taste of salt from her tears. I felt swept along like a leaf on a swift current. I kissed her lips. They were soft. Warm. My hands trembled as I unbuttoned her sweater. It fell off her shoulders exposing a lacy bra. A faint spray of freckles marked the way from her neck to the valley between her round breasts. I unhooked the bra and pulled it off. She leaned against the corner of the horseshoe formica counter as I kissed and touched every inch of her exposed skin.

She pulled my shirt tail out of my jeans. Both of her thumbs worked at the buttons on my 501s. Then she pushed my jeans down over my hips and they fell around my ankles. I chuckled. "Right here in the kitchen?"

"Not in my bed," she shook her head slowly. "Please."

I stepped out of my jeans and took her hand. "How about the couch?"

She followed me obediently into the living room. Leaving her own Levi cords in a heap by the coffee table, she stretched out on the couch and raised her arms over her head.

I knelt beside her and ran my hands over her soft body. I kissed her nipples and stroked the fine moist hairs on her mound.

She opened her legs, like we'd done this a hundred times. The room was quiet. I could hear her breathing. Shallow. Quick. I could hear the first heavy drops of rain on the trailer roof. Flecks of ice gently striking the aluminum window frame. I stretched out on top of her and moved in a gentle fucking motion. From my own warm center I felt the most wonderful throbbing pain.

She rested one leg over my back and braced the other on the floor. I moved down her belly and ate her slowly, lingering over the most exquisite meal. She responded to my tongue, gently rocking and whispering, "Do it. Oh, do it."

She raised her head after a while and asked, "Is it taking too long?"

I stopped. I stroked her glistening vulva and pushed against the pink silken folds. She moaned as the warm flesh gave way and three fingers slid snugly inside her.

"I could do this forever," I said and returned to my dining.

When she came she cried out my name over and over.

I held her, rocking her like a baby, planting small kisses on her face.

At last she said, "Show me what to do for you."

"Erin, you don't have to do anything more," I said. "I'm very pleased as it is."

"Come on," she coaxed. "If we're going to do this, let's do it right."

I was aroused. "Put your leg like this." I straddled it and rubbed myself against her. My pubic bone pressed firmly against her thigh. I felt a feverish friction.

"Does that feel good?" she asked.

"Oh, yes. Yes."

She kissed my face. I felt the tension build inside me, then burst with tingling waves that seemed to electrify even my fingertips. We lay naked, pressed together.

At last she smiled, "This is better than getting drunk."

"It will feel better in the morning too."

She sighed. "Will it?"

"Hey," I said as love for her washed over me. "Nothing has changed here. We're still best friends. Right?"

She nodded in agreement, but I was worried by the time my heart rate slowed to normal. I've heard that once you cross a line you can never go back. Was I being naive thinking that things hadn't changed? What I knew was that I knew a hell of a lot less than I did when I was fifteen.

"Remember when we were kids?" I said tentatively. "And you told me about Joan Baez and Richard Nixon?"

"We've just made love and you're talking about Richard Nixon?" she frowned. "Boy, lesbian sex is sure different than I thought it would be."

It had grown dark. The furniture cast long, soft shadows. The sound of rain was slow and steady. The room was suddenly cold. I pulled an afghan from the back of the couch over us and moved to a sitting position. It occurred to me that what I did and said in the next few minutes could alter my life forever. Events spinning out of control no longer held an allure. I didn't want to make a mistake.

I pulled Erin close and told her. "If someone asked me what the most intimate, most meaningful relationship of my life was, I'd say it was with you."

"I know," she said softly. "Me too."

"Maybe random things happen. Maybe the fact that Richard Nixon and Joan Baez were born on the same day isn't as important as what they did next."

She pulled away and looked at me. "What the hell are you talking about?"

"Choices," I said. "I think we have choices."

She looked straight ahead. I guess she was letting it sink in. After a while she said, "You mean about this?" It was almost a whisper.

"Uh-huh," I nodded, wondering if I was being an asshole.

"You're still the philosophy major who thinks that how you look at things is all there is! That life can be summed up with fancy words." She sounded angry.

"You and I have never been about fancy words," I said. "Making love to you was very special for me."

She watched me, listening.

"You know," I said, "I always admired the way you took hold of life. You ran risks and took chances while the rest of us were making lists and weighing the odds." I rubbed her back. I could feel her muscles relaxing. "I know you're scared right now, but a little fear doesn't make you a coward. Making love to you was the most courageous act of my life. I think this was small potatoes for you."

"You're not small potatoes," she whispered. "You're my best friend."

I nodded. "And whatever happens I want that. I want it to last forever." I sighed. "I just couldn't go on without it."

"Can't best friends sleep together?" she asked, like she thought I had all the answers.

I started to say more, but her sobs cut me off. I held her. After a while I got up and made us both a stiff drink. Our naked bodies were warm under the afghan. The rum burned in my throat. The rest of the world was hard and cold. Around midnight I tucked her in bed, told her I loved her, that I had always and would always love her.

That night when I went home and crawled into bed next to Elsbeth, I lay on my side staring out the rain-speckled window. I watched the cold shadows from the neighbor's yard light reflected on the tree branches. They shone against the dark sky like a photo negative—like an image turned inside out. Elsbeth curled up behind me spoon-fashion and snored softly. I didn't sleep for a long time.

Carol Queen

༄

Sweating Profusely in Mérida: A Memoir

The Boyfriend and I met at a sex party. No, really, this is a true story. I was in a back room trying to help facilitate an erection for a gentleman brought to the party by a woman who would have nothing to do with him once they got there. It turned out later she had charged him a pretty penny to get in. I actually felt that I should have gotten every cent, but I suppose it was my own fault that I was playing Mother Teresa and didn't know when to let go of his dick. Boyfriend-to-be was hiding behind a potted palm watching us. He crouched, eyeing me and this guy's unco-operative dick, which was uncut; it seemed Boyfriend had a thing for pretty girls and uncut men, especially the latter. So he decided to help me out, and replaced my hand with his mouth. That's when it got interesting. The uncut straight guy finally left and I stayed.

The thing about our relationship was that it only really worked when we were at a sex party. But it took us a few months to grasp that, and in the meantime we shared many straight men, most of them—Boyfriend's radar was incredible—uncircumcised and willing to do almost anything with a man as long as there was a woman in the room. I often acted as a hook to hang a guy's het-erosexuality on while Boyfriend sucked his dick or even fucked him. My favorite was the hitchhiker wearing pink lace panties

under his grungy jeans—but that's another story. Long before we
met the hitchhiker, Boyfriend had invited me to go to Mexico.

"Here's the plan. Almost all the guys in Mexico are uncut,
right? And lots will play with men, too," Boyfriend assured me,
"especially if there's a woman there." Besides, he thought it
would be a romantic vacation.

That's how we wound up in Room 201 of the Hotel Reforma in
sleepy Mérida, capital of the Yucatán. Why Mérida? Its popularity
as a tourist town had been eclipsed by the growth of Cancún, the
nearest Americanized resort. That meant the boys would be horn-
ier, Boyfriend reasoned. A fellow foreskin fancier who had stayed
there recommended the Hotel Reforma. Its chief advantages were
the price—about fourteen dollars a night—and the fact that the
management didn't charge more for extra occupants. I liked it because it was old, airy, and cool, with wrought-iron railings and
stairway tiles worn thin by past guests. Boyfriend liked it because
it had a pool (always a good place to cruise) and a disco across the
street. That's where we headed as soon as we got in from the air-
port and changed into skimpy clothes suitable for turning tropical
boys' heads.

There were hardly any tropical boys there, as it turned out. Apparently this was where the Ft. Lauderdale college students who
couldn't afford Cancún went to spend their meager spring break
allowances. And not only did it look like any Mexican restaurant-
with-disco you would find in Ft. Lauderdale, but the management
took care to keep out all but the most dapper Méridans lest the
coeds be frightened by the scruffy street boys. Scruffy street boys,
of course, were just what Boyfriend had his eye out for, and at
first the pickings looked slim. But we found one who had slipped
past security. He was out to hustle nothing more spicy than a gig
guiding tourists through the warren of narrow streets around the
town's central plaza. Instead he stumbled onto us. Ten minutes
later Boyfriend had his mouth wrapped around a meaty little
bundle—with foreskin. Luis stuck close to us for several days,
probably eating more regularly than usual and wondering out
loud whether we would take him back with us. Or at least send
him a Motley Crüe T-shirt?

One night Boyfriend stayed out for hours looking for gay men, who, he said, would run the other way if they saw me coming. He found one, a slender boy who had to pull down the pantyhose he wore under his jeans so Boyfriend could get to his cock. The boy expressed wonder because he had never seen someone with so many condoms. In fact, most people there never had condoms at all. Boyfriend gave him his night's supply and some little brochures about *el SIDA* he'd brought from the AIDS Foundation (*en español* so that even if our limited Spanish didn't get through to our tricks, a pamphlet might).

Boyfriend also learned that Mérida had a bathhouse. I had always wanted to go to a bathhouse, and of course there was not much chance of it happening back home. For one thing, they were all closed before I ever moved to San Francisco. For another, even if I was dressed enough like a boy to pass, I wouldn't look old enough to get in. But in Mérida, perhaps things were different.

It was away from the town's center but within walking distance of the Hotel Reforma. We strolled over one afternoon while the rest of the town was closed for siesta, and Boyfriend went inside. The place looked like a courtyard motel, an overgrown and haunted version of the kind I used to stay in with my parents when we traveled in the early sixties. Through the front door's one tiny window I saw a huge pâpier-maché figure of Pan, brightly painted and hung with jewelry. It looked like something the Radical Faeries would carry in the Gay Pride parade. Everything else about the lobby looked dingy, like the waiting room of a used-car dealership.

Los Baños de Vapor would open at eight o'clock that evening, Boyfriend told me when he returned. They had a central tub and rooms to rent; massage boys could be rented, too. And Mérida *was* different from San Francisco; I would be welcome.

The pâpier-maché Pan was at least seven feet tall and was indeed the only bright thing in the lobby. Passing through the courtyard, an overgrown jungle of vines pushing through cracked tile, we were shown up a flight of concrete stairs to our room. Our guide was Carlos, a solid, round-faced man in his mid-twenties, wrapped in a frayed white towel. The room was small

and completely tiled, its grout blackened from the wet tropical air.
At one end was a shower and at the other a bench, a low, vinyl-
covered bed, and a massage table. There was a switch that, when
flipped, filled the room with steam. Boyfriend turned it on and we
shucked our clothes. As the pipes hissed and clanked in their efforts to get the steam in, Carlos gestured at the massage table and
then to me.

Boyfriend answered for me, in Spanish, that I'd love to. I got
on the table and Carlos set to work. Boyfriend danced around the
table gleefully, sometimes stroking me, sometimes Carlos' butt.
"Hey, man, I'm working!" Carlos protested, but not very insist-
ently. Boyfriend went for his cock, stroking it hard, then urged
him up onto the table. Carlos' hands, still slick from massage oil
and warm from the friction of my skin, covered my breasts as
Boyfriend rolled a condom onto Carlos' cock. Carlos rubbed it up
and down my labia a few times and finally let go, sinking his cock
in. He rode me slow, then hard, while the table rocked danger-
ously and Boyfriend stood at my head letting me tongue his cock
while he played with Carlos' tits. When he was sure we were having a good time, he put on a towel and slipped out the door.
Carlos looked surprised and I had to try to figure out how to say
"He's going hunting" in Spanish so that he'd go back to fucking
me the way he had been. His solid body was slick from oil and
steam, and if he kept it up I would come, clutching his slippery
back with my legs in the air.

That was just happening when Boyfriend came back with David. He was pulling David in the door by his penis, which already
seemed stiff; I suspected Boyfriend had wasted little time getting
him by the dick. He had found David in the tub room, he announced, commenting on his beautiful, long, uncut cock. Boyfriend always enunciated clearly when he said "uncut." David did
have a beautiful cock. He also spoke English and was long and
slim with startling blue eyes. It turned out he was Chicano, second generation, a senior at Riverside High who spent school
breaks with his grandmother in Mérida, and worked at Los Baños
de Vapor as a secret summer job. We found out all this about him
as I was showering off the sweat and oil from my fuck with
Carlos. By the time I heard that he'd been working at the Baños

since he turned sixteen, I was ready to start fucking again. David was the most quintessential eighteen-year-old fuck I'd ever had, except that Boyfriend's presence made it unusual. He held David's cock and balls to control the speed of the thrusting—until his mouth got preoccupied with Carlos' dick, which was ready to go again. David kept his blue eyes open and told me I was beautiful. At that point I didn't care if I was beautiful or not, since I was finally in a bathhouse doing what I had always wanted to do and feeling more like a faggot than like a beautiful *gringa*. David was saying he wished he had a beautiful girlfriend like me, even though I was thirty, shockingly old. This was actually what most of Boyfriend's conquests said to me. But I had a feeling most men couldn't keep up with a girlfriend who was really a faggot, or a boyfriend who was really a woman, or whatever kind of fabulous anomaly I was.

Someone knocked at the door and we untangled for a minute to answer it; there were José and Gaspar, laughing and saying ours was the most popular room at the Baños at the moment. Would we like some more company? At least that's how David translated the torrent of Spanish, for they were both speaking at once. Naturally, we invited them in, and lo and behold, Gaspar was actually gay. So while I lay sideways on the massage table with my head off the edge and my legs in the air, sucking David while José fucked me, I watched Boyfriend finally getting his cock sucked by Gaspar, whose glittering black Mayan eyes were closed in concentration. I howled not simply with orgasm but with excitement, the splendid excitement of being in a Mexican bathhouse with four uncut men and a maniac—a place no woman I knew had gone before. Steam swirled in the saturated air, beading like pearls high in the corner web of a huge Yucatán spider. David's cock, or was it José's, or Carlos' again, I didn't even care, pounded my fully open cunt rhythmically. I wished I had the spider's view.

If you have ever been to a bathhouse you know that time stands still in the steamy, throbbing air. I had no idea how long it went on, only that sometimes I was on my back and sometimes on my knees and once for a minute I was standing facing the wall. When Boyfriend wasn't sucking them or fucking me he was taking

snapshots of us, just like a tourist. Finally two of them were helping me into the shower and the floor of the room was completely
littered with condoms, which made us all laugh hysterically.
Gaspar and David held me up with Carlos and José flanking them
so Boyfriend could snap one last picture. Then he divided all of
the rest of the condoms among them—we had plenty more at the
hotel. He was trying to explain in Spanish the little condoms he
used for giving head—how great they were with uncut guys because they disappeared under the foreskin. And I was asking David what it was like to live a double life, Riverside High to Los
Baños, and who else came there. "Oh, everyone does," he said.
And did they ever want to fuck him? Of course they *wanted*
to. And did he ever fuck them? Well, sure. And how was that? He
shrugged and said, as if there were only one possible response to
my question so why was I even bothering to ask, "It's *fucking*."

The moon was high and the Baños were deserted when we left,
the warm night air almost cool after the steamy room. The Pan
figure glittered in the dim lobby light, and the man at the desk
charged us thirty-five dollars—seven for each massage boy, four
to get us in, and six for the room. He looked anxious, as though
he feared we'd think it was too much. We paid him, laughing. I
wondered if this was how Japanese businessmen in Thailand felt.
Was I contributing to the decline of the Third World? Boyfriend
didn't give a shit about things like that, so I didn't mention it. In
my hand was a crumpled note from David: "Can I come visit you
in your hotel room? No money."

About the Authors

*BLAKE C. AARENS is a lesbian of African descent. Her story, "Strangers on a Train," appeared in *Herotica 2* under the pseudonym Cassandra Brent. She is currently at work on a murder mystery, a screenplay, and a solo performance piece. Her feline companion Sonja approves all of her manuscripts.

*EMILY ALWARD is an academic librarian, the mother of two daughters, and the owner of three dogs. In her free hours she reads and writes science fiction, and her articles and book reviews have appeared in a variety of publications. She edits *Once Upon a World,* a magazine of stories set in other worlds.

LENORA CLARE is a pseudonym for a lawyer and former partner in a Florida law firm. She pursues other interests, including gardening and creative writing. She has been a regular contributor to a regional environmental newspaper.

DEBBIE COHEN lives with her two cats in San Francisco, where she is finding her voice like lint between her toes. She thanks Mary Rose for standing at the vista with her and sharing the view.

CALLA CONOVA, a poet, has spent many years learning the

*Author whose stories also appear in *Herotica* (Down There Press, 1988) and *Herotica 2* (Plume, 1992).

cycles and secrets of nature. She was inspired to write erotica when she discovered that ancient Asians veiled descriptions of anatomy and sexual acts with allusions to nature. This is her first published story.

MICHELLE HANDELMAN, a multimedia artist, resides in San Francisco, "making movies to get in your face, shooting pictures to get under your skin, and writing stories to get you horny."

RUBY RAY LEONARD is the pen name of a happily married doctoral student and researcher from New York City. Her scholarly work has been published in scientific journals. This is her first erotic short story.

*AURORA LIGHT has contributed stories, nonfiction articles, and poetry to a variety of publications, including *Woman's World, Country Woman,* and *Broomstick.* She is a contributing editor for an international Meniere's Disease newsletter and publishes a haiku magazine.

*JANE LONGAWAY was a San Francisco writer and printer.

MARY MAXWELL was raised by wolves. In subsequent years, she has adapted reasonably well to the strictures of civilization.

*MAGENTA MICHAELS is a poet and hand bookbinder. She lives on the California coast south of San Francisco.

*MARTHA MILLER is a Midwestern writer. Her short stories are widely published in lesbian and literary periodicals and anthologies. She writes a monthly book-review column for women and is currently working on her second play, to be produced by Mid-America Playwrights Theater.

SERENA MOLOCH was born in the Bronx and grew up in Queens. "My Date with Marcie" is for the Marcies of her youth, wherever they might now be.

LINDA NIEMANN is a brakeman/conductor for Southern Pacific Railroad, riding the rails on the West Coast. She is also the author of *Boomer: Railroad Memoirs* (Cleis Press) and has a Ph.D. in English.

CHINA PARMALEE wrote "Local Foods" as a member of a college writers group.

---

*Author whose stories also appear in *Herotica* (Down There Press, 1988) and *Herotica 2* (Plume, 1992).

*CAROL A. QUEEN is a San Francisco writer and sex educator whose aim is to create sexually explicit writing that is both hot and truthful about sex, especially underrepresented desires and behaviors. She is an activist in the bisexual, sex work, and anti-censorship communities.

STACY REED is an honors student at the University of Texas at Austin. For money she dances, but her real DJ's a goof. For kicks she writes for various dailies and magazines. Adult education remains her primary work. Stacy dedicates "Tips" to her best friend, Sheila.

*MARCY SHEINER is a journalist/ novelist/ pornographer/ poet whose work is widely published.

GENEVIEVE SMITH is the smut-minded alter-ego of a teacher and writer of scholarly stuff. She doesn't have any pets yet, but she does have lots of interesting friends and family members. She wants to live on the beach, ASAP.

*SUSAN ST. AUBIN is a fiction writer and occasional poet who likes to write erotica as a warm-up exercise. She recently bought a turn-of-the-century cottage from an elderly couple who left behind a riding crop and ten years worth of diaries, proving that stories can be found in the most unexpected places.

LYDIA SWARTZ is a dyke in the prime of her life who has published smut elsewhere, but would rather tell you about marrying the girl of her dreams and being the first queer to announce her marriage in the employee newsletter of the corporation that employs her.

CECILIA TAN, freelance writer, is the author of *Telepaths Don't Need Safewords* (Circlet Press) and the publisher of erotic science fiction and fantasy. She and her overactive imagination live in Boston, even though you can't ride a motorcycle year round there.

*CATHERINE TAVEL creates erotica under a variety of *noms de porn*. She is a freelance writer of fiction, nonfiction, poetry, and screenplays who hails from the concrete streets of Brooklyn, New York. She immensely enjoys exploring the complexities of

---

*Author whose stories also appear in *Herotica* (Down There Press, 1988) and *Herotica 2* (Plume, 1992).

our libidos in the printed word. Her written works have appeared in everything from *Seventeen* to *Hustler.* Her sexy scripts often surface on "adult" cable television channels. With Robert Rimmer, Tavel helped pen porn star Jerry Butler's biography *Raw Talent* and Mistress Jacqueline's *Whips and Kisses* (Prometheus Books).

*PAT WILLIAMS lives in Berkeley. She was born and raised in western Tennessee. At present she is working on her own Black Panther novel, partly as a way of exploring that group and getting past the lies told about it.

SUSIE BRIGHT is the editor of *Herotica* (Down There Press) and co-editor of *Herotica 2*, as well as of the annual *Best American Erotica* (Collier). She is the author of *Susie Bright's Sexual Reality: A Virtual Sex World Reader* (Cleis Press) and *Susie Sexpert's Lesbian Sex World* (Cleis Press), as well as numerous articles and reviews addressing the popular view of sexuality in culture. She is also a connoisseuse of X-rated film and video.

---

*Author whose stories also appear in *Herotica* (Down There Press, 1988) and *Herotica 2* (Plume, 1992).

Plume （0452）

UNIQUE COLLECTIONS

☐ **NEW AMERICAN SHORT STORIES** *The Writers Select Their Own Favorites* **edited by Gloria Norris.** This unique anthology brings together twenty of today's most distinguished practitioners of the short story, including Alice Adams, T. Coraghessan Boyle, John Updike and many others—each of whom has selected a favorite from his or her recent work. It is a rich panorama of the best in contemporary fiction. (258790—$9.95)

☐ **THE MERIDIAN ANTHOLOGY OF EARLY AMERICAN WOMEN WRITERS** *From Anne Bradstreet to Louisa May Alcott, 1650–1865* **edited by Katharine M. Rogers.** Encompassing a wide spectrum of experience and expression, this outstanding collection celebrates the rich heritage of literary creativity among early American women. (010756—$15.00)

☐ **THE MERIDIAN ANTHOLOGY OF EARLY WOMEN WRITERS** *British Literary Women From Aphra Behn to Maria Edgeworth 1660–1800* **edited by Katharine M. Rogers and William McCarthy.** Here are nineteen stunning pre-nineteenth-century female literary talents never before collected in a single volume. Their stories bring to light the rich heritage of early literary creativity among women. (008484—$14.00)

Prices slightly higher in Canada.

Buy them at your local bookstore or use this convenient coupon for ordering.

PENGUIN USA
P.O. Box 999, Dept. #17109
Bergenfield, New Jersey 07621

Please send me the books I have checked above.
I am enclosing $_____ (please add $2.00 to cover postage and handling).
Send check or money order (no cash or C.O.D.'s) or charge by Mastercard or VISA (with a $15.00 minimum). Prices and numbers are subject to change without notice.

Card # _____ Exp. Date _____
Signature _____
Name _____
Address _____
City _____ State _____ Zip Code _____

For faster service when ordering by credit card call **1-800-253-6476**

Allow a minimum of 4-6 weeks for delivery. This offer is subject to change without notice

There's an epidemic with 27 million victims. And no visible symptoms.

It's an epidemic of people who can't read.

Believe it *or* not, 27 million Americans are functionally illiterate, about one adult in five.

The solution to this problem is you... when you join the fight against illiteracy. So call the Coalition for Literacy at toll-free **1-800-228-8813** and volunteer.

Volunteer Against Illiteracy. The only degree you need is a degree of caring.